STRAWBERRY
MOON

To Sheila
with love
Joy
x

Published by Long Overdue LLC

www.longoverduestories.com

Book created through Amazon KDP

Table of Contents

CHAPTER ONE

The French Connection

France – The Dordogne, Saint-Severin,

Dad would spend days away from home, looking for work, much to Mum's angst. However, his perseverance eventually paid off, and he was offered a job as a handyman and overseer to a housing complex in the Dordogne, France, made up of residents from a variety of different countries.

He returned home in March of 2010, full of excitement about what he referred to as 'The Life Anew.'

After months of weighing things out, going over the pros and cons, and trying to imagine what this new chapter would be like, finally Mother, me, and my brother Dan agreed to take a chance on France.

It was early summer 2010, if my memory serves me right, when we started to put our lives into boxes and prepared to leave the only home we had ever known. I was sixteen years old. Dan was a month away from turning 18. Out of the four of us, I'd say Dad was the most on board for this move, I was second, and Mum and Dan were in a distant third and fourth place. They weren't exactly thrilled about uprooting their lives to another country.

Dad loaded the car until it was full to bursting. He drove alone so room was available to take more stuff. He hired a large van at great expense, and his friend (the one who told him to look abroad for work) drove it. They went in tandem and drove for the whole day. It took them a good nine hours to get to Saint-Severin. We travelled behind them, taking the boat across the English Channel, and then hired a car in Calais, yet more expense. It was decided that we would break the journey at the approximate halfway point. We stayed at Le Logis des Tours. Dad made sure Mum had a good map and explained the route thoroughly to her and Dan. Me, being a mere girl, was excluded from this conversation.

The journey was long and I began to feel very car sick. I hadn't experienced this before, so I put it down to Mum's bad driving. She had trouble navigating the country roads. Driving via these bumpy highways was to avoid the tolls on the main motorways. Dan kept on at Mum to let him drive; even though he had only just passed his driving test. And that was after the second time taking it. Still, he felt sure that he could do better than she was doing.

"You have only just learnt to drive properly, and here we have to drive on the other side of the road," Mum said. "You may forget that small detail and kill us all."

"Oh, Mum, don't be so hard on me," Dan argued. "I will be very careful. After all, we don't want to die just as we're beginning this new life of ours, now do we?"

"Get on with it, then, and you just be careful, son, as you have precious cargo on board," Mum said.

That night, we ate far too much of the lovely French food and drank rather more than we should of the cheap wine. Whatever money we saved from avoiding the toll roads, I was all but certain we spent it on that heavy dinner. All of us were suffering from some indigestion that night when we checked into our hotel. This led us to a restless night of sleep in strange beds. The next morning Mum settled our bill and thanked the hotelier, as he wished us bon voyage and happiness for our future life.

Mum finally turned the wheel over to Dan. He actually drove very well, slowly and cautiously. There were no complaints except for the one instance when a tractor had the right-of-way coming out of a side turn; a rule of the road that was unheard of back home. It was quite unexpected. Dan pulled our car to a sudden stop and there was just enough room for the tractor to pass by us. It served as two good lessons for us all: always slow down when driving in these countryside villages. And beware of tractors.

******

As we meandered along the twisting and turning roads towards our new location, I felt the first wave of homesickness. Combine this feeling with some of the remaining indigestion from the night before, plus the motion sickness from the drive, and my stomach was doing some gymnastics in the back seat.

I looked out my window and saw this canal that looked awfully similar to the Hythe Canal, close to where we lived back home. We had lived in Hythe, in Kent, The Garden of England, where time seemed to move at a slower pace. In the late spring and early summer, the hollyhocks were just beautiful. They seemed to spring from everywhere, even poking out of walls and up through some of the cracks in the pavement.

Every chance I had, I was down by the canal with my bike. Come rain or shine, I whistled on past riding my little rose coloured bike, complete with the must-have mini basket at the front, usually full of bits and pieces collected along the towpath. I was a happy child, I'd say around eleven-years-old was when I really got into these scenic bike rides.

There was one day when I was on my way home from school and the weather around me was scary. The sky was darkening considerably fast and took on a kind of reddish, yellowy hue. I'd never seen anything like it before.

"Perhaps it's the end of the world!" a boy shouted as he passed me on his bike.

I stuck my tongue out in response and carried on riding by the canal.

I looked over to the other side and froze in my tracks. There was a man staring back at me; a stranger I'd never seen before. He was gargantuan in height compared to me, and despite being quite some distance away, I could easily make out his face. There was something wrong with it—perhaps it was his skin, it was hard to tell. What I could see poking out from underneath a Stetson hat, was his long, greasy-looking, unkempt hair. He was following me intently with his eyes, as I tried to pick up speed and cycle like the wind towards home.

His large red coat stood out. It was a strange sight for sleepy old Hythe, and his Stetson hat was equally out of place. This strange attire, and his transfixed gaze, made me quicken my pace as my heart began to beat faster and faster in my chest. My breathing quickened as my body prepared for the speed needed to get me home safely. I couldn't quite shake off the idea of the man, though. *Did he know me? Had he followed me back home? Who was he and what did he want?* These questions lingered in my mind long after the sighting and my speedy race home.

After all, I reasoned afterwards, he was just a man, even if he was incredibly odd-looking.

As I dashed into the backyard to put my bike away in the rear of the garage, I heard Mum call out, "Where the devil have you been? It's taken you long enough to get yourself home."

"Well, Mum, I was riding on the towpath and guess what?" I began to tell her. "This horrible looking man was watching me from the other side. I've never seen him before. He was huge, like a giant, and wore this long red coat and on his head sat a cowboy type of hat."

"What have your father and I told you over and over again?" she said. "You need to be careful on that path—in fact, I think from now on, you can come home the long way around."

"Oh no, Mum, please don't make me. It takes ever so much longer that way and the roads are so busy. I could have an accident or worse still, be killed. Then what would you do?"

"Stop your noise, you silly girl. You're just being a drama queen as usual. I've told you what's going to happen moving forward and, from now on, you will not be going down to the canal at all. That's final."

"But, Mum, that's where all my friends go! I shall be OK with them all around me."

"Uh huh, and where were they today? Hm? Go and get changed, your tea is ready and your father will be home soon."

Feeling thwarted in my proposed summer-holiday antics, I rushed upstairs to change out of my school uniform. When I came down, my father was home from work and he looked extremely upset. In fact, I thought he was going to cry. It was the first time I'd ever seen that and it made me uncomfortable. Dad was usually the one to nurture and care for all of us. What on God's green earth could have made him so upset?

"Jack, stop that, you'll frighten the children," I heard Mum say in a quiet voice.

Dan walked in the front door. My brother took one look at our father and asked, "Whatever is it, Dad? You look awful."

"I feel awful, son. I've just been sacked from my job."

Dad worked as a master baker in the bakery in Sandgate.

"Whatever happened for them to sack you?"

"They said I was too old for the job and that they wanted someone who was younger and more reliable. I don't recall being unreliable except last winter when I had the flu."

"For being sick? No. They can't do that. We should take them to court. That's not legal!"

"Dan, you go and tell them that and you'll see what the reply will be, boy."

It's crazy how certain memories can stand out so clearly like they happened only yesterday. I can picture that room. The wallpaper. The wooden calendar we had hanging by the clock. The way my dad sat at the table, shoulders slouched, everything about him looked defeated. Broken. And the way Dan stood up, pacing around like an Army general. In that moment, Dan was the man of the house, the one coming up with a plan. Dad was the dejected child, sitting still as if looking for direction. Dan was left assuring the family that everything was going to be alright.

I began to feel claustrophobic indoors with all the racket occurring, all of this talk about jobs and money and perhaps needing to look at other locations. It made my head hurt and I felt small, like I had no say in the matter. No say in my future at all. All I wanted to do in that moment was get out of the house.

So, I went to get my trusty bike and went back to the canal, deliberately disobeying my Mum's most recent command. En route, I bumped into James. His bike was newer and better than mine; mine was second-hand. James was a good friend to me and was in my class at school. We got along just fine and he would stick up for me when the bullies started. He was big for his age, and towered over the 'shorty's' who were never afraid of giving us girls a load of lip. James always managed to scare them off and put them in their place. All the girls in our class thought of him as their saviour and hero. I felt exactly the same way, but always felt special that he paid more attention to me.

"Where you off to, Maisie?" James asked.

"The canal, of course, there's trouble at home," I told him. "Dad's been given the sack and now we won't have any money coming in and Mum's already starving us on ten almonds a day." This was all about some crazy idea of feeding us correctly, because of the obesity crisis. Mind you we still get sweets from the tuck shop and I've seen Dad going to great lengths trying to make sure his secret chocolate eating remains undiscovered.

"Oh, that's bad news. I'm sorry. Still, not to worry. Come on, I'll come down with you and we can have a race, and I bet I'll be beating you."

We set off to the canal.

"Have you had your tea, James?" I inquired.

"No, not yet. Mum's not home from work till seven; we have to wait 'till then."

"I've not had any food, either, maybe won't get any tonight, because Mum will be so upset over the news of Dad losing his job."

We got to the canal, and it was awash with people walking their dogs. It was a beautiful night. The birds were singing for all they were worth in the huge and numerous trees running alongside the canal. I think they were oaks or larches or something of that line—can't remember what the names are. The birds' chatter occasionally got louder and louder until a scuffle, usually by the big black-and-white birds (can't remember what they were called, either) and it always ended with one of them being beaten by the black-and-white jobs and the victims soaring off into the sky until they disappeared from view.

I completely forgot about the bother back home, being totally absorbed in the goings-on by the canal. I glanced at my watch and lo and behold, reality came rushing back.

"Better not be out too long, James, or Mum will have forty fits," I said. "She worries about us coming down to the canal. Have you seen that strange man? The one who walks along in a long, reddish-coloured coat and wears a Stetson hat? I saw him and I think he was watching me earlier today and it quite put the wind up me. He started to walk along the other side of the canal as I rode my bike on this side. He walked pretty fast, too. He was obviously following me."

"I've not seen him down here. But he sounds like any of the other odd bods who come out at night—surely you know that."

"No, James, you've got it wrong, this was in the daytime. And he was definitely the oddest man I've ever seen, here or anywhere else."

We cycled along for about three hundred yards or so, or that's what it felt like to me, and I said to James, "Must be off for home now, it's nearly seven, and you did say that's when you had to get back, didn't you?"

"Okay, shall we have a bike race?"

"Yes, give me a bit of a start, though."

"Only a little bit. Go on; you can have a bit further than that."

As I turned to get James's approval of the distance between us, I noticed the strange-looking man again, on the other side of the canal, staring at us. I was more scared this time. He was looking directly at me and I could see this creepy grin on his face.

"Look, James! Quick, look over there on the other side. There he is—the Stetson man. Let's get out of here!"

I still felt safe with James by my side. As long as he was there, I'd be ok. But he cycled up ahead of me a good deal and as I cycled along, I looked over my shoulder and saw the man getting closer. He was following me. I peddled faster but he was keeping up with his long stride. Panicked, I turned into an unfamiliar alleyway to try and lose him, but he saw this and followed me. The alleyway had a dead-end and I cowered in the corner, the man just kept slowly walking toward me until he was staring down, looming threateningly over me.

"Hey, what's going on here?" James shouted.

His voice sounded far deeper than normal. He sounded like a grown man, as if it were my dad standing there at the end of the alley. The creepy man turned his back to me and began walking toward James. He slowly approached James and it sounded like he hissed at him like a snake as he approached. James stood his ground and then, in the blink of an eye, kicked the man right in the crotch. He fell to his knees letting out a loud high-pitched squeal.

"Maisie, go!" James shouted.

I pedalled as hard as I could. As I went by the creepy man, he reached his arms out for me and almost hit my back wheel. We kept riding as fast as we could until the man and the canal were well off in the distance. We escaped. And both of us were completely out of breath.

"Are you alright?" James asked.

"Yes, I. Yes. I'm so glad you found me."

"Well, you weren't wrong," James said. "That's certainly the weirdest looking guy I've ever seen. I'm just happy you're ok."

For the next few nights, we watched for hours on end all the comings and goings of the canal. James and I had always fancied ourselves as amateur detectives. We were both avid readers of the Sherlock Holmes books and we'd recreate these little mysteries around town.

James would guide me into abandoned houses and take us on these scary walks through cemeteries or, like now, returning back to the canal in search of a deranged man. James would pretend to be Sherlock and I would pretend not to be nearly as scared as I was.

But this case would remain unsolved. We never saw that man again and after a few weeks moved on to the next exciting (and less scary) mystery around town.

"Earth to Maisie," Dan said from the driver's seat. "You sleeping with your eyes open or something?"

I laughed it off but as I looked out of the window, I had this deep longing to be back home. I missed James, my dear friend and saviour. Always there for me. Who knows what may have happened that day if he hadn't come to my rescue. He was always coming to my rescue and I felt so empty on that drive thinking just how long it might be until I'd see him again.

"Mum, I'm feeling homesick already," I said from the back of the car.

"Never you mind that, love," she told me. "I think we're all feeling unsettled. After all, we have no idea of what we're going to do. Let's think of it as an adventure; one to be enjoyed."

My Mum looked out her window and thought for a second. I could hear her lightly slap her hands on her thighs.

"Well, you two, we have *got* to make a go of it, this trip has taken most of our money," she continued. "We may find that everything is absolutely fine and will settle in happily."

It was as if she was trying to pump herself up as much as she was trying to raise our spirits.

"I think it would be better if we spoke the language," I said. "Dan and I are going to find the school-work hard, at least in the beginning. I can speak Pigeon French. How about you Dan?"

"I don't know any, and I'm not gonna waste my time learning that stupid language," Dan said. He looked more and more confident behind the wheel. "I'll learn just enough to get myself some fine

French ladies. But that's it. And even at that I probably still know more than you do, Mum."

"You're so observant, you two," Mum said. "If you put as much energy into helping a bit more and not criticizing your father and me so much, you might go a long way."

I think Mum had had enough of the journey. However, today it was only to be three-and-a-half hours long, instead of another five, as yesterday. A beautiful day, with glorious scenery passed us by. We were all fascinated to see the golden sunflowers just opening their huge heads; that seemed to follow us as we passed, a sight none of us had ever seen before. The sun continually illuminated stretches of hillside with an almost ethereal light. I couldn't help but think the Dordogne countryside was comparable to that of Kent, quite green and lush.

Finally, we reached our destination, and the sun shone brightly, high up in the sky. Our eyes nearly popped out of our heads. The place that we were now to call home looked like nothing but a pile of bricks, mortar and rubble. Nobody was there to meet us, and the area seemed derelict. We all just stared in disbelief at the crumbled mess in front of us.

The front door opened (it looked like it was going to snap off when it did) and Dad stepped outside with a smile on his face.

"Well, what do you all think?" Dad said. He waived for us to come inside. "Welcome home!"

CHAPTER TWO

Settling In

"The best way to find yourself is to lose yourself in the service of others."
~ Gandhi

The house came with the job; if you could call it a house. To my horror, a part of the place near the back had no roof at all, and a load of buckets and basins scattered around to catch the rain. Of course, the house did have potential, since it was massive with five bedrooms and three bathrooms, but, the place was so neglected that I couldn't help but wonder what must have happened to the chap who used to live here. Dad's predecessor by the name of Henry clearly failed to please the residents and we were fascinated to hear the stories from those who knew him.

When we met some of them, no one had a good word to say about Henry. They were making a number of points directed straight at Mum and Dad. These points could be summed up as, "He was really bad, you better not be like Henry."

All of this took its toll on Mum. A couple days went by and Mum's positivity make-up from the car ride needed some reapplying. She was short with Dad, and most of the things she said were about how dirty the house was, or how unsafe it was, or how he should have done more research. She was short with all of us. I said to her one night, "Hey Mum, I really miss home. Do you think I could call James?" She replied, "Maisie, join the club, alright? We don't need any extra complaining, it doesn't help anything." And she walked out of the room.

Then one night she snapped. I could hear them in their bedroom. The walls were thin in this structure we called a house and the sounds carried very well.

"What the Dickens are we doing in this place?" asked Mum. "It looks as though it's not been lived in at all. How can you have brought us here to live?"

"You know full well the reason we needed to come here and I don't intend going through it with you anymore," Dad said, defending himself. "Anyways, think of the potential for the kids. They'll be bilingual, with loads of opportunities for their future."

"Don't give me that, you old fool! Maisie will probably get married young and as for Dan, well, God only knows what will happen there. He doesn't seem to have any purpose. He never talks about the future or what he wants from life, except for moaning about leaving England. Surely we haven't brought them up so badly that neither of them have any ambition?"

"Julia, please. Keep your voice down. And they are young. Have you forgotten what it was like to be young? All the hormones going haywire and the restlessness that goes with it? They'll settle down— give them a couple of years over here and I think you and I will see a vast difference in the pair. They shall have a far better future and opportunities to look forward to than you and I ever did."

"We shall see about that. I have my doubts. It wouldn't surprise me if we wake up one day to find Dan has left and gone back to England without a word. I think there must be a woman behind his desire to return. You know what he's like when it comes to women. Reminds me of you when you were a young man."

"Yes, and he'll have a new girlfriend in a week. And if you say he's like me as a young man, well, who knows, maybe he'll meet his

Julia over here. Boys marry their mums, they say. I'm told that there are a number of good schools around here where the children can carry on where they left off back home. So, they're not going to suffer because of the move."

Dad was determined to make Mum understand. He began to make inquiries about the schooling available for us. He found that the nearest higher educational establishment was in Ribérac and was called the Vocational High School Armaud Daniel. It was some 13 kilometers from where we were to live. Maybe going to school would start to bring some sense of order and routine to our lives.

A few days after our arrival, we were invited to a meeting of the residents, many of whom were pensioners and would have no idea about schooling for young people, unless they had Grandchildren. We later found out that this was a gathering greatly applauded and laden with hyperbole. Everyone had their chance to speak about their properties; what was right and what wasn't. This was our first introduction to what we hoped was going to be a better life than the one we'd left behind, where they would get to know us and we them. It was meant to be a convivial gathering, where drinks and food was served and everyone expected to join in the conversation, both in French and English, bearing in mind that many residents were English. I couldn't help but think they were just showing off. And taking the chance to complain more about Henry.

"We had so much trouble before with Henry, and how he let us down, with all his lies and troubles. He would tell us what he thought we wanted to hear, and about what he had worked on while we were away and then, when we returned, we'd find he'd made virtually no changes."

The people from number four then started their list of criticisms.

"He had children just like you," the lady said.

I took offence at that, since I was now sixteen—hardly a child.

"When nobody was here, the children used the tennis courts and swimming pool," the lady went on. "We don't want yours to develop that habit. It just makes for additional work. What's more, Henry would never repair any damage his children caused."

Then the rather more up market couple in number two, Mr. and Mrs. Loader started moaning:

"We were just flabbergasted by the way our lawns were cut," the husband told us. "You'd have thought the man had used a rotovator instead of a lawnmower. We never had such trouble with our gardener back in Islington."

At this point, Dad asked, "Can you tell us why Henry is no longer here? It seems that you must have put up with him for a considerable length of time."

"Yes," said the lady from number two. "And the need for him to go to hospital came at a most inappropriate moment, as we were just about to have the matters aired publicly. It was at that time Henry was taken into the hospital with a serious bowel condition. Therefore, Mr. and Mrs. Loader agreed to visit him in the hospital to suggest that we must have help in some form or another, as the place had begun to look uncared for and that was in only two weeks. 'After all, Henry,' I told him, 'we don't want the complex to go to rack and ruin.' He was very upset and only agreed to go, after a suitable financial release settlement **had** been made. He said he would leave Chez Mouzy when he was released from the hospital. After all, his family was now grown up and left home."

Mum, my brother, and I sat listening intently to all of these horror stories. Mr. Banagee, who lived in number 6, did not complain about a thing. He was happy here and he wished us well in our new home, work, and school.

I must say, I felt sorry for poor Henry. After all, his illness was more than likely the reason for his neglect.

We found out that Dad's job would entail:

- Care of the swimming pool.

- Cutting the grass.

- Making sure the complex was safe and secure. (Apparently, there was a large contingent of gypsies in the area, who were renowned for stealing anything they could lay their hands upon.)

- Tree cutting.

- Watering gardens when their occupants were not in residence.
- Maintaining the complex driveways.
- Overseeing the wear and tear of the tennis courts.
- Tree-cutting and gardening, where necessary.

This was a considerable list for just one man to manage, plus, he had the responsibility of looking after seven houses when unoccupied.

For all this effort, he was to be paid the grand total of 600 Euro per month. Not much for 2010.

Mind you, Dad didn't appear to be put off by the residents and their awkward ways of demanding things.

"You know, I feel that you may have had a rather difficult time before, but, I think you will like us and find that if we say we'll do something, it will be done and done properly," Dad said addressing the residents.

"Well, thank goodness for that," commented the man from number five. "Of course, you will be on a trial basis for the first three months, and if at the end of that time we are unsatisfied with your quality of work, I fear you will be let go."

I was mortified to hear my parents being spoken to in this way. How rude and disrespectful these people were. However, Dad seemed to be taking all this capricious nonsense in stride. Dan said little, however, I found all this attitude to be far beyond my family's interpretation.

"My wife will be happy to help if anyone would like housework done," Dad told them. "I believe some of your homes are let out to visitors, so, if you would like her to do the changeovers, she will be more than happy to do it."

I froze as I had heard nothing of this from either Mum or Dad. But I guessed they must have discussed it previously and used their offer to impress the residents. I can't imagine Mum agreeing to this and it must have taken all the effort in her body to look pleasant as these words came out of my Dad's mouth.

Another thing we learned that night: We had no idea of how cheap the wine was in France and red, white, and rosé was imbibed freely by the residents. Our drinking habits by comparison left much to be desired but, to be fair, it didn't take long before ours began to mimic theirs.

The evening continued with more revelations and curses about poor Henry's previous misdemeanors, but, as the company drank more and more wine, the evening softened and we felt happier and more welcome.

But still, we wondered, what were we going to do about our dilapidated home. It really was a disaster zone and a dangerous one at that. Dad called a family meeting to make a long list of what the priorities should be. Our Dad was such a caring, thoughtful, timid man who loved us all very much. I wondered at times how he put up with Mum, who always seemed to be finding things wrong and who had a unique interpretation on negativity.

"Of course, you realize that I shall have to spend a great deal of time working around the residents' requirements," Dad said. "And, Julia, if you're asked to start to work in the houses, there will be even less time to spend helping out in getting this place into some sort of liveable condition."

"If I'm asked. Yeah, funny, I don't remember being asked to do this by you in the first place," she snapped back. "And I certainly don't remember volunteering."

Top of the list of to-dos with our house had to be the roof, where the whole structure had collapsed into the fifth bedroom. It wasn't needed as a bedroom, but the difficulty was that the damaged roof section was pulling the still relatively stable part of the roof down on the far side. Dad spent what felt like ages trying to secure a date and time for the roofers to come and do the job. It made us realize that getting anything done over here, was a bit along the lines of 'we'll do it tomorrow.' And that 'tomorrow' rarely ever arrived.

Eventually, the roofers showed up and it took them over a week to do the job. It cost a fortune that I know we didn't have, and that was to do just about half of what was required.

"I shall need to get a bank loan for all the things that need doing here," Dad said.

"Well, if that's the case, then let's get on with it," Mum told him. "We can go down to the town today and see what the bank manager has to say. Seeing a load of foreigners walk in may put him off lending us money. To be honest, love, I think the place is too big for us anyway. Perhaps we should look for something a bit smaller around here. Something smaller but actually liveable. There does seem to be a huge number of empty places in the area."

Dad ignored her comment and went on with his plan to go to town.

Everything was costing a good deal more than had been estimated and was much more expensive than back home. I became quite morose and Mother was constantly telling me to stop sulking and to pull myself together. That didn't help one bit, in fact, it made me resent her and the place even more.

"You don't need to make such a show of your distaste for what we've come to, Maisie," Mum said to me. "Dad has a job at long last and you, young lady, ought to be pleased about that. Do you hear me? Look at me when I'm talking to you! Did you hear what I just said?"

"Yes, Mum," I replied. "How could I not have heard? I think the whole complex probably heard."

"Maisie!"

Dan kept looking at me sneakily, as if to say: 'I'm right there with you, sis. Bloody hell, what are you and I going to do over here?'

After Mum stormed out of the room, Dan and I walked outside to get some fresh air.

"Way to go, Maisie!" Dan said. He patted me on the back. "You really showed Mum back there."

"I didn't mean to lose my cool," I said. "But we've left all of our friends behind for Dad's trumped-up job with discerning employers, who couldn't give a toss about us. Those toffee-nosed snobs we are expected to kowtow to, won't suit me at all. I just wish we had some friends here. Or someone visited us. I feel like sometimes you need what's familiar to help you face what isn't."

"That was deep, Maisie, really deep," Dan said. I couldn't tell if he was making fun of me or not. "

And believe me," Dan continued. "At that meeting I wanted to punch all the guys there. And go jump in their pool. Take a swim. Take a leak, oh man that would be something, wouldn't it! Would serve them right! I couldn't stand the way they talked about us. Treating us with such disdain. I'm not putting up with that. But hey, maybe things will settle down when the house gets fixed up a bit more. It's so awful, have you ever seen the like of it? It's as though we were living in the dark ages. I tell you, Maisie, I for one won't be staying over here unless the picture improves."

"Dad did see this place before he moved us all over here, didn't he?" I asked.

"Yes, I think so, but he didn't give much thought to us, by the looks of it, did he? Does he really think that you and I will be able, not only to learn the language, but to get work? There doesn't seem to be any work around here for young people anyway."

"Come on, Dan, don't be like that," I said. "You know Dad worships the ground we walk on. Especially you. He's done it to benefit all of us."

"I can't see much sign of that now, Maisie, and as soon as this next year's done, I shall be off. I had just started going out with such a nice girl. She was very pretty and had everything in all the right places, if you know what I mean."

"Gross, I don't want to know about your love life."

"Why not? If you'd like, we can talk about your boyfriend James instead?"

"He's not my boyfriend. Even if he was, that wouldn't matter anymore."

I felt my eyes well up a little bit with tears.

"Sorry. I'm just so, here, let's go for a walk, get to know the place."

We walked a few hundred meters in relative silence.

"Do you think they'll let us ever use the swimming pool, Dan?" I asked. "If we asked nicely?"

"Oh, I'm going for a swim whether they want me to or not. I'm not asking nobody for permission."

"Dan. Please don't. You'll get Dad in trouble."

"Yeah, and? What's the worst that can happen, they send us home? Sounds like a good plan to me."

"Dan. Please don't."

As we continued walking, I looked around and thought how inspiring the place could be. I imagined with a few changes and money spent here and there, the place could be made to look quite splendid, instead of its current semblance of a pile of rubble. There were so many rooms, and we'd never had a scullery before. The bedrooms were huge, with those long Normandy-type windows, and I much admired the lovely Périgord rooftops. Their design was stately and magnificent, shaped like a pyramid but with flat tops. The colour was stunning: a soft light brick orange with tinges of black here and there. A gentle breeze blew as we meandered out through the narrow walkway and away from the complex.

The day, although hot, was proving to be quite an adventure as Dan and I travelled down to the main road between the copious woodland on either side of the lane. We chatted away about everything and nothing.

As we walked across the main road to the other side we found ourselves walking down a progressively narrow lane with hedgerows about six feet tall. We could see the green hills beyond as the day was still now and the vista gin clear. There were a couple of dogs barking in the distance—talking to each other, I reckoned. I glanced at Dan as he walked in front to dash over to see what had moved in the hedges. He had the look of an Adonis, his body lithe and strong, this brother of mine. He liked to pretend that all of this came naturally, but I'm pretty sure he would do push-ups and crunches in secret. I was certain it wouldn't be too long before he found himself a girlfriend who would fall desperately in love with him over here. That might change his mind about going back to England—I couldn't bear it, if that did happen.

The lane became even narrower as we wandered and passed an abundance of better tended grapevines. I was beginning to think this was not such a bad place after all. I realised that Dan and I would have to make the most of it. The option of turning around and going back to England seemed less and less possible.

"You know, Dan, perhaps it won't be so bad once we get to school and begin to learn the language and speak it better than we do now," I suggested. "But I am missing James already. He said that he would come over to visit for the holidays next year. I know he didn't want me to leave. He once said he wanted me to be his real girlfriend, not just a schoolboy and girl crush. I've always liked him, but not in that way. But now I wonder if I do. If maybe I always have?"

"So, he was your boyfriend, huh? Well, maybe it's as well you've moved away from him. You can have a new start over here and you could even meet a Frenchman. Ooh, la, la. You know what they say about French kissing, don't you? Doing that can't compare with what the schoolboys do back home."

"Oh, shut up! You're the one who will likely get caught up with a French tart."

"You mean the patisseries, do you?"

We goaded each other endlessly, when suddenly we came across a farm where a big black-and-white dog was creating havoc. As we moved nearer to the gate, we felt threatened and both of us stood as still as statues for fear of an attack.

"It's okay. He's tied up so he can't get us," Dan said.

The farmer came to see what all the fuss was about. At the sight and sound of his master, the dog stopped his racket. He was a beautiful dog; a bit like a sheepdog crossed with a spaniel, and he reminded me of Soukie, my dear dog from years back, who I'd raised and trained and fed all by myself as a little girl. Tending it on my own, was the only way I was allowed to have a dog. Soukie died after being run over, and that broke my heart. Hardly left my room for ages, except for school.

The good looking farmer approached us.

"Bonjour," I said in my best French accent. Dan stayed quiet and in the background.

"Bonjour. Are you the people who have just moved into Chez Mouzy?" the farmer asked. "I'm sorry about the noise from Benny. He's not only our guard dog but he's also a very good sheepdog, to boot."

"Yes, our parents are there now trying to get the place into some sort of order," Dan told him. "It's so run-down and part of the roof is missing."

"Shouldn't you two be helping them, then?" he replied in perfect English.

"Yes, but we were just having a walk to familiarize ourselves with the surroundings," Dan said. "It's very beautiful here."

"Are you English?" I asked in a guarded way, for I didn't want to antagonize the man who was to be our neighbour. I know I was still only sixteen, but my seventeenth birthday was not far off, and this man was very handsome and reminded me of a school teacher I'd known in the seniors. I'd had a massive crush on him and found it very difficult to concentrate on the lessons when he was teaching our class.

"Yes, I am from England. Would the two of you like to come in and have a look around?"

"Yes, please," I said hastily.

Always in a hurry to jump in where angels feared to tread. I had heard that somewhere once and wrote it out in a journal of mine in the prettiest cursive writing that I could create with a beautiful scarlet ink pen. Mother used to say a far less poetic version when she'd say to me, "You will get yourself into a whole lot of trouble if you don't start thinking before you act, my girl." She was right. Driving aside, Dan was actually the more cautious one, me more of the risk-taker. He took after Dad more and me more after Mother. She was feisty, Dad timid and conservative. But I felt things maybe changing over here in France. Dan seemed more confident and aware of trouble and how to get into it than ever before. He was more prepared to take risks. Some of my confidence had taken a knock without James close by.

"Maisie, I hate to say this, but I think we should be getting back to help Mum and Dad out," Dan added.

"Oh, come on, it won't hurt to just have a quick look around now, will it?"

"That may not be so," the farmer explained, "As this is a large farm and I have two thousand acres. But, come on in, you two. Just peek at the animals and the lovely landscape from the house."

"Come on, Dan, half an hour isn't going to make much difference," I persuaded my brother, and in we went through huge, rusty, black austere iron gates at the entrance to the farmhouse. It was an amazing sight. A gigantic house, traditionally French, with three storeys, a central front door and three sets of large windows on either side of it, on every floor.

"This is impressive, Mr., what should we call you?"

"Just call me Ralph—Ralph Waterman," the farmer replied. "I live here alone, as my wife returned to England. She didn't take to the farming life and missed England so much that she decided to go back to the house we had kept."

"So, you manage two thousand acres all by yourself?"

"No, not quite. I have a couple of local farm hands to help me with the few cattle and my multitude of sheep. They take quite a bit of looking after, what with the anti-fly treatment and the deworming. And, I can tell you it's hard work running a farm."

He showed us the cow sheds and could see numerous sheep in the fields below.

"The animals sleep out in the better weather and come inside during the winter months,"

Ralph said.

"How long have you been over here?" I asked.

"It's been about five years. The farm and equipment were being sold together and it was cheap. My wife Maureen and I had imagined that it would be an idyllic life, compared with the rat race we'd left behind in England. We both worked in the city, in London, and made plenty of money on the stock exchange. But, sadly, our life here together was not to be. Maureen couldn't get her head around the intricacies of running a farm. She liked the peace and quiet but, that was about it. I told her that I couldn't pack up and leave it now, as we would have lost too much money invested in the project. Just didn't work out, but hey, that's life sometimes. How about you two? What brought you and your family over here?"

My brother quickly proved that he still had a voice and piped up with, "Our dad was made redundant and, because of his age, couldn't find another job like the one he'd had. He tried to find other types of work, but was unsuccessful and eventually he started looking in France, and now handles all estate matters at the complex in Saint-Severin. And, speaking of which, we'd better get back and help our parents out."

"Oh, not to worry," Ralph told us. "I may be able to come and give you a hand, and my brother will be over here soon for the summer. He's a skilled craftsman in carpentry and roofing, what a bit of luck that is."

"It was good to meet you both," Ralph continued. "I must pop over and say hello to your family. Perhaps you all would like to come and have a meal here? Do you have a telephone in the house?"

"Yes, we do," I said quickly.

"It's a bit antiquated, doesn't always work," Dan said.

"Works just fine for me," I said. "I can give you my mobile phone number. That would be nice, I'll tell them that we have met our neighbour and that you would like to meet up with them."

Numbers were exchanged and we hurried back to the mess we called a home.

"I think you gave him too much information about our situation," Dan started. "He's a stranger and you were telling him all of our business."

"You're one to talk. When you eventually opened your mouth, you said plenty. Don't be so critical of me."

The date was arranged after Ralph called us the next day. We were so pleased to be asked to go into someone's home and to get to know a bit more about the country and its people. When the day arrived for us to go, everyone was excited and enthralled to be meeting a 'gentleman', or at least that was the impression Mother had of him, without even meeting the man. However, I think Mum was probably correct in deducing that Ralph was a 'gentleman farmer' from what Dan and I had told her.

Arriving after the ten-minute drive, we were welcomed in the most gratifying way. Effusive and genuine platitudes were conducted by us and Ralph. Mum had put on her best dress, but Dan and Dad had refrained from making much of an effort, for which I chastised them both. How could they be so sloppy?

As Ralph took us inside, we noticed the large, beautiful carved wooden inner front door, and the sight in front of us was nothing short of sensational. The room was old and smelled musty, but beautifully furnished in old dark-stained oak wood. The whole of the downstairs area was carpeted throughout with thick piled Persian carpets and rugs of all shapes and sizes. We had a glimpse of the splendour of them the first time we came. The colours were amazing; some multi-coloured and others thick, plain beige, the sort you want to sink your bare feet into. I was mesmerized by the place. We were not shown upstairs. Ralph said he would show us all of that when we came next time. I wondered if he was hiding something up there, he didn't want us to see. But then again, my imagination always did run away with me. I could imagine me and James doing one of our Sherlock Holmes missions, sneaking up there to investigate what would turn out to be nothing special.

We ate and drank the dinner prepared by his housekeeper, Lauren. Drinking alcohol was becoming a bit of a regular habit with me and the family. It was a local custom new to us.

"I'm Ralph Waterman, late of the stock exchange back in dear 'old Blighty'," was how he introduced himself to my parents. He proceeded to tell them all about the reason why he and his wife had come here. I could see my mother fidgeting the way she always did when she wanted to say something yet was having difficulty getting a word in edgeways. Her anxiety was the result of wishing to know more about his private life. I was so relieved when she chose to keep quiet on that front and only asked about his farming activities and how he coped with all of the chores.

After this, we continued to eat and drink. When I looked at my watch, I couldn't believe how quickly time had passed throughout the pleasant evening, in the company of this delicious man about whom I wanted to get to know more.

What was left of the evening went swimmingly, and although I still couldn't gauge Ralph's age, I didn't think I was too young to have a 'thing' with him. As we left, he thanked us all for a fabulous evening and made a promise to be in contact again soon, and to help Dad with the roof when his brother arrived. When he kissed me goodbye on both cheeks, I thought he lingered a bit longer than he had done with my mother. He put his arms on my shoulders as he did it and I certainly didn't feel like a kid. I felt natural and comfortable and I wished to be held in his arms longer. To look into his eyes. To return the kiss, but this time on his lips.

"Come on you two, you've got school tomorrow," Dad said. "It's time for bed.

Both Dan and I looked daggers at Dad for saying such a thing. He made us sound like we were still little children.

CHAPTER THREE

Meeting Ralph Seriously

"With a new day comes strength and new thoughts."
~ Eleanor Roosevelt

I woke suddenly to the sound of an alarming noise coming from under my bedroom window. People were arguing and voices were raised. When I got washed and dressed, I went downstairs to hear more clearly. It was our mother rowing furiously with someone.

"I will tell you now, Mrs. Mountfield, my husband has enough to do without you getting onto him about the state of the lawns. He has every intention of getting around to putting the weed killer and feed onto them, as soon as he can fit it in with all the other jobs he has to do."

"Well, I know he has lots to do," Mrs. Mountfield went on, "but you tell him from me that I shall be expecting them done very soon or the weather will catch up with us and the grass will simply shrivel."

"I shall tell him no such thing. If you want to make trouble, you tell him yourself."

This was just the beginning of troubles between dad and our neighbours, instigated by Mum. Dad always tried to placate the disgruntled people, whilst Mum seemed hell-bent on making things worse, and managed to create havoc.

Dad was pleased that we had met Ralph, who appeared to want to be our friend, as well as our neighbour. We had already been entertained by Ralph, and his hospitality was about to be repaid. He was expected the following day. Mum as anxious to repay the visit as I was to see him. She busied herself for hours on end trying to make the best of the house, that was still only what could be described as 'a ruin'. She was clever with her hands and flower arranging was top of the agenda. Her culinary skills weren't too bad, either, with the exception of when she went on an eat healthily bender and we starved. It was at times like this when she was busy and planning, that she seemed to blossom. I think her main issue was she had not made any real friends since we came over here.

The kitchen was quite small compared to the vast bedrooms, which were abnormally huge. "There is not enough space for two people in my kitchen," she would say, emphasizing the 'my'.

"Get yourself in here and give me a hand, girl," she called out from the kitchen. "I can't be expected to do the bloody lot by myself."

"I thought you didn't want us in *your* kitchen," I said. I'll admit, I had a little bit of attitude in my voice.

"Just get in here, will ya? Like right now!"

"OK, Mum, I'm more than happy to help you. You didn't have to raise your voice to get me there."

"Don't you back-chat me. You're becoming a little brat. You've been real cheeky since we got here and think you are too big for your boots. You're not an adult yet, you know, so mind your tongue."

"Yes, Mum. What shall I do? Would you like me to peel the spuds and do the other vegetables?"

"That would be fine; the spuds are in the scullery."

"Where do you want me to put the veg when I've done them?" I asked.

"Don't ask such stupid questions. Where do you think?"

Her patience with me was clearly running out, so, I thought it better to keep quiet.

"Dan, would you give us a hand here, and talk some bloody sense into your sister," she said.

"I'm not sure I can fit in there," Dan said. "What do you want me to do?"

"You could lay the table for five, for a start," Mum told him.

The place looked like a picture when our guest finally showed up. I don't know how we did it. Mum had put on her best dress and her makeup gave her a new look, a sort of tasteful glow. I was wearing a dress that me feel like a million dollars. One that made me feel like a woman, not a girl. Even Dan made an effort this time, wearing a nice shirt and combing his hair. Dad looked as he always did, having not bothered much. He did have a bath in the old enamel thing which was all we had to keep clean, apart from the huge and deep, square butler sinks. There was no shower, and I reminded Dad constantly that the time had come for one of these to be installed. After all we had passed the three month probation period.

"You will just have to be patient, Maisie," Dad said. "I have yet to be paid and we're still living off our savings."

"When, for heaven's sake, are they going to pay you?" I asked. "It's been more than three months since we came here and you've been working so hard and putting in long hours."

I hated the washing facilities here, and made a statement to my family that I'd be better off back home, where at least we had a decent bathroom, with a shower and a modern bath, instead of the old enamel one here, with bits of enamel missing.

"Just you behave yourself, Maisie," Mum told me. "You ought to know your place by now."

"You're not a child any longer and your father and I have enough to worry about without you causing trouble."

I stayed quiet after that outburst and felt a bit guilty, but not guilty enough to apologize.

"I'm saying to you two younguns, and you Mother, that he will have to accept us the way we are," Dad told us. "We're not putting on airs and graces just for a farmer, and an English one at that. Rare as rocking horse shit, to see an Englishman running a French farm. All seems a bit odd to me."

"Odd for someone to be making a living from his work?" Mum said. I wasn't sure if Dad heard her or if he pretended not to. The doorbell rang and I was the first to dash to answer it.

"Good evening, young lady!" Ralph said. "How very nice you look."

I must have blushed. I had made quite an effort. Not only the best dress I could find in the wardrobe, and put my long hair on top of my head tied with a diamante clip and I thought it looked most sophisticated.

"Do come in, sir," I said hurriedly. "Please come and take a seat in here, the only decent room we have. We call it the sitting room. It's the only place with some semblance of order."

I waited for him to greet me properly. He took hold of my shoulders again and kissed me softly on both cheeks.

"How pleased I am to see you again, sir," my Dad said walking toward the doorway. He held out a hand to shake Ralph's. Mum just smiled and nonchalantly said hello as if this was an ordinary night, an ordinary way for the house and her face to look.

"Welcome to our home, our humble home that needs much tender loving care and repair," Dad went on. "As you will see, there is an immense amount of work to do. I hadn't seen the accommodation when I signed on the dotted line to come and work over here, so as you can imagine, it was all a bit of a surprise when we arrived and were shown our place of residence."

My father was lying. I could feel my face reddening. He told us that he had seen the place when he was over on one of his reconnoitres. He also said he was taken to see it by the agent who employed him. It was so unlike my father to be untruthful. Unless this was the truth and he had lied to us before. Either way, the stories weren't adding up.

Mum came to the fore and said, "I hope you like beef and beer, Mr. ... Oh, sorry I don't know your last name."

"It's Waterman," our visitor said. "Ralph Waterman."

"Do come and sit over here, Mr. Waterman," Dad invited.

"Please, call me Ralph, it's so much less formal."

Ralph revealed a huge bottle of brandy and handed it to Dad. Mum was given a massive bouquet of the most glorious flowers I had ever seen, tied up in a raffia string. There were mauve ones and pink-and-white ones and an array of green foliage—enough for a small hedge.

The French have a penchant for flower display.

The evening was going well until Mum started to get way too personal with Ralph.

"Did you say you lived all alone now, Mr. Waterman? Surely that can't be right for a young man trying to make a go of farming over here. Maisie said you told her that you had no experience in that line before coming to France."

"Yes, that's true, we had no experience at all when we took over the farm, and moreover it was one that was not particularly viable."

"Well, why on earth did you decide to settle on that place?" Mum asked.

"Julia, I don't think you should be asking such personal questions as that," Dad quickly interjected.

"I'm seeing if we can learn a couple things, he can teach you how to make some money."

"Julia, please. Let's ease up on the questions. He is our guest after all."

But Ralph was generously spirited and said, "Oh, I don't mind. In fact, it's rather good to have someone talking to me in a natural sort of way. I only have the farmhands, and a lady that does the house and a bit of cooking for me to converse with. None of them speak much English, so it's a bit of a struggle. Feels nice to hear English again, so ask away!"

"Alright, well, my husband will never ask this because he's got too much pride," Mum said.

"Julia."

"But we need help with the roof. Any chance you could give us an hour or two with that, Ralph?"

"Ralph, sorry, I know you are busy. Please don't feel like you owe us anything or that you have to say yes to this."

"Oh no, of course I will help out. I was planning on it. Do you know the materials required? I don't think it will be cheap, that's why you don't want to get yourself a builder. They are so expensive and sometimes unreliable, sadly that's been my experience. My brother arrives in a week or two and I'm sure he will also lend a hand."

"That's the ticket, Ralph!" Mum said. "Thank you so much. Do have some more wine. Do you like it? The neighbours told us about it. A nice fine red wine called Roche Mazet cabernet sauvignon."

"As cheap as chips from the local supermarket," Dad added.

"I have to say, this is a very good red wine. I tend to go for the specialties, and they cost a fortune, even over here. Mind you, I shall try this one when my brother arrives and see if he can tell the difference between the expensive and this one. He is a wannabe sommelier."

"What's that?" I asked.

"It is a person who specializes and is an expert in wine tasting," Ralph said.

"My word, a gentleman farmer and a sommelier roofer, you certainly are a fascinating pair," Mum said.

"Let's not get carried away," Ralph said with a laugh. "I said he *reckons* he is a bit of an expert with wines. Definitely not certified or anything like that."

I looked over at Mum and for the first time of the night I realized she was flirting with him. It made me angry, not only because of my growing crush, but that she would be so obvious right in front of Dad. I looked over at Dad and again he either didn't care or was pretending not to.

"Everyone here drinks wine with their meals and it seems like they do from an early age," I said, trying to insert myself back into the conversation.

Ralph smiled at me.

"Yes, that's probably true, and the reason why they die young from liver failure."

Dad piped up, "Well, Ralph, we've all got to die of something. Heart disease in the UK is still rife. Many people are needing bypass surgery because they had a heart attack. And furthermore, many don't make it to surgery dying before they get the operation."

"Do pack in talking about disease and death, honey," Mum told him. "Please forgive my husband's rather bizarre attempt at small talk. It's certainly not his specialty. We're here to have a happy evening."

The evening jogged along with a great deal of banter. I hoped that Ralph was not feeling overwhelmed by us, none of our family being shrinking violets. Especially Mum. Even Dad, who was more introverted than the rest of us, had plenty to talk about as the night rolled on. I reckoned he liked Ralph. When the time came to wind the evening up, Ralph offered to help clear the dishes and wash up. Of course, his offer was declined by Mum, who said, "That's what kids are for. Come along, Maisie, give me a hand."

I had never been more mad at her in my life. *"That's what kids are for?"* Treating me like I were 10-years-old right in front of him. He'll never think of me as anything more than a little girl with her little chores to do. I bet he kisses me on the forehead when he leaves. And I'll curtsy like a little girl at a dance recital. I felt my non-existent romance crumbling around me and it was all her fault.

We said our goodbyes and Ralph offered to return the compliment again soon, for which I was delighted. But this time there was no kiss goodbye. I was devastated, but I tried to keep a smile on my face. I waved goodbye when he turned around at the end of the drive. Off he drove in his Mercedes Benz. He had to be the only farmer in these parts that could afford to drive a car like that. I went into the kitchen and picked up one of the dirty plates. I put it under the tap and began to cry.

CHAPTER FOUR

French Schooling

"Twenty years from now you will be more disappointed in the things
that you didn't do than the ones you did do."
~ Mark Twain

We turned up for our first day halfway through the Summer term at the school for senior students. It was all so strange and uncomfortable. Dad had found us a school in Ribérac called The Vocational High School Arnaud Daniel. It was about 13.1 kilometers from Saint-Severin and a sixteen-minute car drive through winding country lanes.

Dan kept on about how daft it was to make him go to school when he only had less than a year to go.

"That's not the point," Dad said. "You may decide to stay on and get decent marks, and even go to university, and then, son, perhaps you may just find yourself a job that actually pays enough for you to survive on."

I think that kind of future was the last thing on Dan's mind. He was more concerned about the girlfriend he'd left behind in England and those he hoped to meet right here. We entered through the massive school gates. They were old and rusty and looked a bit like the ones

Ralph had, the tall gates around the farm gloriously protecting his property. As we walked towards the front door of the establishment, we were greeted by the beautiful Headmistress of the school who looked like a woman you'd find in an advertisement for Dior.

"Welcome to our school," she went on. "I am the Headmistress here. Come with me and I will introduce you to your classes and teachers. We 'av several English pupils here as there are many British families now living in the Dordogne."

When she was out of earshot, Dan leaned over to me.

"Blimey, why didn't we have teachers like her back home?" Dan whispered. "It might even tempt me to stay over here."

"Oh, for heaven's sake, stop moaning about everything Dan."

"I'm not moaning. I just said that I might stay if the women are all like her. Wouldn't mind making her moan, if you know what I mean."

"You grow more disgusting by the day, Dan."

We were taken through a long and windy corridor that smelt of disinfectant. I couldn't help thinking someone must have been sick and the stuff used to disguise the smell. The first class we came to was mine. As we entered through the heavy wooden door, I spotted about twenty desks, each with a young girl sitting behind it. They all stared hard at me, until their headmistress told them to get off their backsides and greet their new classmate. I felt extremely embarrassed and intimidated by the unfriendly looking bunch before me. Not one of them smiled. I wanted to turn around and head straight back to England, where the kids were friendly and good pals of mine. In a moment like this, you forget that back home wasn't perfect. You forget that there was bullying. Those memories are washed away and you only remember home with the pleasant glow of nostalgia.

I was ushered to the only empty desk in the room. As the class began to sit down in their chairs again, making a heck of a din as the chair legs scraped along the highly polished and shining parquet floor. Miss Charente told them to be more ladylike when they maneuvered in and out of their seats.

"Our new recruit is Maisie Patterson, and she is from England. Now, I want you all to make friends with her as quickly as possible. That way, ma cheries, you will learn to speak the English so much better than you do right now."

Dan was standing outside the classroom where she had asked him to wait. As the head left the room, another slim, well-dressed young woman came dashing in past us. In French, she declared how sorry she was to be late or something like it. I was pleased with myself for managing to pick up a few French words said.

He was taken to his class, where there were only a dozen boys all his age and close to finishing their schooling years, and taking three or four Advanced-levels. Some would also stay on at school to complete the Baccalaureate.

I waited for him when the first day was over. "Well, what did you think of that?" I greeted Dan.

"It was OK, I suppose," he admitted. "I'm not really that interested now as I shall soon be looking for work and I won't find it down here."

We walked for a couple of steps in silence.

"Actually, truth be told, I'm feeling quite depressed," Dan said. "I think I should have stayed back home. I should have been stronger and told Dad and Mum that I would find somewhere to live and not come here to this god-damned awful backwater."

"What on earth are you talking about? Dan, you're a bright boy with so much going for you. You will be able to go back to England if you want to. Mum and Dad won't stop you once you've finished schooling. I had a problem with the language today, although the teacher did much of it in English to benefit me, I think. Thank God for that."

"It was the same on my end. The best thing about my class was the teacher. She is well fit with a fabulous pair of legs, and spoke very good English, and she kept smiling at me. I think she fancies me."

"Don't be daft! You know that's forbidden territory."

"Forbidden but fun. Maybe I could take her back to the pool, do two forbidden things at once."

"Your imagination certainly has progressed over here."

"Anyhow, I've decided I still don't like it here. Even if all the teachers are babes. I shall go into town tonight and get drunk. At least the beer is cheap. That's one thing this place has going for it."

"For heaven's sake, change the record. I'm sick of hearing you cracking on and on. Do you think I'm happy here? No. I still miss James. I miss my friends. I miss not having a language barrier. But I'm trying. We have to try to make it work. And my goodness, Dan, you only have to make it work for what, eight more months? Then you can go to University, you can go anywhere in the world. I don't want to hear it anymore."

"Wow, Maisie, sounds like you woke up on the wrong side of the bed."

Mum was waiting at the end of the poorly made-up road. The pavements were risible and you couldn't walk on them for fear of twisting your ankle. The road, if you could call it that, was non-existent, and cars had no respect for pedestrians who were attempting to walk along the pavements, especially the schoolchildren.

"Well, you two, how did you get on today?" Mum asked, grinning from ear to ear. I think that was an attempt to ease the blow of us having to return to school.

"It was okay, Mum, but a good job that the teacher spoke in English quite often, that helped a lot," I told her. "I think I'm going to find learning better French quite hard, but I'm willing to give it a go. There are a few English girls in my class, so that helped. One of them lives where we do. Her name's Helen and I think she and I will get on well."

"That's good love. How about you, Dan? Was it the same for you?"

"It was okay, but I shall be leaving soon, so I'm not too bothered about this late learning."

"What are you talking about, son?" Mum asked. "Of course, you're going to stay on and get your Baccalaureate."

"No, Mum, I've had enough of learning and I'm not so sure I want to stay here. I think I'd be better off back home."

"This is your home, for now anyway. You seemed keen enough to come over and you've not been here long enough to know what you really want. You have to give it a proper chance."

"I was never keen to come over here."

"You were always talking about leaving, Dan. Australia. The United States. Don't act like you were always happy in England. You always think the grass is greener on the other side."

"I never said France! I never said I wanted to move somewhere else in Europe. And certainly not here. There's nothing going on, especially not for young people. Let's face it, you never see a bloody car or van pass by after eight in the evening unless it's visitors coming and going in the complex. It's a deadbeat place and not for young people."

"Dan, I'm going to say this calmly so you can hear each and every one of my words. And if you bark back at me, God help me, you'll really know what it's like to have nothing to do, because you will be grounded. You hear me? Now look, we're all going through it. You think I'm happy? Huh? Your dad still hasn't been paid and he doesn't have the backbone to fight it. I'm in a kitchen that I can't turn around in. We don't even have a proper roof over our heads. And I have no friends here. But do you see me complaining? Do you hear me whining? So zip it."

Dan bit his tongue and sat with his arms crossed. We travelled the sixteen miles home, relapsed into an insulted silence. When we got in, Mum took Dan to one side and told him not to talk that way in front of me. "You will unsettle your sister if you keep on like this. You can do what you like when you're eighteen, but, you're not there yet, so just buckle down and keep your big mouth shut."

Dan told me about this later that night. He was full of rage and still so angry about it all.

It bothered me that my brother was behaving in this way.

"How the hell can I stay here for months, Maisie? It's hard for me to imagine another week here. I'm miserable. Every morning I wake up and don't want to get out of bed. I don't want to do another day. And each hour goes by so slowly. It's horrible! I don't know how

I can do it. I just want you to know that if I disappear one day without saying goodbye, don't be mad at me. It's because I have to. When the right moment presents itself, I shall probably make a run for it."

"Dan, stop talking like that! What do you think you're going to do, run away? Hop on a train?"

"I think it might be the best option at this point," Dan said.

He spoke with confidence and a certainty that scared me. I looked at him and the serious look melted away into a smile. He looked down at me.

"Want to come with?"

CHAPTER FIVE

The Residents

"Be happy in the moment, that's enough.
Each moment is all we need, not more."
~ Mother Teresa

Now, the people living either on a part or full-time basis on "the campus" (as we called it indoors), had a variety of personalities. The seven houses, were bought by 'Brits' and other nationalities. The residents tended to be here during the school term to avoid hordes of children in the towns. Some we had yet to meet.

Those we had met included Mr. Banagee. He was a lovely man, retired and living at number six with his wife. They preferred to rent the house rather than buy it. He told me this was because they didn't want all the hassle of trying to sell the place if they chose to move again. His wife, on the other hand, was a bit of a tartar and treated everyone around her as though they were her servants. The Banagees had obviously been used to having lots of money back in India and would certainly have had plenty of servants.

He always stopped to talk to me. It was clear from what he said about my schooling and future, that he held education in high regard. I was encouraged to work as studiously as I could and to gain qualifications. The only redeeming thing I could say about Mrs. Banagee was that the saris she wore were made of the most beautiful silks and the finest styles you could buy. It was such a pity that her good looks and superb dress sense did not match her personality.

"I think so many of you young people fail to see the importance of qualifications," Mr. Banagee advised. "You know, child, the world could be your oyster if you study hard and with more than one language under your belt, you will go far."

Mr. Banagee had been an academic and was world acclaimed for his studies and the books he'd written about the sacred sites of India. He had a voice on the world stage and was an advisor to UNESCO. I asked him why they had decided to come and live in France.

"Well, my dear, we were in London towards the end of my career and quite liked the UK and France, even more. The sunshine over here swung it for us. We had difficulty facing the British winters and the grey and wet days sometimes even in the summer. We therefore decided to move over here permanently. However, we only rent this house, well, that's how it is for the time being. In fact, the winters here can be very cold, so we tend to hitch up our caravan and head to Southern Spain when it gets more than a couple of 'oldies' can bare."

He was still an educated and studious man and was gathering information constantly to enable him to write yet another book about the history of this part of France and its inhabitants. He said that when it was published he would give me a signed copy. He told me that he always sought out new challenges and loved to learn about areas of which he had little knowledge. His wife would sometimes be heard raising her voice at him. She showed no shame; in her eyes, we were all inferior, because she came from a high caste.

I never heard her husband speak an unkind word about anyone. He treated everybody with respect and kindness, regardless of their background. I became very fond of this charming, mild-mannered man who, to some extent, reminded me of my own father; just with far more wealth and quiet confidence in himself.

It was a different story regarding the couple living in number three: Mr. and Mrs. Mountfield. He had been something in the city back home and she was a retired Justice of the Peace (a Magistrate under English law), until at the age of seventy she had to leave, according to the rules. Both were inordinate snobs. Their home was certainly one of the best on site and they stayed here permanently, only leaving to go back to England for holidays or to travel around Europe and beyond. They were very wealthy. Apart from his previous lucrative city job, I'm told that she had also been a high flyer. They had been left a large inheritance. He was an only child so got the lot, and a massive English estate was also in the offing. It was little wonder that their home was so opulent. There was no worry or jealousy on our family's part, but, they had little time for some residents and were known for occasional rude outbursts. They chose not to mix much with other residents and, to be honest, from the little I'd had to deal with them, they seemed happy that way. Their antipathy to neighbours was fully reciprocated. They were on the corner plot in relation to where the other houses were sited. This meant that to get to the swimming pool, residents whose houses were behind them, needed to go on the grass around their house. They expected a wide berth away from their house and this was strictly adhered to when others needed to swim.

Enough about them. It's good that the only contact we were likely to have was if poor Dad did something to annoy either of them. I don't think she will antagonize Mother again.

Now, it was a completely different story when it came to the two Frenchmen living together at number one, who were thoughtful and concerned for their neighbours. Apparently, they were both from Paris and had trained together in interior design at the Sorbonne. They were young and vibrant and owners of the biggest Pyrenean mountain dog I had ever seen. His name was Brutus, a fitting and stylish name indeed. He was brown and white, and dribbled and growled a lot and stunk to high heaven. I loved Brutus and every chance that came along, I would wander over and ask if I could walk him. They were only too pleased for me to do it, as both worked long hours and were always doing home visits, which took the longest time. I'm unsure if it was me taking Brutus or him taking me for a walk. Our walks became a habit, twice a day during weekends and school holidays, but after school re-started, I only managed to make it once a day. He loved it when I turned up to take him out, he'd get so excited and leap about, almost knocking me over. Then he'd sort of whine, as if to say, 'Thank you for coming' and I would get a slobbery lick and his favourite squeaky toy as a gift. I felt privileged to have been given the front door key. When we first came, both the boys called on us with a cake made in honour of our arrival. They were so kind and generous, giving us a huge amount of information regarding the local infrastructure and information about doctors and dentists, and the library. I couldn't help but think: what a shame Mother Nature had taken out of the running two exceptional and eligible men, as these two were the best-looking young men I had seen in a long time, with the exception of Ralph, of course. Their home reflected their profession. I thought for me, the style was a bit over the top, but then again we all had differing tastes.

One chap called Oliver, was tall and camp, however, his partner, Claude, was medium sized and unless you knew it, you'd never have guessed he was gay. They both had immaculate dress sense. They wore fashionable clothes seemingly bought from expensive shops, and an air of graciousness and authority about them, which I guessed had made them successful businessmen. Dan and I thought it wonderful to have two such fellows living next door. Theirs was the nearest house to ours. Their business was conducted in Perigueux and the surrounding districts. The trappings of their lives suggested success, both of them drove the latest Jaguar cars. Dan, who knew a thing or two about cars, was the one who had told me that they were the most recent Jaguar models. There were no airs and graces or trenchant behaviour from these two most appealing chaps. Both would do anything you asked within reason and with a smile on their faces. We were asked if we'd care to go around to their home and have drinks and nibbles. That was at first. Mother said a flat no. She didn't wish to have anything to do with them. But, I noticed when the cake was given, she had no difficulty in accepting it. After they'd left she said, "I don't like to mention it, but I have to tell you I have no intention of eating it and neither should any of you." Not only did she not mean what she said, but I thought her attitude was so bigoted, and I for one hated it. She'd always had plenty to say about different races and other people who were from a different mould than her own. Dad got mad and told her not to be so naïve and stupid.

"You should be jolly thankful that we have such good people around who are clearly looking out for us," he told her.

"Looking out for us? What, by waiting two months to pay us? Some neighbourly support that is."

With that, Mother flashed back into the kitchen rising like a hornet had bitten her on the backside and hid the cake in some place she thought we wouldn't find it.

Now the Treadworthys at number five, were a completely different kind of people altogether. They were the only couple on the site to have a daughter. Her name was Helen and we were the same age. We were in the same class at school, she wasn't there the day I started, but after being introduced as 'the two English girls' we built up a close friendship. She had been at the school for four years, was more clever than me, especially speaking French, and it showed. I tried hard to keep up with her, eventually succeeding. Mr. Treadworthy was an outgoing sort, in fact, he was going out more than staying in trying not to let his lifestyle become too obvious. He was a good-looking man, probably in his early fifties. He was tall and dark-skinned, with a neat moustache and friendly manner. He had silver-grey hair and always smelt of some strong French aftershave or body spray, or some sort of concoction. He had a job where he was expected to work in various places all over the world. They had been in France for four years, so it was likely that a move would be in the cards within a year or two. Helen told me she thought he was having an affair with a French woman who worked in the Perigueux office with him.

"I don't want to tell my Mum," Helen said. "I don't think it would do any good. Anyway, I don't altogether blame him. Mum is not particularly bothered whether he's home or not. She likes her own space, so I suppose it suits them both to an extent. You never know, perhaps she has her suspicions about him. Mum never seems to show affection to him or me for that matter, she is an undemonstrative woman, chiding him more often than not, about the most innocent of actions. If I opened my mouth about what I thought was going on, heaven alone knows what would happen. She might be straight to the divorce courts or may even leave us. I don't really want to know about their personal lives, as it won't be affecting me much longer. I intend to get myself off to Paris and find work there."

"Oh, Helen, I'm sorry you're going through this," I told her. "It's not good, especially with exams looming."

"Don't worry about me. I keep out of their way, especially when their rowing, which is most of the time when he's home."

"I know. But, whatever makes you think that he's having an affair?"

"He's late home every night, never getting in until eight or nine. Though I do realize the job he does is demanding."

"What does he do?" I asked.

"He's an electrical engineer and in senior management. The demands on his time in this region are colossal. There are still homes with poor electricity supply that often need specialist attention. I also saw him with a woman one day when we went on that school outing to discover the Medieval and Renaissance influence in Perigueux. They were on the walkway down from the huge car park at the top of the town. Not exactly holding hands, but, they might just as well have been, what with all the body language going on. She looked quite young and fashionable."

"You never said a word about it when we were on that visit," I said. "But, I did think you went rather quiet and pale. Do you recall me asking you if you were alright?"

"No, I don't. But, now you know the reason why."

Helen and I looked out for one another.

Mr. and Mrs. Chevalier lived at number four. He was French and she was Swedish. She was on the self-absorbed side, and he was a forty-two-year-old alcoholic. She was older than him from what I saw, by about ten years, maybe more. She was the one who had to work to enable them to live where they did. She was still attractive for a fifty-plus woman; tall and on the plumpish side, but she had the loveliest skin, almost translucent. Perhaps that was down to the make-up used. She also possessed an excellent dress sense.

She was working in one of the 'we sell everything stores' in Ribérac and had been, since her husband was made redundant. Rumour had it that he had been made to leave his last employment because of his bad attendance record and drinking on the job. It was such a shame, since he was a clever man and had had a good job in Perigueux, where he acted as a senior partner in one of the prestigious banks. No one knew why he started to drink heavily, but, I'd heard it said that alcoholism ran in his family and that both his parents were drinkers and both had met an early demise as a result.

I would have thought that might have put him off, however their lives jogged along.

Mum was delighted when asked if she would 'do' for the boys on a regular basis of two days each week and was given a front door key. Her prejudices put to one side.

"I cannot imagine how a house can get so messy with just the two of them in it," Mum declared one night after a heavy day 'doing' for them. However, that was the deal she had amiably agreed to.

The next family along were the Ageleries. They were American, and more-often-than-not, spent at least half the year in the USA. He was a bit brash and loud, but appeared to be a decent sort of man, always interested in other people and their lives. Not in a nosy way, but in an 'I'm interested in you as a person' way. And, Mrs. Agelerie, was just delightful, full of caring and hope for the future of the world, even after the terrible events in America, when the Twin Towers were hit and so many lives lost. She loved everyone, at least that was the impression I had. They oozed money, with their home, their lifestyle and their generosity. I remember the day an old-fashioned tinker came onto the site. He was a raggedy old man, slightly bent over, and in the heat of the day he was sweating and continually wiping his face with a red and dirty white handkerchief.

Annie opened her door, invited him into her home and gave him a cool drink. She then handed the man a few notes. He went away smiling and a much happier chap than when he'd first arrived. I watched all of this from the garden, and thought, "Wow, what a lovely lady." I overheard one of the neighbours say that her husband was from Dallas, Texas and his money made in oil. She was a potter and had had her studio built in the garden. She was often to be seen working away on one of her splendid designs. These were developed in the brightest of colours, some she gave away to her friends and some she sold at the Friday Ribérac market, mostly the large more commercial pieces. When we first arrived here we were presented with a bright blue, speckled bowl adorned with little bits of silver. She was never to tell us what materials she used. I had my suspicions it was the real McCoy.

Some of the other residents were jealous of the Ageleries. Not me, I was completely overawed by the sight before me when I was invited into their home. They had a cook, and a cleaner, a well-established local lady who came to work for them on four half-days a week. Sadly, that meant Mum was out of the running. She would have loved to have work in this astounding place. They lived in the only stand-alone home on the site. They were middle aged, both intelligent and aware of their surroundings. It was a magnificent building built to their own specification. As you entered the hall, you discovered that it was just the smaller of two hallways. The second one was found on the other side of two exquisite oak wood doors in between, which were adorned with spectacular light purple-coloured glass. On entering the second hallway, one could imagine it was designed for the purpose of partying and dancing. I don't think that such events ever happened, as we would have been aware of them. There were three living rooms and a vast dining room, which could seat a dozen people around their grandiose mahogany table and chairs. The largest kitchen I had ever laid eyes on was positioned at the front of the house, and every surface available was of Italian marble. The kitchen, overlooked the astounding Périgueux countryside. It had recently been fitted with the latest of white and black kitchen design and must have cost a fortune. The grand and wide staircase cascaded upwards, separating into stairs dividing half way up, leading to the different sides of the house and many bedrooms. The campus. So many different types of neighbors. All with more wealth than I may ever know in my life. I wouldn't say I felt completely at home yet, but these people were starting to feel like my little eclectic community.

.

Chapter Six

Revelations

"Challenges are what make life interesting.
Overcoming them is what makes life meaningful."
~ Joshua J. Marine

As luck would have it, we hadn't experienced much rain up until now. The trouble was, when it did rain, it came down in torrents. We'd been told it could last for days, causing chaos and disruption. Residents told us sometimes the water flowed down between the houses on the unmade sand and stone pathways, taking on the resemblance of a river. It removed all the beach stones that made up the roadway into huge piles you could not see over. This was clearly the reason the Dordogne was so rich and green.

Ralph paid us a visit. Dad was delighted to see him and arrangements were made for another dinner date with him. He was clearly a man who liked to entertain. This was fine by me. He looked even more handsome than I recalled. His tan had darkened and his thick dark brown curly hair had taken on a reddish blond appearance. It must have been the effects of working outside in the sun.

"Hello, Ralph, how are you?" I asked.

"Well, young lady, I'm fine, how about you? Are you beginning to settle into school and your new home?"

I much preferred "young lady" to "girl" but I still wished to hear him say something more adult. I didn't want to talk about school with him, feeling that this was only a reminder of our gap in age. I wanted to talk about wine or art or something that made me feel like an equal. But I continued anyways.

"Yes, I suppose I am, but, I miss my old friends."

"Cherie, you will make new ones here."

"They're a bit standoffish at the school. I like Helen, she's in my class and lives near with her parents. She's English and we have become good friends. The best thing is that my French is improving and faster than I would have thought. But, I'm anxious to leave school and make my way in this big wide world."

"There you are, then. A new friend who is your neighbour. What more could a girl ask for? A young lady like you won't have any trouble getting on wherever you decide to go, Maisie. I think you have the personality and common sense to make it in life, whatever you choose to do."

I could tell him what more I could ask for, but, thought better of it. I'm sure I blushed profusely as I felt my cheeks redden and my mouth dry. He was paying me a compliment, what was I to say in return? The answer was not much. I giggled embarrassingly, then managed to utter, "That's kind of you to say, Ralph. Thank you. Perhaps on the next break from school I can come and help out on the farm."

"Well, that's not far off if I recall correctly," he told me. "In the weather leading up to Christmas we need to get the animals sheltered. That's when we could do with a hand."

Sheltering animals in the winter had never sounded more romantic. Later in the day I was talking to Dan, and told him I was infatuated with Ralph. I told him I was going to help out on the farm to be around him more.

"You're mad," he said. "He's got to be in his thirties or even forties, and that's more than twice your age. He wouldn't give you a second glance. You'd be just a baby in his eyes."

"Just you shut up, will you?" I snapped. "That's the last time I'm going to tell you anything. You're such a rotter."

And, as it turns out, he was a complete and total hypocrite. It was late September when I found out that my brother was having an affair with a married woman living in Ribérac. He didn't tell me. I found out through another girl at school. Not just any woman either...

"She's the mother of one of the boys who's in the infants," I was told.

I wondered if I should bring the subject up with Dan, scold him for telling me I couldn't date someone older then he goes out and does just that! Or should I keep quiet and hope it will fizzle out. It probably wouldn't last. He was a bit flippant with his girlfriends and had had plenty of them since the age of thirteen. His flirtatious nature and good looks, with his big blue limpet eyes—the kind that sucked you in when you looked into them—made him a sought-after catch. He had also developed a splendid physique, made possible by the exercise paraphernalia he'd acquired. I chose to keep quiet for the time being. I didn't want to fall out with him. We had enough on our plates trying to live in this virtually 'unliveable' house. Mum had made the place as cosy as possible with her limited means, however, she had begun to clean--reluctantly--for number four, where Mr. and Mrs. Chevalier lived. They didn't seem to be as well off as some, but they found the money from somewhere to pay Mum for four hours work a week. She called the latter a 'real snooty cow who considered only herself'. She expected a great deal from Mum, who was then nearly fifty and not as fit and sprightly as she used to be. She had asthma and we were warned before she came over, that the countryside in France was not the ideal place for an asthmatic, the harvesting, seemed to have been going on since the day we arrived and undoubtedly exacerbated her condition. But, on she went coughing her way through, looking after us, as well as the people at number four and the boys.

This evening Dan had followed his usual routine, leaving the house straight after supper, and Mum and me alone. I helped clear up the dishes and put things tidily in their places. We had purchased a beautiful French chiffonier: a tall mahogany piece of furniture that held all the kitchen paraphernalia we owned. Found it in an old antique shop in Verteillac, a small village not far from Chez Mouzy, it stood proud in our kitchen.

After we sat down, Mum looked me straight in the eyes and asked: "What's your brother up to, Maisie? I know something's going on but I can't put my finger on it."

"I don't know, Mum," I lied.

"Well, he goes out nearly every night and stays out 'til very late. Surely, he's not drinking all that time. He doesn't come back drunk, so I don't think it's that."

"You're right, but you've always known how well he can hold his booze and, come to think of it, I can't remember him ever being inebriated, can you?"

Quickly changing the subject, I started to talk about the house.

"Do you think we shall get the place into some semblance of order before the winter, Mum? We must get that roof fixed. Ralph said his brother was coming over to France and that they would give Dad a hand to do it. Do you think we should get in touch and chivvy things along?"

"No, I don't, that's the last thing we should do. Ralph offered their services out of the goodness of his heart. The last thing we want to do is upset the apple cart and put him off helping us. We are going to meet his brother on Saturday night, and don't forget that he has a farm to run and no woman to come back to with a hot meal waiting after a hard day's work. I don't think your father would be happy coming home to no wife and no food waiting for him, any more than you and your brother would."

"Do you think it a bit odd that he doesn't seem to have much to do with the residents, Mum? We've yet to see him visit or invite any of them to his home. Has anyone said anything to you about that?"

"No, they haven't. Maybe he's upset them. It's possible that he's only got friendly with us because of the meeting with you and your brother so soon after we arrived. Perhaps there's some shyness involved."

It worked well, her attention now away from Dan. Maybe the time had come when I should talk to him. The gossip was beginning to spread effectively around the school, and I thought he should know about it. I decided to talk to him the next day. Knowing this wouldn't be easy, I had to pick the right moment. He sometimes went into the town after school, probably to the girlfriend. Luck was with me as that day he was waiting beside the front school gate.

"I'm glad you're here as I have something I want to talk to you about," I began. "It will have to wait until we get home, as I don't want Mum overhearing anything."

"Sounds a bit serious, kid," he asked me. "Are you pregnant?"

"That's impossible as I don't have a boyfriend, and you know it! Just wait 'til we get home, Dan, I'm gonna give it to you!"

"Ooh, Ooh, I'm scared, don't hit me, will you? You know I'm not allowed to hit you back 'cos you're just a little weak and feeble girl." He uttered as he jigged around me grinning from ear to ear. After that remark, I tried to whack him with my satchel.

The chat continued after Mum arrived to collect us.

"You should take advantage of what you have the opportunity to do now," I said to him. "You'll only regret it later and the moment will pass and you will have moved into another dimension of your life, one without the spoils that education can bring. You don't need me to tell you that."

"Just listen to you. Since when have you been such an academic?"

"I don't profess to be that," I told him. "But, I do know that without studying, there won't be much open to us in the future. You aren't so stupid that you don't recognize that fact, surely?"

"Why don't the pair of you just shut up and think sensibly instead of arguing all the time?"

Mum interrupted. "Dan, you listen to me now. You will stay in education until your father and I tell you the time has come to leave. Do you hear me?"

That did it. Dan shut off totally in that moment, pulling up the stone walls of silence he was capable of building up around himself. I thought any chance I'd had for a talk with him was gone. Mum drove home in a bad mood. I decided that I would take a chance and talk to my brother before supper. I called to him to come into the yard for a moment. We went out together, and the September sun still shone brighter than ever and the early autumn air was deliciously hot. And Dan looked so handsome with his gold hair shining like diamonds.

I turned to Dan and said, "I've got to tell you the gossip at school. You're my brother and I love you and I don't want to see you get into trouble. She's married, isn't she?"

"What on earth are you talking about?" Dan answered.

"You know exactly what I'm talking about. It's all over the school, your affair with that woman in town. For heaven's sake, stop it Dan! She's no good for you. Get yourself someone who's available and your own age."

"Mind your own bloody business, Sis, it's got nothing to do with you or those plebs at school."

"You had better think what you're going to do about it soon or Mum and Dad will find out. I've never known you to be this stupid before. You seem to have lost all sense of reason."

After I said that, he walked back indoors, leaving me to ponder what had just been said.

"Have you two been at it again?" Mum asked Dan. "You never stop fighting these days. I don't know what's come over the pair of you. Now go and get me some beans from the garden. And tell your sister to come in and lay the table for supper."

Dad came home a bit later and we all sat down to eat. As always seemed to be the case during dinner, the phone rang.

Mum was all aglow when she returned from the hallway.

"That was Ralph!" she said cheerfully, smiling all over her face. "His brother is there and he says we can meet him on Friday and that the roof can be discussed. Dan, make sure you're around that evening, won't you, love?"

"Yes, Mum, I will," Dan said grudgingly.

"Right, it will be grand when the roof's back as it should be. He says they'll both come and help with the repairs. Bit of luck, that, and we shall have it all finished before the winter takes hold. I believe it can get very cold here in the winter," Mum said.

Dad was quiet these days, and looking older than his fifty years. I worried about him, as I think he was finding the job a bit difficult and more involved than he'd been led to believe. But, knowing my father, he wasn't going to give up on it yet. His theory was that you had to give things a go before you threw in the towel.

"You know, Dan, it wouldn't hurt you to give me a hand with some of the jobs around here," Dad said to him.

"How can I do that when I have to go to school most of the time?" Dan replied. "Not much time left for jobs around here."

"You are on the Summer break right now so that won't stop you giving me a hand will it, son."

At this point Dan felt our Father's plea and looked a bit guilty. Dad rarely asked anything of either of us.

"No worries, Dad, of course I can give you a hand. In fact, I'm here tonight. What would you like me to be getting on with?"

Dad's face was a picture. He beamed from ear to ear. "That's fine, son. Can we cut the grass together? I will use the sit-on mower, and perhaps you wouldn't mind having a go at the other side with the hand mower."

In that moment it seemed like Dan might turn things around, might focus on being a good son rather than being the married woman chaser. I wondered if maybe I should do the same. Put the Ralph fantasies behind me. Focus on school. Enjoy my time with Helen. Maybe meet a boy, go on a date.

Then I thought about the boys around me, their oily faces, their acne. Their skinny arms. None of them could compare to Ralph. He was a man. I watched Dan walk outside trailing my Dad and thought that if it was this hard for me to give up on Ralph, and we hadn't shared anything more than a kiss on the cheek greeting, then how hard will it be for Dan? There was probably no way Dan was walking away from his older lover. I looked out at him starting the hand mower and felt this strange feeling come over me as if I felt sorry for him. As if I knew things would turn out disastrously with his French affair.

CHAPTER SEVEN

The Meeting

"For God is not the Author of confusion but of peace"
~ 1 Corinthians 14.33

Mum rang Ralph to make sure of the time we were expected for supper. News must travel very fast out here, because it quickly became known that we, the family of hired help, had befriended and were cosying up to the 'landed gentry' at the farm. The local gossip was ubiquitous in the complex. Coffee mornings or afternoon teas were rampant with the news. We found out about it when Mum was 'doing' for the Mountfields. Mrs. Mountfield said to her, "I hear that you are invited to go to the farm of Mr. Ralph Waterman and that you are going to meet with his brother."

"Yes, that's right, and it won't be for the first time, either. How do you know about that, Mrs. Mountfield?" Mum asked.

"It seems to be all around the complex—I think everybody knows. Mind you it's no one's business but your own. However, I'm curious as to how it came about that you got to know him in the first place."

"That's down to the teenagers, you know what young people are like, or have you forgotten?"

"I hope you aren't intimating that we are too old to know how young people think and behave?"

"Of course not, madam. Do you want me to clean the brass and silver today?"

"Yes, please. I have also heard that Ralph Waterman's brother is a bit odd. Have you heard the same?

"No, as a matter of fact I haven't. Now, I'd better get on or I won't get all the jobs done you want doing today, now will I?"

When Mum came home she was furious.

"Those nosy Parkers wanting to know how we knew Ralph, almost suggesting that we weren't posh enough for the likes of that family," she fumed. "How on earth did she know about us going to supper with him? Was it you kids trying to show off?"

"No, Mum," I told her. "It wasn't me and I don't think Dan could be bothered to get involved with such trivia, do you?"

"No, as a matter of fact I don't, but I'd like to find out who did spread the word. She told me that Ralph's brother was odd. Have you heard anything like that, Maisie?"

"No, I haven't. But, if he's as good looking as his brother and available, that would be rather nice, would it not, Mother?"

"You should be ashamed of yourself running after old men," she told me. "Why don't you find someone your own age to be your dreamboat? There must be plenty of those around the school."

"I'm partial to the older man. There's nothing wrong with that, Mum, they could well be rich and exciting and I'd never have to worry about living in poverty or struggling from day to day, wondering how I was going to feed my family. I quite fancy the idea of being a spoilt lady of leisure."

"Stop your nonsense," she replied. "Ralph and his brother, are certainly not going to be interested in a scrap like you. You're so skinny and have no dress sense."

"You are too kind, Mother. You really make me feel good about myself. Maybe I would have some dress sense if I had any sort of money to go shopping with. You wonder why I might want to be with someone with some means."

"Don't be so soppy! You know I'm only teasing you."

"You shouldn't do it even if you don't mean it, as It could affect me psychologically for the rest of my life," I said tongue in cheek.

"Oh, is that so? But you can call me and your dad poor? Is that how this works?"

"What about me being skinny?" I asked her. "I hate being called that. I know I'm thin, but, I can't stuff anymore than I already do down my throat. Perhaps I should put it down to your cooking, Mum."

"That's enough! You have always had the best food we could afford to buy, so don't go down that road."

Mum ended the conversation there, walked out of the room. I wanted to scream. SHE was the little girl, I was more like the adult. SHE was the one who wasn't mature enough for Ralph, not me. Why is it always about age? What is age if you don't act it? What makes her more mature than me? I was so mad. I'd never tell any future daughter that she was a scrap. A skinny, bad dressed scrap. I wouldn't say that to my worst enemy, let alone someone I was supposed to love!

Friday evening arrived, I was desperately trying to find something to wear that was both nice and was going to make me look a bit fatter. I thought that maybe I should pad my bra and wear a full skirt. That would do it. I bought some new make-up in town after school. Mum was going to be late to collect Dan and me, so I had some time on my hands. The French do have a way of looking chic in knowing how to apply the paint. The girl in the pharmacy spent ages explaining to me how I should be putting the stuff on and what I should buy to suit my complexion.

I wasn't used to putting make-up on so I didn't have much of a clue. My hair was long now and was a silky medium-blonde colour. I washed it and brushed it to enhance the shine, then I applied my heated tongs to give it a ringlet curl. I must say I was overjoyed with the end result. I never usually had time to give myself that much attention.

When I came down the stairs on the night of the dinner party, all of the family was waiting at the bottom. I felt like Meggie descending the stairs to face Ralph in the 'Thorn Birds' in her rose pink frock.

"Gosh, is that really you, Maisie?" Dan said. "You look so different!"

Dad quickly interjected before he had time to go any further: "You look lovely, darling, doesn't she Mother?"

"Yes, you look so grown up, love. I think you're filling out a bit, too," Mum said with a slight glint in her eye.

"I'll go and get the truck round the front, you lot be ready and waiting," Dad told us.

Mum always did this with me. The days when she made me the most upset were usually followed by nights when she said something that blocked out the memory of how bad I felt earlier. Mum had put on her best dress, which was all flowery and feminine, and that lovely violet, misty blue flowered pattern, nicely understated, and now very popular with ladies of a certain age. Dad had put on his one and only suit...the one he was married in. Dan looked atrocious as normal. Unkempt, hair askew, torn jeans and unshaven. He must have made more effort for his lady friend. Dad told him to go back in the house and shave, and that it was disrespectful to our hosts if he didn't. Dan made an afforded protest but was unanimously overridden and did as he was asked, coming out looking fresh and presentable.

It was a lovely late October evening, and the sun still shone at 21.00 hours. We arrived to find Ralph waiting at the gate with his loyal dog and friend, Benny boy.

"Hello, you guys, how good it is to see you again," Ralph said. "It seems like ages to me. Let me open the gate and you can drive straight in."

We alighted from the truck and were greeted by Ralph with a kiss to Mum, on both cheeks of course, very French. Benny was running around me and Dan wagging his tail incessantly, vying for our attention and in return getting it. When Ralph got to me he took hold of my chin and lifted it with his hand. Smiling down he kissed my mouth briefly. I was embarrassed and hoped my parents weren't looking. I'm sure I blushed and kept my head bowed until we were all inside Ralph's hallway. We were led into the huge lounge, with the three gargantuan leather settees that sat three to four people.

I couldn't believe it, he kissed me! I didn't feel like the stupid girl with a crush anymore. For the first time I felt like there might be something on the other side. You don't kiss a girl on the lips by accident. He was in this game as much as I was. I glided into the house, the happiest I've ever felt.

We were invited to sit down, and then Ralph's brother walked into the room. I was shocked when I first set eyes on him. Every feeling of happiness from seconds before vanished. I looked at him again and thought I was going to faint. I had to breathe deeply to prevent falling.

"This is my brother, Gangees Waterman."

I tried hard to be as stoic as I could, but there was a look about the man that seemed distantly familiar. He stepped forward and came over to where I stood, took my hand and kissed it before he went anywhere near the rest of my family. That was odd for a start. Close up, he smelled of whisky or some sort of alcohol and tobacco mixture. He held out a massive hand to the others and time was spent in the delicacies of introduction. I don't know what made me do it, but I found myself taking in all his features and demeanour. He was ugly in comparison with his brother. I wondered if he had the same set of parents. His shifty narrow eyes and his protruding nose were quite disarming and he was tall with huge feet and hands a bit giant-like. When he spoke, it was like an intimidating forthright, loud speech. I needed to get away from this man and walked back to the settee to settle down in its comfort. I'm sure I know you from somewhere, I thought. Fortunately, my parents and Dan took centre stage at that point and I could relax. *How do I know you?* I kept asking him in my head.

"Maisie, can I get you a glass of wine?" Ralph asked. "I have a very good red or maybe a white. Most of the white wine in this region is dry."

I settled for the white wine. That was the first time I'd been able to speak since meeting Gangees.

There was a great deal of laughter emanating from the adults. Edifying talk about wines ensued, including discussions of the various advantages of certain wines, and the few that were not so advantageous. Gangees sat himself directly opposite me with his hawk eyes staring in my direction. After about five lengthy minutes of this, it dawned on me where I thought I'd seen him before. The vision I'd left behind five years before on the Hythe canal, was right there in front of me. He was still dressed peculiarly, but, without the Stetson and long coat. His hair was shorter and not the greasy hue I'd remembered. His eyes were just as I recalled and they were staring again, following me around the room. I left to visit the toilet, to avoid the constant stare.

It was him, there was no doubt in my mind anymore. But how could it be? The man I wished to hold again, kiss again, lose days looking deeply into his eyes, how could he share the same blood as that monster, someone whose eyes I can't even look into for more than a second without feeling all of the terror and ugliness that just exudes from his being. Ralph, the one who I longed to kiss again. Gangees, the one who cornered me in an alley. Brothers. Together under the same roof.

When I returned, Gangees watched me until I was seated. Then, suddenly, like turning off a light switch, he turned all his attention toward Dan, Mum, and Dad.

"Gangees, that's a very unusual name," Dad said. "Where do you live now?"

"I live in England at the moment," the peculiar character said. "The trouble with me is that I never stay in one place for long. I'm a restless spirit you could say. But, I'm always welcome here with my brother. Is that not the case 'bro'?"

Ralph ignored that question and Gangees continued to say, "Ralph was born in the UK but I was born in India close to the river of the same name. I think the river came first. 'Gange,' that's my nickname, and it trips off the tongue. Our parents must have been having some kind of joke when they named me."

"I hope that everyone likes beef," Ralph interjected. "Of course, you do, I forgot we had it when I came to you. Everything is fresh and my housekeeper has helped us with all the preparations. She brought an armful of vegetables in from her allotment today. That's something the French people love to have, an allotment and very smart they are, too, not like those back home, with old bits of timber and slate strung together and a dirty old water butt beside them. The amount of ground allotted to families is quite large over here. That's because there's plenty of it."

By this time everyone, especially me, was a little bit drunk. Dan, on the other hand, was a regular sot. Mum and Dad would chide him, even though they were unsure if he was sober or not, and say, "Before long you will be an alcoholic, and then you'll know what dependency is all about, son!"

"It's nearly ready," Ralph announced. "Would you all care to sit up at the table in the dining room? I know the table is a bit over-the-top, but the previous owners left most of the furniture here. It's very old and heavy. How it got here in the first place, I have no idea."

The kitchen was just off this huge, high ceilinged and rather chilly, dark room. I couldn't help thinking, it's a good job it wasn't mid-winter. The fireplace was massive, but the wood burning stove not lit. I wished it had been as I was feeling cold. When we came to eat the first time we were in the smaller far-cosier kitchen.

"Do you burn wood from your land in the fireplace?" Mum enquired.

"Yes, there's plenty of it," Ralph replied. "But, it takes a lot to heat this room so we don't often use it, and especially not in summer."

"I have been thinking of having a wood-burning stove put in," Dad told him. "They are most effective and so much cheaper to buy over here than back in England."

"Like we could afford that," Mum said with a laugh.

Ralph and Gangees were popping in and out of the kitchen, which was off this great room and bringing in a variety of terrines. I could not believe my eyes, as yet another awe inspiring, veritable feast was presented. The room was so long it looked like a banqueting hall and had a table that would seat some twenty or more people.

We all sat in the middle part of the table. The setting was delightful. At one end, a display of apparently freshly-picked flowers stood at the end of the table. Those beautiful chrysanthemums with large varied shades of gold-and-white heads, adorned the vast Italian looking, porcelain, vase. At the other end of the table, stood a naked bronze female figure in a seated position, holding a pitcher of water.

"That's very old and valuable and was also left by the previous owners," Ralph explained, referring to the bronze figure. "I think they had more money than sense. They had this place as a country escape from their supposedly luxurious flat in Paris. I dare say money was no object. I had her valued and she's worth over thirty thousand euros. I really must get her insured."

"God, have you nothing better to do than to hold onto old rubbish like her?" Gange uttered. "She's not even beautiful, and she's extremely dirty. I thought you had better glorifications to spend your hard-earned money on, brother."

Ralph chose to ignore his brother's remark. I had the impression that he was used to such insulting barrages.

Gange. Or Gangees. Either way, what a terrible name for a man! Then, I wondered if maybe that was why he behaved so oddly. If he was born a rotten apple and that was just what he was destined to become. I was surprised that he hadn't attempted to change that name. He embarrassed me to no end the whole evening, as his attention to the others was far less than was his attention to me.

We ate a bountiful feast and drank a great deal of wine, to such a degree that Dad could not safely drive us home. Mum drank more than all of us. She was drinking far more in France than she did back home.

"Leave your car here and I will take you back," Ralph said.

"But you have had quite a lot to drink as well, Ralph," Dad declared. "In fact, we all have had too much."

"Well then, you all must stay the night," Ralph answered. "I've got plenty of room here."

"No, no way can we inconvenience you like that," I interjected.

"It's no inconvenience whatsoever," Ralph said.

"I must get back," I continued. "There is so much to do at home and we all have to work tomorrow. I help Mum now with some of the house cleaning in the complex. Mum and Dad are expected to do so much for the people there."

As we were about to leave, Ralph said, "Gange and I can come and help finish off the roof for you, Jack. When is it convenient to come, and do the job? It should take no longer than a day or two."

"I'm always working," Dad explained. "But, perhaps I could get an afternoon off, though, and give you both a hand. The materials you required are all at home."

"That's fine. Let us know when and don't leave it too long, or deep winter will be here, and you will be living in a cold abode. Come on now, can you all manage to walk to the car?"

"Of course, they can," Gange said. "We've only got through three bottles, haven't we?"

"And the rest," came the reply from Dad.

Thanks, were said all around, with Mum making a fool of herself by hanging around the necks of both Ralph and Gangees. Dan thanked them fondly and shook hands, as did Dad. I stood back, badly wanting to grab hold of Ralph, but kept myself under control. I was reluctant to have anything to do with his weird brother. The moment came to thank and hug Ralph, when Gange left the room to go in the kitchen, and I slipped surreptitiously out into the courtyard towards Ralph's waiting Jeep. Mum, Dad and Dan had stumbled across the yard and somehow got into the car. I think I must have been the one who was the soberest of us all, as I concentrated hard on walking in a ladylike fashion across the yard in my high heels and into the back seat of the waiting car alongside Dan.

I looked over at my brother, who was nodding off intermittently and said, "You know who I think that Gangees bloke is? Don't you remember me telling you about that man I saw on the canal bank back in England? You know, the one who had a Stetson hat and wore a long red coat, and how his eyes followed me as I shifted along riding my bike on the opposite bank?"

"I don't know what you're talking about" Dan muttered. "I'm drunk and tired and just want to sleep."

Ralph got into the driver's seat and drove us all back to the house.

"We were so scared," I continued. "He chased after us. You've never seen two children cycle home so fast in all your life."

"Please. Maisie. Quiet. Shut up will ya?" Dan told me.

My brother had changed recently, ever since he'd been seeing that woman. He was always in a bad mood, angry most of the time. One would have thought a new relationship would have made him happy, even if it was a clandestine, forbidden one.

CHAPTER EIGHT

The Befriending

"Sometimes you need what's familiar to help you face what isn't."

Ralph and his brother arrived on Sunday to pick up the car. As they both alighted, I could see Gange looking over our property, eyes darting everywhere to avoid missing a trick, and from my bedroom window I heard him say to Ralph, "Do you think they'd mind if I look around?"

"I shouldn't think so," Ralph said. "After all, we shall need a close reconnoiter when we come to do the roof."

I saw Dad standing in the doorway and they were having an extended conversation about the roof and all its foibles. I breathed a sigh of relief, as this gave me more time to have a sluice down and get dressed. I threw on a reasonably new dress and went downstairs. Dan was still in bed, while Mum and Dad had apparently been up for quite some time, however, both were a bit the worse for wear. I could smell the coffee, a smell I'd loved since being small. It was the main drink of our household and seldom was a brewing pot unseen. We had bought a new French percolator which Mum thought to be the bee's knees, and she was a dab hand at making coffee to perfection.

I had forty fits when I realized it was almost lunchtime.

"Crumbs, Mum, why didn't you call me?" I asked her as I flew in through the kitchen. "Just look at the time!"

"You must have needed your sleep, love, so we thought it better for you to stay in bed and recover from last night. Ralph and his brother are here, did they wake you?" She said all this with a slight slur to her voice.

"I was just stirring and I heard the car draw up."

"Your Dad's outside showing them around the place. Do you want some breakfast?"

"No, thanks, I'll just have coffee."

Mum poured it out then I slowly wandered to the outside kitchen door, holding onto the hot coffee as though it was mid-winter. There was indeed a definite coolness to greet me, the temperature must have taken a dive, even though the sun shone brightly.

I really did not wish to see Gange, but a glimpse and chat with Ralph would set me up nicely for the day ahead. Little did I know what this day would bring.

"Hello, Ralph, is Dad showing you around?" I said briskly.

"Good morning, young lady, and how are we today?" he said as he came over to me and picked me up. My feet came off the ground, as he swung me around, just once, fortunately, since any more swinging and I would have vomited. That would have ruined this nice little romantic moment.

"We are fine, thank you. I definitely had too much to drink last night. I can see it has affected Mum more than the rest of us, but Dad seemed OK."

As I said that, Gange came around from the back of the house, obviously nosing about to find out what he could.

"Where is your brother?" Gange asked me. "I quite took to him last night. We had long chats about my time in the Navy. He seemed to be keen to join, and said he'd be making enquiries about it."

"Did he now?" I replied. "He's never said anything to me about going into the Navy."

"Well, you're a girl, he probably thought you wouldn't understand manly stuff like that."

At that point, I felt sick. He said the words in such a pompous, arrogant way, that it completely disarmed me. He was doing the staring bit again, and he was strangely weirder in the cool light of day.

"Come on in," Dad said. "Julia's got the coffee on and perhaps you could eat a bit of lunch?"

"No thanks, Jack. It's kind of you but I have a lot to get on with. I still have a field that needs ploughing. Are you coming, Gange? I could do with a hand."

"I think I'll hang about here a bit, take another look at that roof," his brother replied.

My heart sank.

"I also want to chat a bit more with Dan," Gange said. "Is he here?

"He's still in bed," replied Mum, who was slowly but surely beginning to sober up. "Shall I call him for you?"

As we went to see Ralph off, I noticed a couple of the residents straining their necks to try and see who was visiting us. I was horrified to think that this ghastly man was going to be around for the day.

Fortunately, he wasn't, because he invited Dan to go with him into town. Being ecstatic about that arrangement, I flung myself into helping Mum with the washing and did a pile of ironing that had been hanging around for days.

"You shouldn't do so much at your time of life."

"There's nothing wrong with my time of life! I'm still pretty fit and could give you a run for your money any day. But, I've been thinking about a trip back to England soon."

The rest of the day ran smoothly. Mum went out for her usual early evening walk, I finished preparing supper, which the three of us ate at about 8 p.m. Late for us, but we'd waited long enough for Dan to get back from town and hunger got the better of us. As the evening drew on, I noticed Dad getting restless.

"What's the matter?" I asked him.

"I think I'll give Ralph a call and see if his brother and Dan are back yet."

I daren't say too much, but had an inkling as to where that Dan was. Dad called Ralph and was told that Gangees was back home. He said that he left Dan hours previously. He had offered him a lift, but he'd said he had to go and see a friend from school and they were probably going to the movies.

Of course, I knew differently, but was not going to stir up trouble for the brother I loved, even though we spent most of our time these days arguing.

"Dad, he's almost certainly walking home as we speak," I started to lie on his behalf. "The picture house doesn't close until late and I dare say he has met up with friends and they're drinking in some bar."

"I have never known your brother to come home this late and he's got school in the morning," Dad said.

Mum didn't say much, but she was clearly worried, as well. She opened another bottle of wine and was almost through it when Dad returned after about an hour. After an hour, Dad returned alone. The hours passed and there was still no sign of Dan. Dad took off in his car about 11 p.m. to look for him. He returned a few hours later.

"I looked everywhere," Dad said. "Where on earth can he be at this time of night? I went past the cinema and it was closed. There was a chap walking away from the place who I asked what time the bars shut and he told me at midnight."

It was now one in the morning. Should I say where I thought he might be, or should I keep quiet, I wondered? That was a question only me and my conscience could answer. Weighing up the pros and cons, I decided it would be better not to keep quiet.

A restless night was spent by us all. In the morning, Dad took the truck out early to see if he could find Dan. He had no luck, so went on to the police station in Ribérac to report him missing.

When he returned, once again alone, he told us they were less than helpful. Even though the sergeant spoke English. All of our senses were running rampant with fear and theirs were clearly not.

"Oh, I shouldn't worry about your boy, he is young and sowing his oats," the policeman told Dad. "You remember how that felt when you were seventeen, surely Monsieur?"

"I'm very worried," Dad repeated. "This is not like him at all. He may often be late home from school and at weekends, and yes, of course he wants to be with friends, and that we encourage. But this is different. He has never stayed out all night since we came to France."

Dad was most upset about the lack of interest shown by the police, and said to Mum and me that he would go down again later in the day.

"Dan has changed beyond recognition since we came here," he continued. "He's not happy and misses his friends back home. To be honest, Julia, I think we made a mistake dragging him over here. Perhaps we should have listened to what he said he wanted to do, instead of using the heavy-handed approach."

"No good having those recriminations now," Mum replied. "What's done is done."

I imagined all manner of things that could have happened to him. Had the husband of his lover come home and caught them together? Was he lying in a ditch somewhere having been beaten up? My imagination was running wild and I felt very agitated. Again, I thought about revealing the truth. I found it hard to imagine what our parents' reaction would be to the fact their beloved son was having an affair with a married woman.

"I must get off to school now," I told them. "Mum, will you take me?"

"Gosh, just look at the time, you'll be late girl. Are you ready? Come on then, I won't bother to change." She came out to the car in her dressing gown and slippers.

When I arrived at school, I found it hard not to say anything about Dan to my classmates. I hadn't even mentioned that Dan was missing to Helen. But, the whole day was a disaster anyway. I should have stayed at home instead of being there, unable to concentrate on the heavy lessons that were now all being taught in French. At last the day came to an end. I rushed out to the school gate to find Dad waiting to pick me up.

"Hello, love," Dad said. "I went down to the police station again and reported that Dan still hadn't come home. They were a bit more receptive this time. Fortunately, I found the one who spoke reasonable English and I could explain everything to him without fear that it would not be understood. They told me they would send some officers to look for Dan."

I was trembling as I was deciding whether to tell Father about the married woman and Dan's association with her. As we drove along I plucked up the courage and told Dad.

"What did you say, Maisie?"

"I said that Dan's been having an affair with a married woman who is a good deal older than him."

"Oh, my God! How long has this been going on? Does your mother know about it?"

"No, Dad, you are the only one I've told. Best not to say anything to Mum yet. Let's wait 'til Dan gets home, then we may get away without telling her."

"Do you know where she lives?"

"No, I don't. It's in the town somewhere, but I don't know the address."

"We shall need to tell the police about this. Do you know her name, Maisie?" Dad was getting more and more agitated as he spoke to me.

"I don't know her name, Dad, Dan never told me. The only thing I know is that she has a child in the infant section at our school."

Back to the police station we went. Dad blurted out what I had told him. I felt so remorseful for divulging Dan's secret. But the stakes had changed now. He had been missing for over 48 hours. Fortunately, the same officer was on duty—the one who spoke reasonably good English.

"Oh, well that puts a different slant on things now, does it not?" the officer said. "We shall start to make some enquiries. You say that there is a child in your school who is the woman's son?"

"Yes, that's correct, but I don't know her name," I explained.

"Well, I dare say we shall find that out in due course. Our officers are back from looking around the countryside and they have not had sightings of Dan. Dan, who, by the way?"

"Dan who?" my dad repeated.

"Yeah. I mean what's his surname?"

"Patterson," Dad said at speed.

Are you kidding me? Why didn't they know that already? Some police force this was.

We were asked to go home and try to get some rest, as we'd been up most of the night and were feeling the strain of it all. I was overcome with fatigue, while Dad said nothing at all. I realized how worried he was not knowing Dan's whereabouts.

As we pulled up at the house, I jumped out of the car to rush indoors to the upstairs toilet, where I vomited up the meagre amount of food I'd eaten that day. I stayed there awhile in the hope some good news would be coming our way later. I prayed, something I wasn't in the habit of doing, but, in the quiet of the bathroom I asked God to help us find Dan and make everything the status quo.

"Mum, how are you?" I asked when I was back downstairs. "I know it's worrying, but thinking more clearly about it, don't you think he might have taken himself back home to England? After all, he kept on threatening about going back."

"Maisie, I don't think that Dan would leave us without saying a word," Mum replied. "He's a sensitive boy, aware of how painful it would be for us if he just up and left without a word."

She was right. Dan was a sensitive young man and however much he hated life here, he would never have just up and left without saying something.

The atmosphere in the house was now one of desperation.

"Come on, let's go down to the farm and talk to Ralph and Gangees. Maisie, did you give the police your mobile number?"

"Yes, Dad, I did. They will be able to get hold of us if needed."

Dad had phoned the farm earlier and had told Ralph that Dan still hadn't been seen anywhere since he had been with Gange, two days before.

I changed my clothes, as the weather was still reasonably warm. Even though it was the beginning of November, I'd sweated profusely during the day and stank to high heaven. So did my father, but we had more on our minds than body odour. He still hadn't told Mum about Dan's secret.

The journey took forever. When we got there and Ralph heard the car, he came rushing over to us and asked, "Is there any change yet? Have the police tracked him down?"

"No news, yet, Ralph," Dad said anxiously.

Ralph indicated for us to go into the sitting room. The old dark and rancid-smelling place was not the best area to sit in. Benny had been allowed indoors and came over to where I sat and started to nudge at my hands asking for me to stroke him. It's amazing how comforting stroking an animal can be.

"Jack? Julia? Would you care for a drink? Whatever you want I probably have it."

"A brandy wouldn't go amiss, Ralph," Dad replied.

"Make that two," Mum hastened to add. It was the first comment I'd heard her make since we left home.

"What about you, my dear?" he said to me.

At this simple kindness, I felt the tears well up in my eyes, and had a devil of a job stopping them from running down my face. I knew he felt our pain and he said, "I will get you a pick-me-up as well, Maisie." Then he touched my arm with such gentleness that I wanted to hug him right there. I thanked the Lord for small mercies and the fine friendship of this man and his lovely dog.

"Where's your brother, Ralph?" Mum asked.

Dad interjected: "I want to talk to him about Dan, what they did and where they went. He may be able to shed some light on what's happened. I think he was probably the last one to see him."

"He's down helping get the cows up to the shed for milking. It's a job he likes to do each day around this time. He shouldn't be long."

"Have the police been up to talk to him?" Dad asked. "They said they would do that within a day or two."

"No sign of them yet."

He walked away to the kitchen and poured large Remy Martin brandy into his beautiful Edinburgh crystal glasses. We slowly sipped the strong alcohol. I had not tasted brandy before and it was having a considerable effect. My head began to spin and as I got up, I went back down causing a racket by breaking one of the expensive glasses. I apologized profusely, saying I'd pay for it.

As the conversation slowed, my mother said with a tremble in her voice, "What on earth could have happened to him?"

At that moment, Gangees made a dramatic entrance, knocking a wooden chair over in the kitchen as he tried to get his boots off and walk at the same time. He was uttering words of comfort as he came through the door into the sitting room. Dad got up but Mum remained seated, and I was afraid to move for fear of causing trouble.

"How dreadful that the boy hasn't come home yet," Gange said. "Where on earth can he have got to?"

"Never, never in a million years, would Dan purposefully put us into this situation," Mum declared. "He is not that sort of child, and would never have left without telling us if he intended to go back home. But, now I wonder if that maybe exactly what he's done."

"Well, there we have it, that'll be where he's gone," Gange said.

Had the man not heard what my mother had just said? Was he naïve enough to think that Dan could behave that way? He did not know my brother, so how could he be so stupid as to make such a declaration?

I had to butt in: "You don't know him well enough to make any assumptions as to what he may or may not have done."

Dad told me to be quiet, which I immediately was, for I didn't want to make a horrible situation worse than it already was, even though I hated this bloke with a vengeance. His smarmy ways were revolting and I didn't trust him at all. In fact, I vehemently thought he was behind what was going on.

"Gange, you were with Dan last Sunday afternoon," Dad said. "Do you have any idea of where he went?"

"No, not really," came the reply. "I left him in the pub, as I'd had enough to drink and we'd finished our conversation about him joining the Navy. He told me that he wanted to stay in town, as he had to get in touch with a friend."

My mobile rang at that moment and made us all jump.

"Where are you, Madam?" It was Victor, our policeman who spoke good English. I told him where we were and he said, "Please get yourselves back here immediately. I have some news for you."

With that, I grabbed my jacket and told my parents we must get to the police station, as they want to talk to us about Dan."

I didn't know what to think at that point. The policeman's voice didn't sound particularly scary or concerned. Perhaps they had found Dan and wanted us all together, to give us the good news.

CHAPTER NINE

The Revelation

"Last Thing.
So, when you close your eyes to leave me I'll close mine."
~ Vander and Bloom.

It was Sunday, November 21st, 2010, when Dan went missing. That night there had been a full moon, a beautiful pinkish, reddish colour. At first, I thought it was a strawberry moon, but that was impossible as they only come late in June. That name, strawberry moon, I loved the story of how it came about. It was the early American Algonquian tribes who gave it this name, as this particular moon heralds the start of gathering ripening fruits.

Ralph came with us to the police station. Dad went to the desk in the corner of the room, where two distinguished looking gentlemen sat. They wore full gendarmerie uniforms.

"We had a call to come to the station," he explained anxiously. "It'll be about our son,

Dan, who's been missing for several days now."

"Oh, yes sir," one of the men replied. "Will you come this way, please?"

I grabbed Mother's arm and called Ralph over to my side as we were instructed to follow the officer and Dad along a dark corridor with walls that had been freshly painted in a pretty lilac. I didn't understand the reason I'd been taking in such detail, when we were all so worried about Dan. He walked us over to a closed door and knocked on it.

A voice from inside called out: "Entrée!"

Inside there were three solemn looking men who were not in uniform.

The only one who could really communicate with us in English was a young bright-eyed, tall officer in a very smart grey pinstriped suit and pink shirt and black tie. He told us that he was the Chief Officer of the branch and said: "Please, will you sit down."

He offered us seats in front of the desk that partially hid the other two officers, revealing just their heads and shoulders.

"We are so sorry to have to tell you that your son has been found dead," the police chief said in his broken English. We think he has been murdered. He was found late last night."

Mother screamed and ran into Dad's arms and stayed there holding him and no words were spoken. Dad just sat, staring at the officer and I put my hands to my face in total shock and disbelief. Never had I experienced such a painful emotion. I couldn't take any of it in. What were they saying? My brother? He can't be dead! I didn't know what to do or say. I stood for the next few moments, feeling shaky and wanting to shout out: "No! This cannot be true! What are you saying to us?"

But, the words never left my mouth. Dad and Mum were being consoled by one of the officers. Mother was in such a state and screaming out: "No, no, no! It cannot be true! Not my son, not my lovely boy!"

Dad was making a futile attempt to comfort her. No one seemed to be taking much notice of me until a uniformed policeman who spoke good English, came over and said, "Is there anything I can do to help you, my dear? This must be such a terrible shock for you."

"Where is he? I want to see him!" I replied in desperate tones.

I had no thought for my parents in that moment. I found it hard to try to comprehend what was going on around us. There were cups of tea and a brandy bottle appeared and added to the table where cups and glasses stood. Suddenly, I found myself weeping uncontrollably. What had we just heard? Surely this could not be true? They must have found the wrong person. I mean they didn't even know his last name a few days ago.

I sensed many people standing around us now, uttering words that sounded as if they were attempting to be sympathetic, which meant absolutely nothing to me and my parents. The shook was all consuming. The stoical presence of Ralph, who was now beside me, was the only thing making any sense.

I flew into his strong arms and wept onto his shirt. I remember he smelt of farmyard. I don't think I shall ever forget that smell.

"Ralph, what are we to do? What are we to do?" I repeated, over and over again.

"I'm here, Maisie, let's see what we can find out," he tried to reassure me.

Dad went down to the morgue with the man who'd broken this dreadful news to us, to identify the body. And yes, it was our beloved Dan, my brother, not quite eighteen years old. When he returned, we were told to remain in the room. Two more police officers entered and spoke to us in French, interpreted by Hugo, our English speaker. The words were coming through thick and fast.

"Your son was murdered," he pointed out. "We can't tell you how at the moment, however, what we can tell you is that we think we have the person in custody, he has been arrested."

"Who could have done such a thing to our boy?" Dad asked. "He had no enemies."

"Unfortunately, we are not at liberty to give you any information yet. We cannot tell you anything until many more investigations have been carried out, steps have been taken and a post-mortem conducted."

"Never mind steps being taken!" Dad half-shouted at him. "We are his family and have every right to know what happened, when and by whom!"

"Now, now, sir, I know this is all very upsetting, but, you should all go back to your home now and we will speak with you later."

My God, such insensitive behavior directed at us! Surely, they could appreciate what this news had done to us, the impact it had on us. It seemed wicked to send us away without any more information than the little given so far. Ralph was with my parents, trying in vain to comfort them.

He said, "Come with me and I'll take you home."

What a sad journey that was, the saddest journey of my whole life. When we got back, Ralph helped us from the car to the house, since none of us could even walk properly, the stink of farmyard smells from over the road and from Ralph, stuck in my nose and made me feel sick.

Dad turned the key, opened the door and said to Ralph quietly: "Come on in."

We all sat in silence. I looked over at my Dad. His face seemed to transform back and forth from denial to shock to anger.

"I need to see the body again," Dad said. "I was too upset. I didn't get a good look. Maybe it is somebody else."

None of us said a word. His face transformed to shock.

"Who could have done such a thing as this to our boy?" Dad said. "Dan was such a gentle, kind soul."

Still silence. Cold, dreaded silence. The shock heated into anger.

"He shouldn't have got involved with that woman! The husband must've found out, that's what this has to be."

Mum turned towards Dad.

"What woman? What husband? What haven't you told me? I've had a feeling for a while after seeing you and Maisie cosying up and talking quietly. If I came into a room where you were together, you'd both shut up. That's enough to make anyone suspicious."

"They haven't told us who they have locked up, Mother," I told her. "But, I think it may be the husband of the woman Dan was having an affair with."

"What? What are you saying about my son? He would never do a thing like that!"

"Well, Julia, he was having an affair with a married woman," Dad told her. "And Maisie has known about it for some time, but only told me after Dan went missing."

"And you both knew this and chose not to tell me about it? How could you!" Mum yelled.

"What difference would it have made?" I said. "There is no way any of us could have done anything to stop him. I tried to, Mum, and I told him he'd be in trouble if he didn't look out and end the affair."

"I cannot believe the two of you connived behind my back," Mum mumbled. "How could you do it?"

How could you do this? How could you do that? We fought with each other. We went quiet. Ralph left. We all went to separate rooms. I cried. I stared at the ceiling. I cried again. We went to bed, woke up, then we did it all again. Denial to shock to anger and accusations.

Mum could not comprehend the magnitude of it all. None of her coping strategies kicked in. She had always enjoyed her wine, but, what we were beginning to see now (and what lay ahead), was unimaginable. Her drinking was about to take on a new dimension. She would begin first thing in the morning, before Dad and I were up—clearly trying to hide the habit from us. Then she would continue to drink furtively until late at night. Dad told me that he found endless empty vodka bottles. She had tried hiding her secret by going into the woods close by and distributing them in the undergrowth around the trees. Her speech was always slightly slurred and she shied away from meeting people. It seemed to be the only way she could carry on after Dan's death; to drink herself into oblivion.

Dad was reluctant to say anything to her at the time. I recall one dreadful day when she went out at about eleven one morning, no one had seen her, she'd not left a note to say where she was going, and the car was missing. We were so worried, that we enlisted some of the residents to help us search. Dad called Ralph, who came straight away. The folks helping took their cars down to the village and out into the countryside. I was amazed at their kindness, a quality not seen before, except by Mr. Banergee, and his extraordinary nature was proving to be of great help to me in particular. I remember when we were first told of Dan's death, he came to see us, bringing a hamper of good food, and he was unrestrained with his caring platitudes.

The day was cold, with an occasional glimmer of sunlight, then it started to rain, not heavily, but enough to make me even more concerned as I saw Mum's coat still hanging on the stand. It was awful to be going through such overpowering emotions yet again.

Ralph said to Dad and me, "Get in the van. Where does she like to go around here? Is there a special place?"

"Not that I know of," Dad said.

We got in the van and spent more than three hours looking for my distressed, desperate mother. When we eventually found her some four hours later, sitting on a bench by the River Isle just staring into space, I jumped out of the van, dashed over to her.

"Oh, Mum, we've been so worried about you."

Dad and Ralph came over and Dad lifted her from the seat and took her into his arms and said, "There my dear, thank God you're okay. We have been so worried."

"I'm sorry," she cried, "I couldn't face staying indoors a minute longer. I just had to leave. I didn't mean for you to be so worried about me. I'll be OK now."

But, of course, she wasn't. And, when we arrived back indoors she opened a new bottle of red wine and drank the lot.

Desolation had laid its hands on us.

Chapter Ten

The Confrontation

"I have learned over the years that when one's mind is made up,
this diminishes fear."
~ Rosa Parks

On the last day of November, I made up my mind to go first into town and talk to the woman who had been having an affair with Dan. I asked around school, figured out who it was, where she lived.

I realized I was on what could be a troubled and dangerous mission, but was possessed with the need to try to find out who could have done this terrible thing to my brother. I said nothing to Dad about my intentions, as I knew he'd try to stop me.

Dan's lover's husband had a reason to want revenge and were he the violent sort, then it was possible that he had killed Dan, despite what the police were saying. We had been told they had no reason to think he was the killer, because of his alibi and lack of evidence.

My heart ached. What on earth was I going to say to her? What if she wasn't alone? These thoughts kept darting through my mind on the way to her house. I had taken Dad's truck as I could drive that. Even though I hadn't passed my test, I was prepared to take the risk and hoped I wouldn't get stopped by the police. I would be taking my driving test soon and had taken a few formal lessons with one of the local driving instructors.

As I knocked on the glass-and-oak door, I felt scared. My mouth went dry and the butterflies were having a wild party in my stomach. I wasn't sure what I would say if her husband was at home. I had taken a chance going there, however it was daytime and with any luck he would be working.

I heard someone coming towards the door, but I couldn't make out if it was a man's or a woman's footsteps. A woman opened the door and she looked horrified when she realized who was standing in her porch-way. I have no idea why it was that she seemed to know who I was.

"I'm Dan's sister, Madam," I began. "I think he was a friend of yours."

I think she understood a little of what I had said but not all of it.

"You come inside," she urged me. "We talk inside."

I was surprised that she invited me into her home. She ushered me to sit down, which I did, and felt most comfortable on the large, soft cushioned settee (the type I loved because it seemed to embrace you as you fell into its welcome). I was overcome by the aroma of her strong, cheap-smelling perfume that remained in my nostrils throughout the rest of the day. She was very attractive, though, and I could understand why my brother found her so alluring.

"What are you doing here and what do you want to know?" she asked curtly.

"I would like to know if you can possibly give me any sort of clue as to who my brother's murderer could be."

She looked me straight in the eye and said, "How you expect me to know anything?"

"Well, your husband was arrested at the time as one of the main suspects, surely you remember that. I know it was a while back, but surely you could not have forgotten something as serious as your lover's death."

"How you know he my lover? Who tell you this?"

"He told me this, Therese."

"How you know my name?"

"There was a lot of talk at the school about the two of you. So, I confronted him. He was very angry that I did, telling me to mind my own business and keep out of his. I didn't want to interfere, but I tried to make it clear that I feared for not only our parents finding out, but, also your husband."

"He could not hurt a fly," she told me. "He's a big man but he not got a violent bone in his body. I knew from start that he not does it. I told the police this, but, of course they had to investigate and all. Found that he was with a friend in a town near here and that he stood up and said so. So, he gets away from prison. I felt bad for what I done and to think this boy so young got killed, maybe because of me."

"Why do you say that?"

"I say it because I know other men and they can get jealous. I don't think any knew 'bout Dan and me, but as you say, there was talk, so maybe they hear it and want to hurt him. I dunno. I feel so bad 'bout what 'appen. Now you go now, I know nothing else."

"Thanks for telling me that, Therese. Can you think of anything that might help me in looking for the person who did it?"

"The only thing is that the day he died he was 'ere with me. We do nothing as my husband was to be home very quick. I had a job to get rid of Dan. I kept on tell him he should go. Eventually he go, and I know they pass each other, him and my husband, as he keep on asking who it was at our house."

"Oh? Well, that's new information to me," I said.

"I go out after a while when husband asleep in chair—he tired after hard work and big meal. I tried to contact Dan on 'is mobile, but he have it turn off. I walked into the town and onto the route I thought 'e might take. I see Dan and it seemed he walking away from Ribérac and a big car stopped beside him and he got in."

"Therese, did you tell the police any of this?"

"No, I forget 'till now. Didn't think important. I went to find him to say all alright and he no need worry, but even though I call, he no turn round and see me."

"Thank you for your help. I shall not bother you anymore. Just one last thing. Did you see what colour, what type of car that was? And, do you remember what time it was?"

"No, it was dark, may 'av been about eight in night. But, I notice it was a very big wagon type of thing. Something like farmers use."

This was all I needed to be able to take things further. I would tell the police what Therese had said.

It made me even more certain of Gangees' involvement.

CHAPTER ELEVEN

James Arrives

"Start by doing what's necessary,
then do what's possible and suddenly you are doing the impossible."
~ St. Francis of Assisi

I finally found James' number in one of my drawers in the old dresser that made its way to my bedroom when we came to France. I felt exhilarated when I found it and asked Dad to make the call. He told me it was up to me to get hold of James as he was my friend and not his.

"Hello James, it's Maisie here," I said in a disconsolate voice.

"Is it really you, my little friend? how are you? What are you doing now - I'm so pleased to hear from you Maisie. Is all well? You sound a bit down?"

"I have the most terrible news James, it's Dan, he's been," I could feel my heartbeat pounding. I was starting to lose my breath. "He's been murdered! And I don't know what to do. And I'm scared. And lost. And I—can you come over here? Oh please come over here James. I'm going crazy."

"Hold on. What did you just say? This isn't some kind of sick prank call is it? You're making some sort of dark joke aren't you?

"They killed him, James. Dan's dead. They've opened a case and everything. I wanted to call you but I couldn't find your number anywhere. Oh James. I can't eat. I can't sleep."

"OK, OK. Slow down. Slow down. Deep breaths. So, alright. Do they have any leads? Who could have even done such a thing--- have you any idea?"

"Yes. I think I know exactly who did it but they won't listen to me they think I'm hysterical."

"How are your parents doing? Oh my God. Look I've got some leave coming up, I wasn't going to come to France, but I will now. I promise. I'll sort it out my end then call you and let you know when I'm going to get over. I'll be there as soon as I can. Is there someone who can collect me from the airport?"

"Of course, absolutely, that's the least of my worries. Oh my gosh, thank you James. Make it soon, James. Please, I think I'm going out of my mind here. The whole world is turning upside down. Mother's drinking is out of control and Dad has shut off to some extent. He's walking around like a ghost."

A couple of weeks passed with excruciatingly slow momentum, then James got in touch and told me he'd be arriving at Bergerac airport on the Friday at the end of the week. I told him dad would collect him and that I would have a meal ready for when he got here. I reckoned it would be about six p.m.

On seeing my friend from school back home I blurted everything out with the very definition of wasted energy.

He stopped me in full flow and pulled me into his arms and held me there, crying bitterly. When he released me I uttered through unveiled tears enquiring about his journey.

I blew my nose and tried to regain a degree of composure.

"Did you talk with my dad at all?"

"Sort of. Your Dad didn't say much though. I tried to make banile conversation but it fell on stony ground I'm afraid."

"No, he's not himself at all these days, little wonder, what with Mother and the lengthy business of trying to get the police more in tune with finding Dan's killer. We barely get any news and it's all so frustrating. James you won't recognize Mother. She is drinking herself into oblivion. Try not to be to shocked when you see her. James, you have got so tall, and you're better looking than I recall. You look so grown up."

"Better looking than you recall? Gee, what did I look like before? Well, you don't look so bad yourself Maisie. In fact, you are quite beautiful. Course, I recall that always being true."

That remark did a lot to cheer me and help boost my confidence. I could feel myself even blushing a little; feeling the innocence of a childhood crush.

"I think it goes without saying, it looks like you have way more on your plate here than you can handle alone. No one could handle this alone" he said quietly to me.

He looked off in the distance and I could see he was debating whether to ask this next question at all.

"Are you happy here, daft question right now, but what I mean is before the tragedy did you feel as though you'd settled here?"

"No, not really."

"Do you have, um, a boyfriend or anything like that?"

"I fancy a bloke, a farmer, years older than me so I doubt anything will come of that. But I have been homesick and missed you so much, James. I felt as if you should be here too and we could be out on our bikes playing those daft games we used to make up. Do you remember being Sherlock Holmes to my Watson when we tried to do a bit of sleuthing to find out more about that bloke who scared us so much. And you'll never guess what James. I have to tell you he's over here. I know he is. And I think it's him who had something to do with Dan's murder. He was the last one to be with Dan on the Sunday he disappeared. Gange, as he's called short for Gangees, daft name if ever I heard one. He is the brother of the bloke I fancy, you know the one who is so much older than me."

"Woah, slow down Maisie. That's a lot to take in. I'm not even sure where to start."

"See, you're going to tell me I'm hysterical just like everyone else. But I know it's true! I've seen him up close, and this Gange guy, I'm telling you. He was the guy we saw!"

"I didn't say you were hysterical. I'm just overwhelmed by it all, it's hard for me to even process that Dan is gone, let alone try and solve the mystery.

We moved out of the kitchen and into the living room where mother was muttering to herself about a lot of nonsense. I couldn't help but see James' face out of the corner of my eye. His look was contorted as if some horror had beset him.

It was lunchtime, she had left her bedroom, come down and grabbed the first full bottle of booze she could lay her hands on.

James went over to her, held out his hand to shake Mother's. She backed away saying "Who the hell are you?"

"Mum, it's James, you remember James my school friend from back when. We used to hang out together when we were younger."

"I don't remember nothing, now bugger off."

I beckoned to James to follow me out of the room.

"I am so sorry to see this Maisie, you poor girl. You're living in a nightmare. I take it this stuff with your mum has all happened since Dan's death?"

"Yes, she always enjoyed her wine, but now it's anything she can get her hands on and totally out of control. She needs help, not sure how we're going to get it. How long can you stay James?"

"I've got one week of leave, looks like we have plenty to keep us occupied. Our childhood experiences could come in handy, what do you say my dear Watson?"

I didn't laugh but not because I was offended, my mind was just racing a mile a minute and I didn't really hear him.

"I'm sorry Maisie I didn't mean to sound flippant," James apologized.

"What? Oh, no. I just got lost in my head. Sorry. I want to tell you everything. I think we could solve this, I really do. You're the only one that can help."

"Tell me as much as you can about it all and what have the police done so far."

"Precious little as far as I can tell. Dad's always going to the station asking for information, and little is forthcoming. I have been to see Dan's lover, that was difficult as I was scared she would send me packing, however she invited me in and gave me some new snippets of information."

"I have a friend back home, not really a friend but a guy I'll share a pint with from time to time, and he is always on about getting transferred around the world. Apparently encouraged now in the British police force as they reckon it broadens their horizons and helps to build better understanding and character. I wonder if he'd come here? He's a smart guy, hard-working guy from all I can tell."

"Here, come and sit down in the garden. I'll tell you everything."

I relayed everything I could recall, which was most of it including the mundane minutia. And I told James how and why I was so convinced that Gange was the culprit. He now knew that Dan's girlfriend's husband had a brother in the local police. I told him I thought that fact would make it easier to get the evidence we needed, but that had proved not to be the case. In fact he had been closed lipped most of the time and when he did speak it was clear he wanted the whole debacle over and done with as soon as possible.

"James, I want you to come and meet this Gange bloke. I think that's where we should start."

We went in silence, arm in arm. It didn't take us long to get to the farm. Suddenly out came Benny who made a beeline straight to me. He jumped up so pleased to see me and sniffed around James as if to say, "If you're a friend of hers, then you're alright."

"Hello, this is a nice surprise," came a voice from behind us.

"Hello, Ralph, this is my friend from England the one I used to be at school with." James held out his hand to shake Ralph's.

"Well a friend of yours is a friend of mine I'd say. Come on you two, come on in I've got some fresh coffee on the go."

"Hope it tastes better than her tea," James said.

"How could you say that you've only had one cup of it?" I added.

"That was enough to know you can't make tea."

Benny raced us into the courtyard

"Ralph, is your brother around? I was hoping to introduce James to him."

"Gange will be here soon, he's just gone into town to get some odds and ends."

"What are you doing for work now James?"

"I'm in the newspaper trade. It's hard work, but I love It. Must get a place in some university or other. Probably in the U.K. everywhere I go people say that a U.K. university training is the envy of the world. I think that's likely to be true. Do you think so Maisie?"

"I don't know, what I do know is that Helen and I will probably go to one in Paris."

"That will be a good move, now that you speak fluent French," Ralph said. "I think the choices in France can rival anything in the U.K. No offense, James."

I saw the look that said, "Wow" on James' face at that remark. And then, suddenly, like a gust of Mistral wind had blown him in from the South, came the miserable bloke we'd come to see.

"And who do we have here?" Gange said. "How are you Maisie? You look a bit pale. Are you quite well? What are you doing down here?"

The questions just poured from his mouth. And when he wasn't talking he had that smug grin like an angry vulture on his thin lips.

James stood mouth open, then he turned to me as if to say 'you're right, that's him.'

"Hasn't my brother offered you something to drink?" Gange said. "What will it be tea, coffee or something stronger?"

"Yes," I uttered. "We've been drinking coffee."

"Better still, why not eat with us? What's for dinner Ralph? We can muster a bit more up for these two skinny kids now can't we?"

"Thank you," said James fidgeting with his watch.

"We don't want to be any trouble, but thanks."

Ralph rustled up some cheese and fresh bread with salad. James and I began a light interrogation of Gange. We interrupted him often trying to find out where Gange was six years back and what he was doing. It worked and he came out with a load of tosh about being abroad in Japan. Gange began to get suspicious and kept on deflecting the questions back to us until we both became more confused than when we started. When Ralph sat down with us, he remained quiet and seemed to want us to shut up given his silence and occasional grimace. Eventually he told us something that made it possible that he was in the U.K. at that time. He slipped up by telling us how he came home for his brother's wedding and then after that his parents returned to England when his Father was diagnosed with cancer. He would visit him in Berkshire.

He came out with these facts without realising what he had said. We were catching him in a trap.

Ralph took me to one side when the opportunity arose.

"What's going on with you two? Surely you don't think Gange had anything to do with Dan's murder."

"I'm sorry, but we don't know. He is so strange, Ralph. He stares more than is comfortable and, after all, he was the last one to be with Dan on that Sunday."

"Yes, but the police have interviewed him and nothing has come of it. And I don't think that you and James are equipped to be acting on supposition."

"I haven't told you all of it. There's not time to go into that right now. But I will tell you what happened to me back in England one day."

"My curiosity is running wild, you have to tell me Maisie."

So I did. I recounted the story about Gange wearing his coat and hat chasing after us, cornering us. All Ralph did was laugh.

"I'm sorry love, I don't mean to be unkind and I'm sorry you were so frightened, but my brother would never be as stupid as to try and frighten children."

With that remark I walked away, hoping that James had taken the opportunity to have kept the pressure up on Gange.

On our way home James and I decided we would follow Gange one night to see if anything suspicious came about. We chose the Monday as James was returning to England the following Wednesday. I made our supper then we let Dad know we were going for a walk.

"Make sure to take your torches and how far are you planning to go?"

"Just round and about Dad. Won't be long."

"Wrap up warm, the nights are getting quite cold now."

Down we hurried, torches lighting the way. As we came near the farm we heard raised voices coming from the yard. It was Ralph and Gange having a heated discussion. I hoped that Benny was shut away for he would undoubtedly have given the game away. It was so dark and difficult to see clearly. But when the men parted company, we had our chance to follow Gange at an appropriate distance. He kept going back and forth In and out of one of the barns. It looked as though he was taking small items, not usually seen in a farm yard and he appeared to be hiding them. All of a sudden he dashed into the house then re-appeared suitably clothed for outdoors, got into his Jeep and drove off at speed from the farm. We just managed to avoid being seen by hiding behind a huge rhododendron bush.

James went home and I wish there was more to report from our endeavours, but truthfully not much happened while he was here. Our sleuthing, had not got us far with the exception of James promising he would see if his friend the detective could come over and help matters.

James told me he had a strong suspicion there was a police cover up going on.

As the days progressed, few curt remarks were made by Ralph, he eluded to James being just a child with childlike behaviour and comments. I think this came because Ralph picked up on the fact that we had his wayward brother in the frame for Dan's murder.

CHAPTER TWELVE

Neighbourly Kindness

and Sisterly Love

"Kindness is a language which the deaf can hear and the blind can see"
~Mark Twain

It was now the second week in December, almost a month since Dan's murder and Christmas just around the corner. This Christmas was one that would likely go uncelebrated and one to be remembered for the rest of our lives. Mother's drinking had increased and was a source of our great concern. She drank when and where she wanted to, she'd stopped trying to hide it from us. Dad said nothing. I think he knew it was no good reacting to her distressing habit, as it appeared to be the only thing that kept her going.

Ralph had come over to see us as he did regularly these days. Dad had spoken to him about Mum's drinking. When he arrived, Dad said, "Best to just stay quiet and not say anything to her about it."

We watched her sway back and forth to where whichever bottle she'd opened stood. It was no longer just vodka, but whisky, and anything else she could lay her hands on. We were terrified when she got into the car to take off to Ribérac. She was in no fit state to walk, let alone drive. Dad and I did all we could to dissuade her from leaving, saying that she was a danger to all others on the road and that if she wasn't careful, she would end up killing someone. It fell on deaf ears and off she went.

Ralph didn't say much, he just tried a few comforting words now and then. It was dark and past six and the continuous, all-consuming sorrow was relentless, no place for a visitor to hang around. Ralph stayed with us as long as his fortitude could take it, until reality called him and he left us saying, "I'm sorry, but I must go. The animals need tending to."

"Where is your brother, Ralph?" I asked hurriedly.

"I think he's at the farm—at least he was there when I left. I called out to him to see if he would come up with me, but I couldn't find him. He must have been down at the lodge end of the farm and he would never have heard me calling."

Mother eventually came back home, more sober than when she left. No new leads were available yet and it appeared the police were in no hurry to find Dan's killer. As we were wallowing in our distress, there was a loud bang on the front door.

It was Sylvi Chevalier. I hadn't liked her much until that night. She was the Swedish lass who I considered to be a self-centred individual who kept to herself and was married to an alcoholic. Now we had something in common.

"I've only just heard the news, Mr. Patterson, as I've been away in Sweden for a few weeks," Sylvi explained. "It's dreadful. Do you know anything more yet?"

"No," Dad told her. "We contact the police almost every day. I went down there yesterday and they haven't any more news for us. I think they're getting a bit fed up with our constant enquiring. 'We will get in touch when we know anything,' is all they ever have to tell us."

Sylvi came over to where Mum and I were sitting. "My dear girls," she began, "What can I possibly say to you, that would make you feel any different to how you're feeling right now?"

"There is nothing, don't worry about it," I reassured her. "No one can change what's happened or can say anything to make us feel any better. It is what it is and we must live with it. I so hope that as they say, 'Time will heal'."

"Please let me know if there is anything I can do to help you," she urged us. "If there is, please don't hesitate to call me."

"Would you care for some tea?" I asked. "I'll go and make it." I went off to the kitchen without waiting for the reply. It must have been difficult for her to come over and bother about us. How do you react when visitors who you don't know too well come around, desperately trying to find the right words to say, to try and empathize with your loss? How can anyone have any idea of the pain we feel? I'd taken to Sylvi on that night.

She cared enough to stay with us, and we all drank tea until we felt as though we were drowning in it. It clearly diluted Mum's booze, as for the first time in a while she appeared to be sober, and seemed quite happy talking with Sylvi and even smiled once or twice. Sylvi left us at about eleven that night and reiterated that if we needed her, she'd be on hand. Dad saw her to the door. She turned to us and said we should try and get some sleep. Not that I thought we would, for we hadn't managed much sleep since Dan went missing. Our nights were fitful at best and often one or the other would spend the whole night wide awake. Mum was usually out cold drunk, and Dad paced the floor endlessly.

The sleeping situation had become chronic for me and Dad. I decided to speak to a local pharmacist in an endeavour to get something to help us catch up with so much sleep loss. We were starting to malfunction. I told him of our situation and the resulting effects. He was both helpful and sympathetic, advising that we should take a sedative drug to get us through this difficult time, but to make sure that we didn't use them for too long, as they were addictive.

The evenings had drawn in and the nights feeling colder. The weather was appalling with rain lashing down on us as if to say: *Get out of here.* With the bad conditions came the musty smell that seemed to permeate from the ground, as if winter as releasing all the moulds it could muster in one foul swoop. My poor mother; never had I imagined she would behave as now. She barely acknowledged that Dad and I were in the house. Dad fared almost as badly, but he had the instinct of a husband and father needing to try to keep up the morale of his family.

Dad had been in touch with a relative in England, as we were clearly in need of help. It came in the guise of Mother's sister, Aunt Mary. She was a formidable character with a no-nonsense approach to life, but we needed direction and support. Aunt Mary lived in Somerset, a long way from where our home used to be. Dad picked her up from Angouleme Airport. I think her presence helped us put a sort of perspective to it all. She told us that time would heal our wounds, although I failed to see how, in that moment. She spoke from the depths of experience, as she had lost a child when he was only four years old—he'd drowned in their garden pond.

"But, Auntie, how can that compare with murder?" I asked.

"I'm not trying to draw comparisons, Maisie," she pointed out. "I'm just trying to assure you that time is a great healer." She enlightened me, but I knew it would take more than time for me to get over losing my brother, who I so loved. Mum was trying to make some sort of effort at being normal and not taking in quite so much alcohol. She shouted from the kitchen for me to come and help her prepare lunch. As I got up from my seat, the one I spent so many hours sitting in, the doorbell rang. It was 'Gange'.

"Do you want to stay for lunch?" Mum asked him. "It's only a stew but there's plenty of it and you're more than welcome."

"Thank you, Julia, and yes, I'd love to," he replied.

Dad took Gange into the lounge and introduced him to Aunt Mary. As usual, I felt uncomfortable around him. I was still convinced that he was the odd bod I saw by the canal back when. Today, Gange was on his best behaviour and did not do the usual 'staring' I'd become accustomed to. However, my family, including Dan, had said that his staring was in my mind, when I told them about what I thought of him. We sat down and ate the food, none of us being particularly hungry, but we ate as best we could for Mum's sake, who was trying hard to be brave in front of her sister.

Dad said he was going to the police today. "I want to see if there's any more news," he announced. "We don't even know how Dan died. I think at least they should tell us that."

At that point, Gange said that he and Ralph would like to do some work on the roof. "We need to get it finished before the winter really gets a hold," Gange stressed. "We planned on doing it much earlier, as you know, but fate took over."

That was the closest this man got to saying anything about Dan and he mentioned nothing about how we were feeling. I wanted "fate to take over" in the form of the cops showing up and putting him in handcuffs.

A short while after lunch, Ralph arrived and I just ran out and hugged him. He meant so much to me—in fact, now more than ever. I hadn't much experience with the opposite sex, but all I knew now was that I wanted to be around him more than before. I'd always fancied him, but now I felt this urgent desire to make love with him. How could I be thinking such things when my brother had not yet been buried, and he still pervaded my everyday thoughts? It seemed like sacrilege. It was wrong of me, surely, but, I could not shake off the rage I felt inside. He seemed to be embarrassed by my clinging to him for so long and slowly pulled away and took my arms from around his shoulders and held my hands.

He looked me straight in the eyes and said, "I know how you're feeling, Maisie, and no words of mine will ease the hurt. Try to be strong, my dear." With that, I began to cry. Everyone in the house tried to comfort me, but to no avail. I just took off to my room and wept there for what seemed like hours. Eventually, I fell asleep and when I awoke I went to the bathroom and washed my swollen red eyes and tried to make myself look a bit more presentable. When I came downstairs the house was so quiet, no one was about. I looked up at the ceiling in the large extension where the rain had been coming through, to see that it had been completely repaired.

Where was everybody, I wondered? I put the kettle on to make myself a hot drink and with that I started to wander over the house and found myself entering Dan's room for the first time since the incident. I began to look through his things and opened a drawer, where to my amazement I found his mobile phone. I thought the police had taken most of Dan's stuff. Curiosity overtook any other feelings and I began reading the text messages he had written to his lover and those she sent him. I was left in no doubt after reading these that their affair had been a serious one, and that they may even have been on the verge of eloping or running away together. It became clear that Dan had persuaded her to leave Ribérac with him and go back to England. I wondered about their intentions regarding her little boy. The messages were very personal and erotic and as the clarity of their deep passion sunk in, I stopped reading, placed the phone back where I'd found it, and gently closed the drawer. I hadn't realized what a sensual man my brother was, but these messages described a different man from the brother I knew. Why had the police not taken or asked us for Dan's phone?

I went back downstairs, having pulled myself together. My parents and Aunt Mary had just returned from the police station. Dad was angry. I could see the anger in his body language and facial expression. Mum was very quiet and came into the living room.

"Well, God help us with this bloody French policing!" Dad raged. "They are absolutely useless. Might as well not have bothered to go down there. All it's done is upset your mother."

Anger was now setting into the processes of our grieving.

"Dad, did you see what Ralph and Gange have done?" I asked in an attempt to cheer them up a bit. "They've finished the roof."

"That's one blessing," Dad replied, "But I'm not sure, Maisie, that we will be staying here now that this has happened. It won't be the same without Dan."

"That's certainly the truth, Dad, but it won't be any different wherever we go—the feelings aren't going to go away. Being back in England, if that's what you plan, will be just as bad. Running away is not the answer."

"We shall see. Your mother doesn't want to live here, but, it is all too fresh for us to make rash decisions."

"Did they tell you if they've locked anyone else up for Dan's murder? And how did he die, Dad?" I wanted so much to hear the answers. I was bereft at the thought of how my brother had died.

"As you know they arrested the husband of that girl he was seeing."

"Well, I think they have the wrong person," I muttered.

"What on earth makes you say that, Maisie? Do you know something we don't?"

I had to think carefully right now. I couldn't let my parents, or anyone else for that matter, know who I thought had killed Dan. So, I mumbled some sort of excuse like, "Well, I have no idea who could hate Dan so much to want him dead." But I really believed that the culprit was Gange. He was a very strange man and was the last one to have been in Dan's company, so we thought.

Everyone was tired through lack of sleep, misery and grieving. Then, the phone rang. It was one of the boys, asking us all to go to number one for drinks that evening. I know they were trying to be kind, but to be honest, any form of socializing was the last thing that any of us wanted to do.

Dad said, "How kind. What time shall we come over? And will it be alright if my wife's sister comes along?"

"Yes, of course, bring her along, the more the merrier," was the reply. "Make it 6 p.m. There will be a few nibbles as well, so you won't have to worry about cooking."

Worry about cooking! Thinking about food was the last thing on our minds. Anyway, Dad said it would be good for us to go out and have a change of scenery.

When we arrived, only a few of the local residents were there to greet us. There were not many folks over at this time of year. Most spent Christmas back in 'Blighty'. People were kind and considerate, especially the boys, with the exception of Mrs. Treadworthy, who came out with, "When are you going to finish off the grass cutting and clipping the shrubs back ready for the spring, Jack? The grass is too long and time's getting on. Soon it will be too late for the cutting back. You know it weakens the branches of the shrubs if it's not done at the end of autumn."

How my father kept his cool and chose not to react to this ghastly woman, I'll never know. But, he stayed calm and I was so proud of him. We only stayed for a couple of hours, by which time Mum was absolutely pie-eyed and we had to half carry her over the gravel back home. Then I helped Dad put her to bed. We caught each other's eye with a look of sheer desperation.

I continued to have great trouble sleeping, even with the help of the sleeping pills and was seeing things at that stage of sleep when you're drifting off and then suddenly awaken. I would see all sorts of people, always dressed and close to my face. That was the scariest part of it. They were always standing or kneeling by my face next to the bed. It was never anyone I knew, just faces close to me, and this went on for ages. I saw the doctor who gave me some drug or another, and that made the visitations worse. I got to the point when I was afraid to go to sleep. When the visions came, I often screamed out and grabbed the light switch to the lamp by my bed, usually sending my glass of water flying. Sometimes I would scream out so loudly that Dad would come rushing in to me. Never Mum.

Dad was always trying to show signs of sanity. I know deep down he was grieving as much as we were over losing Dan, but, as he said, we had no choice but to keep going.

Aunt Mary wanted to go back home before Christmas came. She said she had much to do and could not possibly be away too long. She did have a little dog, a Jack Russell terrier, who was being cared for by a kindly friend, and she missed him. But, I thought that it might strike her that being with her distraught family at this critical time might just be a bit more important than a Jack Russell terrier.

Anyhow, it was not to be, home she went, saying that she would come again after Christmas.

CHAPTER THIRTEEN

Toby—My First Love

"The rule of the universe is that others can do for us what we cannot do for ourselves; and one can paddle every canoe except one's own."
~ C. S. Lewis

As Christmas got closer, there were no further leads on Dan's murder. We just couldn't believe that nothing had been done or that no new evidence had come to light. There were no other suspects on the horizon.

The police had not kept in touch with us and the only time we had any news was if Dad went down to the police station. There was a glimmer of hope after the last visit though. A young detective by the name of Tobias Roi, an English police officer had been assigned to our case and to act as family liaison officer. James had worked his magic. He met with Dad and asked numerous questions about Dan, and all the family's whereabouts at the time of the murder. The next time Dad went down, I insisted on going, too.

When I first met Tobias, my distinct impression was what delightful eye candy. He had that swarthy sort of persona, he was young, and handsome, tall and dark with an air of mystique. He was working in France on a temporary assignment, to gain experience of how other countries' policing systems work. His mother was English and his father French (she had come over to France about ten years after the Second World War, working as a nursing assistant in a large hospital in Rheims … met and married his father, which explained the reasoning for his French surname, Roi, meaning 'King'). Toby was in his mid-twenties and born when his parents were well into middle age. It was such a relief to be working with an English detective who understood everything we said and how the grief was affecting us.

I was instantly attracted to him, as I now seemed to be to most men I met, whether they were young or old. Maybe those erotic letters I read of Dan's had something to do with it. I'd reached my seventeenth birthday back in November, and was now becoming very aware of my femininity. I had developed a girly kind of figure, where all the curves appeared to be in the right places. I was taller than most girls my age, reaching a full five-feet six inches and enjoyed and entered every sporting event available, both in and out of school. To be honest, it was the one thing I could do that gave me a break from my mind wandering off into the depths of darkness and despair.

The morning Toby came to the house, he knocked on the door with a commanding sort of knock, an urgent one that said: *I'm here and let me in right away*. We were all anxious to have more information about Dan, and most concerned about the length of time everything was taking, which was affecting us badly.

Tobias spoke at length to Mum and Dad, and didn't seem to notice me. That made me nervous and fidgety. I just wanted him to take some sort of notice of me. He didn't, and appeared not to want to talk to me at all. *I'm Dan's sister*, I thought, and I have as much right as the next man to be involved with all this. I was too reticent to insist on being involved in the conversation. I'd never been the 'pushy' type, I would always rather wait to be spoken to before I spoke or made a move. Strange as it seemed, this aspect of my personality had intensified as I got older, and I'd become less confident and shyer. I'd thought it was usually the other way around.

But, I could bear it no longer and plucked up enough courage to walk right over to where they all sat and said in a very loud voice: "It was my friend James who mentioned to me that you might come over and help us and I would like to be involved in this conversation, if you don't mind."

Dad said, "Don't talk like that, Maisie, there's no need for the aggressive tone. The detective is just explaining a few things to us about what is going on in the search for Dan's killer."

I realized that my statement had come out all wrong—trust me to mess up the first advance to someone I wanted to impress.

With that, a lovely long arm came out to mine and shook my hand with gusto and strength, forcefully enough to break a finger or two.

"Maisie, what a lovely name that is," he said in a dulcet tone. His persona was gentle and I felt very drawn to this mild mannered, softly spoken man. *What a beautiful velvety voice he has,* I pondered. Just adding to all his other assets.

"We are doing all we can in the search for your brother's killer, Maisie," Toby explained. "It's not easy, as there are so few clues. What we do have is some evidence we can provide to forensics, a science which has come on so fast over the last few years, and it will enable us to compare samples with any suspects we have on file. There are a few of them lined up, and we'll be taking samples of saliva, and other body fluids for testing."

"Well, you won't have far to look," I announced. "I know exactly who killed Dan."

As soon I had said it, I was horrified that I had come out with what must have sounded so immature and idiotic. My mother came over to me and said, "What do you mean, 'You know exactly who killed Dan'?" Mum had been interrupted when Tobias arrived so hadn't had much time to get her drinking under way, and appeared reasonably sober.

"What the hell are you talking about, you stupid girl?" Mum went on angrily. "If you know something that we don't, you'd better tell us right now!" She was understandably furious with me and I felt nothing but risible embarrassment for opening my big mouth in front of Toby.

Dad broke the silence that followed my outburst. "We need the officers help, Maisie."

Toby turned to me and said

"I think you'd better come down to the station and we can have a chat about all this, Maisie."

"Tobias, do you know how my brother died? No one is telling us anything and it's so frustrating not to know."

Tobias didn't answer readily, only to say: "We know a little and have our suspicions but little evidence, yet." He told us that there was to be an inquiry held because Dan's murder had occurred in a public place, and when foul play is suspected or evident, then the 'judicial process' is initiated. This was referred to the examining Magistrate (Judge D' Instruction). It would be he who conducted a full investigation and might call witnesses and ask for further investigations by the police. Tobias told us that the system was different in France than in England, and that it could take many months to complete.

He explained that the public prosecutor remains in overall charge of investigations. The investigation remains confidential and third parties are not allowed to have any information about the case. If later we wanted to know the details of Dan's murder, we would have to apply through a lawyer to the court for these. We had already been told all this, but it clearly hadn't sunk in very well with any of us. Did we really want to hear all this drivel, it meant absolutely nothing to me or my parents.

Leaving the room with Toby, I was thinking I couldn't wait until I went down to meet with him in town. As he left he said to me, "I have heard a lot about you from James. He said you were not reserved and I see that is so Maisie. He also said he was very fond of you and said how beautiful you were. Give the station a call. Here's my card with all the details you'll need to get hold of me."

"Thank you," I told him. I was overwhelmed by what he had just said to me. "I'll call you soon."

I went back inside to find my parents sitting, one either side of the log fire, and the pine log burning smell was intoxicating.

"What on earth made you come out with that remark?" my father asked. "Who do you believe killed Dan? You'd better talk to us before you go down in your gooey-eyed way to see that copper. We all need to be on the same page."

"I shouldn't have said what I did, but, it was out before I had time to stop it. Dad, you know that horrible 'Gange'? He's such a weirdo and he's the last person to have seen Dan alive, apart from the murderer, that is, assuming it's someone else. Don't forget that they went out together on that Sunday."

"Don't you think the police would have followed up that line of enquiry? Surely, he'd have been the first person they thought of? Of course, they've accounted for him as a suspect."

"But, the pair of you must agree with me, he is an oddball," I persevered. "You've got to admit he's so strange. He stares at me when he comes over here or anywhere that we're in his company, and I find it so embarrassing. Also, many years ago, I'm sure that it was him who saw me and chased us on the Hythe Canal."

"What are you on about, girl?" Mum said. "You've never said anything about someone following you when you were younger."

"Yes, I did, Mum, you've obviously forgotten. But, I did talk to you about it, remember, and you wanted to ban me from going down there anymore. Don't you recall that?"

"No, I bloody well don't! How do you expect me to remember what happened all those years ago?"

"Only seven years, Mum, it's not that long."

"Here she goes again, trying to get one over on me!" Mum snapped. "Clear off, get out of my sight, you crazy little girl! Your imagination runs away with you, and it always has. You're seventeen years old now and you ought to start acting like it. I'm going upstairs. I've had enough of this morning. The whole lot's just turning into the worst nightmare and we're no closer to getting to the killer, are we?"

She left us to go up to her bedroom that she no longer shared with Dad. Along the way she went into the kitchen to start on the first drink of the day, then took the bottle up with her.

Dad stepped in to help. He took hold of Mum's arm and led her upstairs and probably put her into bed. That was the last we saw of Mother that day.

When he came back down, looking daggers at me, he said, "You know you shouldn't antagonize your mother like that. She's in no fit state to cope with it, Maisie."

Maybe Dad would have a better memory. Perhaps seven years ago when I told Mum, she would have told him. I quickly put that right, recounting what happened on the canal bank in Hythe when I first was intimidated by the sight of the man wearing the Stetson hat, and how on the last incident, James came to my rescue.

"The only difference now is that he's wearing sensible clothes," I pleaded. "Back then, he was dressed peculiarly and looked like an oversized tramp. Surely you remember, did Mum not tell you about it?"

"Don't start that with me, Maisie, it's bad enough you do it with your mother." He instantly changed the subject, saying, "I'm off to work. Make yourself useful round here, will you?"

The Storm

"Keep your face always towards the sunshine and shadows will fall behind you."
~ Walt Whitman

That night was horrible. I couldn't sleep and kept thinking about Dan. Why, oh why, did we ever have to come to this godforsaken place? The night proceeded with fitful sleep or insomnia and I was ready to fight the world and all the regular visitors who were continuing to haunt me. It must have been about three in the morning when I decided to go downstairs. A terrible storm had begun to rage, a storm such as I'd never encountered before. A loud crack of thunder got me out of bed, and over to the window, looking out the trees were blowing like fury, and I wondered if any could fall onto the house. Thank God the roof had just been fixed. It howled like the soundtrack from the film the *Hound of the Baskervilles,* the one James and I watched over and over.

I went downstairs to the kitchen and sat at the table. It was the only bit of furniture I loved in this place. It was handmade of oak, and felt so smooth when you ran your hands over its top. It was old and had an almost indescribable patina. Dad got it at a flea market when we first came to France. Strange how a bit of furniture can have such a powerful effect on you.

The kitchen was lovely and cosy with the warmth from the Aga. I stayed there, cradled in my fluffy dressing gown and ski socks. The Aga had been kept alight since the day we first arrived. I wallowed in its comfort until morning came, drinking hot coffee and eating yesterday's leftover croissants.

When Dad appeared I said, "How the hell did you sleep through that storm. And I think I've got a cold coming. My throat is sore and my headaches? It was awful and the thunder and lightning scared me so much, I've been down here since three this morning."

"Gosh, love, that's strange, didn't hear a thing," Dad said. "Must have been so tired that we slept right through. It looks as though the roof held up, though. We must thank Ralph and Gange for that. What a good job they've made of finishing the work off for us."

That was enough to set me off.

"I see your sticking up for that dreadful man again!" I snapped. Then I sneezed several times on the trot. "I feel so angry I can't even mention his damned name! Don't go sticking up for him or anything you think he's done for this family. The only thing he's done is to *murder your son, and my brother!*"

And out I went, with the intention of never returning. I felt so irascible. However, I soon jumped back, as I needed to get into some proper clothing as I was still in my nightclothes. The storm had abated, leaving the whole complex battered and torn.

It was horrible outside. Branches and twigs thrown everywhere, even the little bird bath made of concrete that was left in our garden by the previous owner was on its side. I decided to walk into Ribérac, try to see Toby, hoping it would be a working day for him. There were at least four fairly large trees blown over, a couple partly onto the road. The rain started again and the roads were beginning to freeze over, making the journey both treacherous and dangerous. I was not perturbed and my resolve to get to town was even stronger. I felt more and more poorly as I went.

I carried on walking, not wishing to return home after my outburst, I found it hard to believe the French system could be so cruel. Compassion didn't appear to be their concern. And as I thought about this, I was about to find out that the ice on the sidewalk was about to be my concern as I slipped and went flying on the ice. I lay on the ground for a moment summing up the damage. I thought at first I'd broken my ankle, however I got up and managed to hobble. I was continually blowing my runny nose now and the cold was getting much worse.

If a car came by I was going to thumb a lift; I was quite prepared to take the risk. I eventually arrived, soaking wet and freezing cold, and my ankle hurt and was swelling. And my head felt as though it would explode. I had on a thin dress and coat that were neither warm nor waterproof. I stood shivering, then asked the desk officer if Tobias was at work. The reply, in broad French, was, "I don't know, but will go and find out." I had learned enough of the language to understand every word he said to me. As I stood waiting for Toby, I observed many notices on the walls, which of course were all in French. I was more familiar with spoken French than the written, strange, but, when I saw the one about Dan's murder, I managed to understand every word.

I was overjoyed to see this in a way that meant at least things were happening. The situation was being taken more seriously ever since Tobias came to town. A reward was being offered for any information people could give. I looked up from the notices and saw this good-looking man coming towards me, following the desk officer along the long corridor.

"Hello, Maisie, and what can I do for you?" he asked. He was fluent in French and I knew that he occasionally broke off into it, in the middle of a sentence. "I didn't expect to see you again quite so soon. What a nice surprise. Just look at you, you're soaking wet! And you don't look so well, are you okay? Come into the kitchen where it's warmer over by the range."

"I don't feel so good I've a bad cold taking hold."

"Then what on earth are you doing out you silly girl?" Toby said in a concerned voice.

I was relieved to be offered comfort there, and the heat being emitted was just divine, but I was still unable to stop shivering.

"Thanks," I told him. "Well, I thought I must come down and make a formal statement about my brother's death. Everything seems to move so slowly, Tobias, and I'm truly worried about that."

"Let's get you warmed up and we'll get you a hot drink. And do call me Toby, Tobias is so formal, don't you think?"

We walked through an amazingly long corridor, which was draughty and smelt of disinfectant, and I still shivered. "You haven't warmed up yet, have you?" He was full of concern for me. "I shall find something to put round you to keep you warm."

He saw I was limping and asked why. I told him of the fall and he wanted to take me to hospital, but I refused.

"It's ok, Toby, there's nothing broken. I'm sure."

The corridor led close to the smelly cells, apparently, and the disinfectant may have been necessary to clear up inmate's detritus. There were more notices pinned to boards clinging to the corridor walls. It struck me that the French were keen advocates of the poster.

When we reached the room where I was made comfortable, a drink arrived. It looked rather like coffee, but smelt like tea. It was coffee after all, however unrecognisable. I realized that this man was no expert in the making of hot drinks.

"If you're warmer now, we can go to my office and I'll take your statement?" I was reluctant to leave this comfortable place and hoped he would do the interview right there. I had determined not to make a fool of myself, to be grown up, factual, and completely rational.

"Right, come this way Maisie, just follow me," he advised. We went further down this never-ending corridor until we came to a staircase. Up we went three whole floors and eventually came to his office. Most corridors were dark, narrow, unwelcoming and musty smelling. I asked if there was a lift. "No, sorry, we don't have one of those, the pity," he apologised. "Still, we shall keep fit, now won't we?"

"Let me get something to write with," Toby said as he fumbled around trying to find a pen. "I have hundreds of these and manage to either lose them or people come and borrow them and I never get them back."

"Oh, I know all about that, my friends in school do it all the time. Have this one of mine," I handed him a pen which I'd drawn from my portmanteau of a bag along with yet another paper tissue.

"Right, now let's start at the beginning," Toby looked at his watch and started his interview. "You said that you thought you knew who killed Dan. I have to take down all the details of why you feel that way, Maisie, and who it is that you imagine is responsible."

That word imagine stung to hear. He probably thought I was crazy too. And, as if reading my mind, he corrected himself.

"Or who do you think did it. Think. Suspect. Imagine. Whatever you want to call it."

That felt better to hear. I dived right into my account.

"That Gange bloke went out with Dan the afternoon of the day he was killed. He says he left Dan in the pub drinking. I, for one, don't believe it. I think he's making things up to mislead."

"Maisie, we have spoken to other customers who were in the pub that afternoon, and they have all made the same statements that Gange, as you call him, was there, but he left after about an hour-and-a-half to two hours."

"Didn't you know that his full name is Gangees? Apparently, he was named after the river in India, near where he was born. And, it's normally shortened to 'Gange', for damned good reason if you ask me. How could anyone's parents be so stupid to call their son the name of a river?"

As soon as I'd opened my mouth, I thought *here I go again, acting like a child. How was I going to get this man to take me seriously if I carried on this way?* I quickly pulled myself together and started to behave more appropriately. Even though I needed to blow my nose continuously.

"Yes, I knew about the name. To be honest, Maisie, you will have to come up with some more factual evidence than your feelings towards him."

I continued to tell Toby why I felt as strongly as I did about Gange. "Toby, he is creepy. Whenever we, that's my family and I, are in his company, he never seems to take his eyes off me, and they seem to follow me wherever I go in the house."

"Well, how can you blame the man for that? You're a good-looking girl. Surely it's a compliment when a man behaves that way."

"It's not normal. And there's more to it. When I was around ten back home in England, my friend and I used to play along a canal in Hythe, the town where we lived. I saw Gange there several days running and so did James, the chap who got you to come over here. He dressed oddly and walked along the other side of the canal, staring at us as we rode our bikes. This was very scary for us children, and then he disappeared. The point is, Toby, I believe this 'Gange' bloke is the very same person we saw on the canal bank."

"You can't arrest or suspect a man of murder on the strength of what you've just told me. Surely you don't believe that he waited for you to grow up and then followed you over here to France?"

"I don't know. I just feel that there are too many coincidences for him to be innocent. I know, too, that it all sounds overly dramatic. James met him when he was over here recently, he saw him and felt it could possibly be the same man. Did he not confirm the story of the canal bank and the weird bloke who followed us back then?"

"Not that I recall," Toby replied.

"You were ten years old when all that happened and the mind can play tricks, you know," Toby warned.

"Yes, and that was only seven years back. Not so long as to play tricks on my recollections." I then told Toby of my visit to Dan's lover in town, revealing all the minutiae of what she had told me. He didn't seem particularly surprised, and said nothing.

Then, with a dismissive tone, he said, "I need to get on with some detecting work now, Maisie, so I'm afraid we shall have to part.

However, I would like to see you again, aside from when we're working on your brother's case. Would you care to go for a coffee or a meal with me one night?"

That took me back a bit, as I had no idea that he liked me enough to ask me out. "Yes, I would. When were you thinking of?"

"How about in a couple of weeks. I'm busy right now, we have a lot going on, and not enough staff to deal with it all. There's been a lot of problems in Bordeaux, what with the elections coming up."

"That will be fine. Will you phone me?"

"That I will," he said, smiling. "Til we meet again, fair lady." And with that said he took hold of my hand and kissed it. *Very French* I thought. "I shall get one of the lads to run you home. And get yourself to bed with a 'hot toddy' just wait here, someone will be up in a minute."

I noticed Toby didn't write much down when I'd told my story. I don't think he was taking me seriously. Nevertheless, he did ask me out, and that had to be a result.

The excitement I felt waiting for Toby's call quite overwhelmed me. When it came, I was over the moon. This guy was going to be my first real date, how cool was that? I had hoped that Ralph would take my obvious feelings towards him more seriously, but, that was not to be.

Mum's behaviour was too vacuous right now to be aware of anything going on, and if I was going out with somebody a good deal older than me, or even leaving the country, she wasn't interested.

It was sad to see her in such a state, a state I had a feeling was going to be her life for rather a long time.

CHAPTER FIFTEEN

The First Date

"Do an act of kindness every day and your soul will be in constant bloom."
~ Anthony Douglas Williams

We went out to dinner for our first date.

"There is this fantastic new restaurant that has opened up in Perigueux," he enthused. "It's Greek. Makes a change from the French stews and bourguignons we're all so familiar with."

"That sounds wonderful, Toby," I replied. "When do you want to go?"

"How about Friday?"

"Yes, that will be fine. I shall pick you up at about seven, will that be OK? And, how about your parents? Are they happy for you to go out with me?"

"Dad keeps on about the age difference, and Mum is so out of it I don't think she could be bothered either way. After all, I don't think you're that much older than me, are you Toby?"

"I'll come in and have a word with your Dad before we leave. I understand his concerns. After all, there is quite an age difference between us. He probably thinks that I've got a wife or girlfriend tucked away somewhere, but I haven't, just so you know. And, by the way, I'm twenty-seven."

"I never dreamt that you would have a wife or you wouldn't have asked me out, now would you?"

Oh, that was naïve of me, how stupid, I thought. I resolved to start acting as a grown-up and use common sense. I hadn't told him that he was the first boy I'd ever gone out with on a proper date because I thought it might put him off. I'd had a few flirtations, but nothing much came of them. I had a thing for Ralph, though. That thought made me sad, as when I first met him, I was convinced he fancied me. If that had been the case, I surely would know by now. Maybe a relationship would have developed between us if our lives hadn't taken such a dreadful and traumatic turn.

When the day came for the date, I couldn't stay still. It was now a week before Christmas and school-work was building up. We were in preparation for some major exams, all of which would need to be completed in the French language. I put that thought behind me for the time being. Toby came to the door, and when he knocked quietly, I made a dash to answer it, almost slipping over on the raffia mat strategically placed in front of the door.

"Do come in, Toby," I invited. "Dad is waiting to have a word with you."

Mum was nowhere to be seen, as was usual. With an outstretched arm, Toby went over to where Dad was sitting.

"Good evening, young man, good to see you again," Dad greeted. "Are you any further forward with Dan's case?"

"Sadly no, sir," he told Dad. "You will be the first to know as soon as we do have any more information."

"We want to be able to have a funeral and some closure, which we can't because things remain as they are."

"I know, Mr. Patterson. It's the most awful time for your family."

"Now, son, I hope your intentions towards my daughter are responsible. She's very young. I'm relying on you to take good care of her and bring her back home safe and sound. We don't want any more disasters occurring."

"Of course, I will, sir. We're going to Perigueux for dinner and then I shall bring Maisie straight home."

The thought of that disappointed me.

I'd imagined a romantic dinner, plenty of wine and after we left the restaurant, we would stop off at a concealed spot for a bit of canoodling. As we drove over to Perigueux, I kept looking at Toby. He was better looking than I'd originally thought, particularly when seen from the right side. He drove safely and slowly and we passed virtually no cars. It was the capital of the Dordogne, somewhat unbelievable when you think of how few cars we passed on the road.

It was a different story when we got closer to the city. The time of year made the place even more difficult to park in this place.

We eventually found a space, but then had a twenty minute walk to get to the main narrow street and then on to the restaurant.

It was not as cold, as I'd anticipated. We had recently experienced a bitterly cold snap and I had dressed appropriately for it, as a result I was beginning to sweat. On the walk to the restaurant, Toby turned to me and said, "I'm so glad you agreed to come out with me. I wondered if you might see me as too old."

"Indeed, no! In fact, I prefer older men. They are so much more sensible than boys my own age."

"That's good. I think I'm sensible enough, also your father seemed to approve of me, so that helps, doesn't it?"

He took hold of my hand and gave it a squeeze. "Come on," he said, "I don't know about you, but I'm starving."

This was my first introduction to Perigueux's nightlife. It was a medieval town with a population of approximately 31,000. The little main street was narrow and well-lit and an exciting, mystical place to be. It was a part of history I had learnt about in school. One of our teachers was inclined to teach her students only about French history. Her degree being in the subject. Therefore, I knew a good deal about this magical place.

The town was situated near the River Isle and had been in existence since Neolithic times.

One of the delights of the area, was the renowned pâté de foie gras, a gastronomic delight that was produced on a commercial scale in the Périgord region.

The Place de la Vertu was one of the prettiest squares in Perigueux and the one that Dan and I sometimes came for coffee and gateaux.

We finally reached our restaurant, after me tripping several times along the cobbled street because I'd worn the most stupid red high heels to impress Toby. I thought I was the business when I wore them. It was just as well that Toby held my hand, or I would undoubtedly have fallen flat on my face or ricked an ankle.

I turned to him as we were about to enter the restaurant. "Are you religious, Maisie?" he asked.

"I wasn't, up until Dan went missing. Since then, I've spent a lot of time praying to God and thinking long and hard about religion. Now I find I'm thinking about Him and all that goes with Him far more than before, that of course is if He is a He. My parents don't go to church, but they are good people. Mum has lost her way right now and my worry is I don't know how I can help her."

"We will concentrate on getting Dan's killer first and then see what we can do to help your mother. Now let's get inside, it's cold out here."

How kind and thoughtful that last comment was, and I wondered why he would ask if I was religious. We entered and the place was welcoming. It was made to look like a Greek tavern. I'd never been to Greece but had seen pictures and read a lot about the place. It was top of my wish list of places to visit. Each time I read about foreign climbs, I knew I wanted to travel and see the world.

Everywhere paper decorations were strewn in the colours of the Greek national flag. There were huge posters showing golden sands, and clear ice-blue water and scantily dressed women. Those that fascinated me most were the ones where the soldiers stood on guard at the palace in Athens, where the Prime Minister resided. They wore bright white uniforms with coloured braces, skirts and large black hats, with a pom-pom on each black shoe. All this alongside Christmas paraphernalia.

We were greeted by the head waiter and taken through the main corridor to a quieter, darker area further to the back of the place, where only four tables were laid for those who intending to eat. The tablecloths were red-and-white check, covered with a white paper one, and the menu written on a large paper placemat.

Toby, being the gentleman he was, came around and pulled the chair out for me. I sat down and was immediately told about the specials displayed on a blackboard standing on an easel. The menu in front of us was vast, full of food I'd never heard of. Toby was better informed than me, obviously having eaten here before, as the waiters appeared to know him.

"Do you come here much, Toby?" I asked.

"I've been here a few times, the food is delicious, that's why I've brought you here. I hope you enjoy it, too. If I'm honest, it does have a French flavour along with the Greek."

We enjoyed the meal and drank a bottle-and-a-half of the house red wine, which was excellent and intoxicating, being 13 percent proof. Fortunately, Toby didn't appear to be the worse for drink, which was just as well, as the French gendarmerie were acutely aware of drunk driving. They would stop you even if your driving was within the speed limit if they had an inkling you'd been drinking, a breath test followed along with a halted journey. Worst of all is that they issue you a fine on the spot. If you didn't have enough money on you to pay it, you'd be escorted to the nearest cash dispenser. We finished eating and Toby said, "I think it's time we were on our way back. It's ten, I told your father I would have you home by then. And, it'll take us an hour to get back if we don't want to hurry."

I took that as meaning he wanted to dawdle so we could have a kiss and cuddle en route. I thought it best not to open my mouth and put my foot in it by saying something I'd live to regret. We walked back along the pebbled street and up the centre walkway of the tree-lined avenue until we reached the car park. Then, horror of horrors, we couldn't find the car!

"For the first time in my life I didn't look for a landmark," Toby remarked. "I always do that, as I know how busy and full it gets here." We searched for ages, then suddenly Toby said, "I know where it is!" And, we ran together like the wind, back to where we started. I remembered seeing a large poster saying: *Come to the bowling alley on the 05 January 2011 for a night of fun, laughter, food and bowling, plus fireworks.*

It didn't take us long to find the car after that. We were silent until he asked me if I wanted to find a place to stop for a while. Without hesitation, I agreed, then added, disappointedly, "But, you said we were late as it is."

"We can stop for five minutes. I'll make up time when we're back on the road home."

We pulled into a lay-by that was well off the road. Not that anyone would have seen us. The car came to a stop and I found that I was nervously fidgeting and rubbing my hands one over the other. I began to sweat again, the last thing I wanted, it doesn't quite go with kissing. I didn't know what to expect or what to do, with my limited experience. Toby leaned over to me and said gently, "Don't be afraid, I'm not about to do anything you don't want me to."

With that, I bent towards him and kissed him full on the lips. It was clumsy and he didn't expect it.

"There's no need to rush anything, Maisie, we have all the time in the world to get to know each other. You are still so young and I don't want to spoil it."

"Actually, Toby," I admitted, "I'm quite happy for you to take advantage of me."

"But, this is a bad time for you to start an affair, you're so vulnerable now. What with that and your mother showing all the signs of being an alcoholic, the last thing I want is to add to your troubles."

"You won't be doing that. Toby, I need someone to love me and make a fuss of me."

With that remark, he came right over to my seat, held me tight and kissed my face all over.

"Maisie, I would love nothing more than to take you onto the back seat and make love to you properly, but, I'm not going to. And, I think we should be making tracks." He continued to hold my hand all the way back home and when we arrived, he looked at me and said, "You are the most beautiful, lovely girl and I hope to see you again."

"How about tomorrow?" I interjected.

"I can't tomorrow. In fact, the days I have off will be spent back In England with my parents."

He leaned over again and held me tightly and I loved it. We had a long kiss goodnight. "Off you go now, gosh, just look at the time, it's 11.30! Your dad won't be pleased with us."

I left him waving as I went to the front door. When I got inside, Dad was waiting for me. "Bit late, isn't it dear?" he remarked. "I was getting worried about where you'd got to."

"Dad, I was in safe hands, I think you know that."

"Did you have a good evening, love?" he asked. "I must say you look happier than I've seen you look for ages. After Christmas I think we ought to get your Aunt Mary back over here for a bit, what do you think?"

"That'll be fine, Dad, she did say that she wanted to come back again soon. Her company will do Mum some good. We won't be doing that much celebrating for Christmas, will we? I'm so worried about Mum, Dad, is there anything we should be doing to help her?"

"Every time I mention her drinking, she goes off the deep end. I wonder if she'd be better off going back to England."

"Do you know if they have an Alcoholics Anonymous place over here?" I asked him.

"No, but I think I will look into it. The difficulty will be getting her to go," he replied.

"Well, we can both put a bit of pressure on her. She can't carry on like this, Dad. If she's not down here drinking, she's in bed doing so. She's lost all of her zest for life."

"I must say I'm surprised that she's come to this. Of all the people we know, I never thought your mother would end up the way she has."

"Well, she has, Dad, and I think we ought to act soon or it may be too late. After school tomorrow, I'll go into town and see if I can find anything out. Come to think of it, Toby might know of somewhere, although he's not been over here that long, so maybe not."

I went to bed after giving Dad a hug and kiss goodnight. My father, so stoical, just amazed me. No one outside of our home could possibly understand what he must be going through. I'm sure he now felt that he'd not only lost a son, but, also a wife.

I had another restless night, and when I did fall asleep I dreamt of this new person in my life, and it was so good, giving me some respite from all the trauma going on around me. The thoughts I had of what the future held, kept me in a permanent state of rumination.

I was getting a lift to school these days with Helen Treadworthy's mum. Mother no longer worked for her or anyone else. I walked down to the end of our road, to wait for my lift. I noticed how lovely it was, even in winter, as you could see the grapevines in their state of flux awaiting the minute green buds to appear among the soot-blackened old brown ones come the spring. I didn't know which month they would start to spring back into life, but was anxious to find out.

Helen and I had become close, she was most patient and kind to me. As we walked through the school gates and towards our classroom, we started talking about our favourite subject: boys. I began to tell her about Toby and my first date.

"Oh, Cherie, he's a bit old for you, don't you think?" she asked.

"I suppose he is, but, I like the more mature man much more than the daft immature boys in our class," I replied.

"Yes, I do know what you mean, there's not one of them I would want to date."

That was all the time we had for chit-chat. We got down to our learning for another edifying day. The lessons went well. Helen and I were reasonably confident about passing the pending exams. My French may have been good, but I needed to get down to more serious study to make sure that it was up to exam level.

After school that day, I went into Ribérac to try and find some kind of support group for Mother. I told Helen I would be able to get a lift home. During my search for help, there didn't seem to be anything available. I asked around, not giving the game away about Mum. More than one person told me to try the church. In all my years, I'd never known my mother to go to church. In fact, she would say she was a non-believer, and there was no doubt about that since losing Dan.

CHAPTER SIXTEEN

Help for Mother

"Tis not for mortals always to be blest. 'Tis not too late tomorrow to be brave."
~ John Armstrong

Toby took me to Perigueux to see the doctor he knew.

"Is he a shrink?" I asked.

"Well, if you mean does he help people with mental illness, then yes he is, but, the doctors here are excellent at what they do and care for all sorts of mental disturbances, routinely. In fact, I'd go as far as to say that most of them specialize in mental illness. Many visitors to France are known to have breakdowns when on holiday. Their guard is down, when out of the normal routine and the relaxation of it makes their troubles come flowing out."

"It will be a miracle if we can get Mother from the house to see anybody. These days, as I think you know, she just stays home drinking. I would do anything to be able to get her out and rekindle her old interests; not that she had many." I paused to consider it. "I think we shall have to ask him in the first instance to come to the house, so she's on familiar territory, don't you?"

"Yes, that will be the way to do it. But, prepare yourself, Maisie, for seeing your mum like we did yesterday. I think she'll need to be hospitalized—I really don't think any other treatment is going to fit the bill."

Toby made us an appointment to see a Dr. Renout. He was a general care doctor who specialized in *'care of the mentally affected,'* beautifully inscribed in italics. These were the very words written in French on a golden plaque attached to the wall by the Doctor's front door. We rang the doorbell of a grand looking house of four storeys, in a tree-lined avenue called Avenue de Perigueux. The trees were huge and their boughs met in the middle, making a sort of archway of green leaves on skinny branches, giving shade from the summer sun. Neither of us knew what type of trees they were.

The door was opened by a little woman, who reminded me of Mrs. Overall in a comedy show on British television called *Acorn Antiques*. The character was played by the talented, catholic actress, Julie Waters.

"Yes? What do you want?" she asked in a brusque way.

Toby replied in perfect French, "We are here to see Dr. Renout. We have an appointment at three."

"Come in here and sit down. You will have to wait, as he's still seeing a patient."

"Thank you," Toby said.

We walked over to the plush chairs that looked as though they were covered in a gold silken material, that appeared almost too good to sit on. We did, however, and they were as hard as rock, clearly designed to discourage people from lingering. In fact, I preferred to stand. I was feeling nervous anyway, and the hard chair made my back ache. It seemed like a long time, an hour at least, before the doctor opened his consulting room door. A distinguished looking, tall, middle-aged man, with greying sideburns greeted us with gusto, then ushered us into a large official type of room, his consulting room.

Toby began the conversation and told the doctor about my family and the sad details of our loss. Then he introduced me, "It's your turn now, Maisie. Tell the story of what has happened to your mother over the last few weeks."

I began to tell the Doctor about Mum's habit and managed to get the points over that I had intended. After about thirty minutes of talking, I felt the tears welling up. The doctor was so kind he came over, put his hands on my shoulders and surprisingly, spoke to me in broken English.

"My dear girl, fear not, you have had so much to cope with for someone so young. It's not right that you have suffered this way. You don't have to tell me anymore. I get the picture, and the good news is, I can help your mother. She will need to come into the hospital and may be with us some considerable time. But, I assure you, it's highly likely she will be cured. Very often we see the effects alcohol has on people and how they become estranged from the rest of their family and friends. It's not at all uncommon, although I haven't seen too many people with such a background as yours."

"Now, the plan will be that I shall come out to visit with her soon," he continued. "I believe in creating an atmosphere of trust and so I will need to gain her confidence before we take her into the hospital."

I interjected to say that I thought it would be difficult to remove her from the house without a fight.

"Don't worry yourself about that part of the treatment, Maisie. We have our ways of persuasion."

I couldn't help thinking that he would need a ton of drugs and a team of white horses before he'd be likely to remove Mother to anywhere she didn't want to go.

After our session came to an end, I felt a sort of peace come over me. It was a strange feeling I'd not experienced before. It was as though a great weight had been lifted off my shoulders, and it felt good. I was feeling drained and hungry.

We chose one of the larger restaurants, not as posh as the one we had gone to on the last date. However, Toby said the food was good and more along the line of burger and steaks, with lots of chips and salads. The wines were to die for. Beautiful wines from Bordeaux and also delicious Burgundies. The wine list indicated a fine range of champagne too. Toby was partial to champagne and knew what he was ordering. As for me, I was beginning to learn about wine and indeed getting a taste for the expensive stuff.

"How come you are so familiar with all the fine liquor, Toby?"

"Don't forget that my Dad was French and we lived over here for some considerable time, in a little village near to Rheims, up in the south-east aptly named Bouzy, where Champagne was produced in vast quantities. If you were in the know as we were, you could get the good stuff cheap, we used to drink it most nights. I loved it then and I love it now. Shall we order a bottle?"

We had to wait a little before we were shown to our seats. It was a popular place and mainly occupied by young people. We were taken to a booth and, as I slipped into my leather seat, looking out onto the main restaurant area, I noticed a good-looking chap acting rather oddly. We spent time checking the menu, then both ordered steak and frites, then Toby asked to see the wine list. He chose an expensive champagne, which I consumed on an empty stomach. As we waited for our food to come, the man who was acting oddly was staring into space, not looking at anything in particular. I judged him to be in his twenties, pale skinned, with abundant curly long blond hair enough to make any girl jealous. For most of the evening he was putting on and taking off a green woollen hat, and as his food was served and he began to eat and drink, you could tell that he was thoroughly enjoying it. I said to Toby, who was sitting opposite me, and unable to see the action, "Come on over here with me, so you can watch the entertainment."

"What on earth are you on about?" he asked.

"Come round and sit here, you'll see what I mean." I felt a bit unkind to be making fun of the blond character, but, the whole time we spent there was just a hoot. The man had a bottle of pink champagne, being kept cold by the plastic container with ice and water. He would grab his glass, then stand and toast his imaginary partner several times. Sitting down again, he took his fork and started to push what looked like a dish of snails around for about five minutes. He then took hold of his empty glass and held it like an earphone, first to one ear and then to the other, laughing the whole time.

Toby told me to stop looking at him, as every time he caught my eye, the theatricals became overzealous. I burst out laughing and the man stood up and toasted me.

"There you are, what did I just say?" Toby ticked me off.

"Well, I suppose we could move to another seat, but mind you there aren't many available now." It was 18.30 and the place had filled. A few couples had moved away from sitting opposite our clown, and I understood why. Then he walked over to a couple of men who sat almost opposite him and they clearly were unphased by it all, and they all started laughing and joking together. This went on for about ten minutes, then he went back to his seat and ordered a brandy. When it arrived, the salutation to his imaginary companion began all over again.

I can't remember when or what I ordered that evening. Toby was less amused by it all than me, especially my reaction to this chaps behaviour, but, I almost fell off my seat when he went out with his Capstan cigarettes and matches under his arm, then proceeded to do a little dance on the pavement, especially for the folk who were seated outside the restaurant. They began to clap, and the more they did so the funnier he got. His woollen hat continued to be pulled on and off, then pulled down right over to cover has face. I thought the whole episode was a delight and I couldn't stop giggling.

"For goodness sake stop it, Maisie! You're embarrassing me," Toby said coldly.

That made me pull myself together a bit, but when our comedian re-entered the place near where we were sitting, I just erupted with giggles and fell onto the seat beside me, as he took a long and low bow for my benefit.

"That's enough, I've had enough of this," Toby commanded. "Come on, eat your food. It's probably cold now. You're just a child really, aren't you?"

That was enough to sober me up and fast. The champagne had truly kicked in. I was not used to drinking it and certainly not in the quantities I had that night.

"For goodness' sake, where's your sense of humour?" I argued. "I'm so sorry, but I just couldn't help myself. You must admit he was hum … hum…. humour … humourous!" I couldn't get that word out very well and made a number of attempts trying to do so.

CHAPTER SEVENTEEN

Loss

"Unless you cross the bridge of your insecurities,
you can't begin to explore your possibilities."
~ Tim Fargo

There was no stopping for a kiss and a cuddle on the way back home that night. I was rather disappointed but also very drunk. It must have been the champagne along with the evening's entertainment. I was dropped off sharply, not even helped to the front door.

"I shall be in touch," were the last words I heard him speak. I almost fell in through the front door.

Dad was waiting up for me. "Oh dear, what have you been up to?" he asked.

"Dad, I think I've overdone it and I think it's over." I went on to explain to father all about the evening's antics and about the doctor who was going to help Mum. "And, I think I've lost Toby," I concluded. "He has no sense of humour and didn't find anything to laugh at the whole time tonight. To be honest, Dad, I'm better off without him. He's far too stiff and starchy for me." I had been wrong in my initial favourable judgement of Toby and as I went upstairs, I thought I would put it down to experience.

"Never mind, love, you get off to bed and I'll see to locking up," Dad called up to me as I staggered the stairs.

I wobbled into my room. Mum came out onto the landing, took one look at me, and went right back into her bedroom without saying a word.

It didn't hit me until the next day that I had probably lost the man who I thought just may be the love of my life. What on earth could I do to make things right again, I had very different feelings now to those of last night, when I wanted to be rid of him.

I recalled him telling me 'I was still a child', so for that reason alone, he probably wouldn't want any more to do with me. But wait a minute, I reasoned. It had been Toby who took me to see the doctor who was going to help mum. Surely, he wouldn't just leave without helping Dad and me to see it all through?

Why, oh why, am I so stupid, I thought? It seemed that I had a talent for ruining everything good in my life.

It was almost Christmas and I was curious about what Dad and I should be doing. There was so much to think about. Mum would likely be going away for treatment. You never know, I thought, perhaps Toby would turn up with news about my brother's killer. But that was wishful thinking. Dad was out working and I decided to go to town and do a bit of Christmas shopping. I went up to Mum's bedroom—she was half in and half out of bed.

"Mum, what are you up to?" I asked her. "Do you want to get up? I've come to see if you still want Aunt Mary to come over for Christmas."

"Oh, I don't know, why are you bothering me with such stuff, girl," she bit back.

"Mum, it's not nonsense, it's stuff we need to discuss and I want to do so before you start drinking today."

"How do you know I haven't started already? You know nothing! Now clear off."

I thought it better to avoid having yet another row with her. So, I made my mind up that I was not going to let her affect me, and I caught the bus to town. I had a good time looking around the shops and seeing all the festive bibs and bobs, there was so much to see. The French really did go to town when it came to celebrations. The streets were brightly decorated and the fairy lights glittered and were hung between the trees where they swung in a gentle breeze. It was cold but welcoming and everyone I passed spoke and wished me a Bon Noel. I brought a few decorations to brighten up our sad home. I hoped I might bump into Toby. If I did, it would only be in a professional capacity. I reckoned he meant what he'd said. I'd blotted my copybook.

School was over for the holidays and I met a few classmates as I wandered the streets. They were happy and excited about the Noel preparations. "What are you going to do for Christmas, Maisie?" my friend Suzie asked. "Do you want to come over to ours for drinks?"

"That's very kind of you, Suzie, but I'm not sure how much celebrating we'll be doing," I thanked her. "I'm not sure if my aunt is to come over or not. Anyway, I'm getting some presents right now, so, see you later."

And with that, I was on my way. I brought Dad a nice warm scarf made of wool and it had the lovely greens and browns of a Scottish tartan—I knew he'd like that. Mum, I was less sure about. I ended up getting her some special and suitably expensive bath oil, made by the perfume factory in Grasse, Southern France. This perfume was very famous for being used in the basic oils of so many expensive products, such as Chanel and Lancôme. This shop was such a find. The wonderful aroma greeting you as you entered was heady and divine. I could have stayed there all day, surrounded by lovely smells, but knew I should get back. Dad would possibly be home, and I was aware that leaving Mum for any length of time was unwise.

I didn't see Toby, but a few of his colleagues passed me and tooted their horns as I waited for the bus. The bus was so infrequent and unreliable, however, it eventually came. When I got off the bus I started to walk up our long lane and was about halfway up the trek to home when a large car came up behind me. It stopped and startled me, and as I turned to see who was there, a man got out and called over to me, saying, "Would you like a lift, young lady?"

I hesitated at first, saying that *I was almost home so no thank you,* when he said, "I'm looking for Chez Mouzy."

"Well, you're going in the right direction," I told him. "Just carry on up this road and turn at the second turning on your left and you're there."

"Thank you, my dear, let me give you a lift."

It took me a few seconds to realize it was Dr. Renout. "Thank you, Doctor, I've only just realized it's you. Have you come to see my Mother?"

"Yes," he replied. "I'm sorry I didn't call but I was in the area and thought I'd take a chance that you'd be home."

"I'm not sure about Dad, but Mum's there and she's probably quite drunk by now."

"Never mind, dear, that's what I'm here for—to help her get better."

I got in his car and we drove up to the house. I hadn't seen Ralph or Gange for over two weeks, but would you believe it, there the two of them stood, side by side and right outside our front door.

"Fancy seeing you two here," I said to the brothers.

"Hi, Maisie, we've come to see how you all are," Ralph said. "We haven't seen you for some time and a visit was long overdue."

"I'm always glad to see you, Ralph, but now is not very convenient. This gentleman is Dr. Renout, and he's come to see Mum."

"Oh, we'll leave and call another time then?"

With that, Dr. Renout came over to me and said, "Shall we go in, Maisie?" It was an obvious attempt to stop the men from interfering in our business. Although, Ralph knew what was going on. When we went inside, Dad was upstairs with Mum. We met him coming down the stairs and looking annoyed.

"Where have you been?" he demanded. "I thought you'd be looking after your Mother this morning. That's why I went to work!"

"Dad, we didn't make any arrangements last night and it's nearly Christmas and there's stuff to do. Anyway, this is Dr. Renout, you know, the doctor who I told you about. Remember me saying that Toby and I had a meeting with him, and that he would be along to meet Mum some time?"

"Yes." Dad turned towards our visitor. "Good day to you, sir, my wife is upstairs. Could I have a word with you before I take you up to see her?"

"Of course, Mr. Patterson," Dr. Renout assured him. "Where shall we go?"

"Follow me." But then Dad saw the men standing outside, and Ralph was already halfway through the door.

"Hi, Jack, is there anything we can do to help?" Ralph asked.

"No, thanks lads, I'll give you a call later."

And with that, they left.

"Now Doctor, I expect Maisie has told you all about my wife?" Dad began. "It started when our son was murdered and we still have no clue as to who did it. The police don't seem to be interested in us any more, we never hear a word about their enquiries into it. I also want you to know that she doesn't think there's anything wrong with her. She tends not to recognise people she knows well, and has become aggressive."

"I understand all you say," Dr. Renout assured my Dad. "This behaviour is typical of someone who has experienced great trauma in their life. The trauma of something as terrible as this in a family, is enough to tip the strongest minds over the edge. I'm sure it isn't true regarding the police's inaction. Maybe they have temporarily run out of leads. I do understand how this has happened, Mr. Patterson, and I can promise you that we will be able to make her well again. Shall we go and see her?"

"Yes, come this way please."

Dad led Dr. Renout upstairs and into the bedroom. I followed closely, not wanting to miss anything. Dad introduced the doctor to Mum.

"Hello, Mrs. Patterson. I'm Dr. Renout and I work at the clinic in Perigueux."

So, saying, he held an outstretched hand to her as she lay prostrate in bed with only a thin nightdress to protect any dignity she might have left. Mum said nothing at all in reply.

"May I sit on the bed and have a chat with you?"

"Sit where you bloody well like. What do you want anyway?" Mum snapped.

"Your family is worried about the amount of alcohol you're consuming now."

"It's got nothing to do with them, or you! You should all mind your own bloody business! Anyway, clear off! I'm tired and want to go to sleep!"

Dad and I looked at one another with a look that said *how on earth is he going to manage that one?*

"I can't do that, Mrs. Patterson, because I'm here to have a chat and talk about a plan we need to make together, to get you well again."

"You can just sod off. There's nothing wrong with me. None of you should be interfering with me."

"Well, we have to, or you are going to kill yourself. You and your husband have lost one member of the family, and your daughter is most upset seeing you like this every day."

"Like what? What are you going on about anyway? Who are you? Get out of my house! Who is he, Jack? Get rid of him."

Dr. Renout got up from the bed and said to Mum, "I will leave you now, Mrs. Patterson, and look forward to seeing you again soon."

We all went back downstairs. The doctor announced grimly, "I'm afraid I shall need to take her into the clinic as soon as possible. She is too far gone and needs urgent treatment. Can you tell me for how long she has been as forgetful and aggressive as now?"

"It's been getting worse over the last month. She always liked a drink, but started drinking more since we've been over here in France." Dad said. "I think that could be the reason, along with Dan's murder."

I said little, as it was all happening so fast and I felt afraid of what lay ahead. The doctor then announced that he would send an ambulance for her tomorrow and that it would be best if we didn't say anything to Mum about it.

"How long will you keep her there?" Dad asked.

"As long as it takes to get her well again. Good day to you both. Try not to worry. When she has recovered, you will look back on this time and it will all be like a bad dream."

Dad and I hugged each other after he left. I knew Dad had tears in his eyes and was trying so hard to be strong for me.

"It'll be alright, Dad," I tried to reassure him. "It's the best thing for Mum. We couldn't continue as we were, with you not being able to work and me missing school at times to take care of her. I'm sorry I went out this morning. I wasn't thinking straight. Have you spoken to Aunt Mary about coming over again? I think it will cheer Mum up to see her, even if she's in the hospital."

"I think you're right, love, I'll talk to her tonight."

Dad phoned Ralph first, and spoke with him for ages. I indicated that I wanted to talk to him and when we spoke he was so kind and sympathetic. "Ralph," I said, "it's just so awful. All this on top of losing Dan."

"I know it is, love," Ralph sympathised. "Why don't you come over here after Julia is in hospital? It's the school holidays now, I believe, and there's lots you could help me out with here. Your father will be able to go back to work and I don't want you to mope around and be lonely."

"I'd like that, Ralph. At the moment, I don't know how I'm going to cope, I don't want Dad going under as well."

"That won't happen, Maisie. Your dad's a tougher guy than you may imagine. He'll come through it all OK. I'm more worried about you."

******

Dad called Aunt Mary, who agreed to come over but not until after Christmas, probably in the New Year, as she had too much to do at home. Glory alone knows what she had to do. There were no children there, her husband was long gone. I think she was making excuses. She and Mum had their moments and often disagreed.

I had spoken to my doctor in Ribérac about the 'visitors' I was continuing to have at night. He told me to cut down on alcohol if I was drinking a lot and never to have coffee last thing at night. The doctor said that the hallucinations were a manifestation of all that was happening in my life.

He was so right. That night I had more 'visitors' than ever before. I had become accustomed to the odd one here and there, but nothing to the extent I was now seeing. The people coming into my bedroom were always smartly dressed in some sort of costume, men as well as women. There were clowns and jugglers, then a plethora of people all dressed as though they would be performing. The last straw was when the whole circus came in procession, in through the door, through my bedroom and out through the window. I was especially disturbed when some of these visitors came too close to my face. I leapt out of bed, shouted at them to bloody well leave me alone and almost ran downstairs in fear. I hoped I hadn't woken Dad, for he needed his rest. After I went back to bed I tried to settle down to sleep, but the nightmares that followed were horrendous. In one of them, Mum died. In the next, Gange came to live with us. Lastly, but by no means the least and the worst of all, was when Dad left home and went back to England and I was left in France.

CHAPTER EIGHTEEN

Changes

"Be happy in the moment, that's enough.
Each moment is all we need, not more."
~ Mother Teresa

I woke the next day to the sound of my mother shouting at Dad at the top of her voice:

"What are you doing, you stupid man? Why are you packing a case? Where are we going? Are we going back to England, Jack? I think that's good, yes, I'd like that. Don't do that. I don't need you helping me, just bugger off and leave me alone, I need a drink and I'm going to have one."

"Listen to me, Julia," Dad told her. "You remember the doctor who came to see you yesterday? Well, he wants to help you get better. He wants you to go with him to a clinic in Perigueux."

"I'm not going anywhere with any doctor. They treat people who are sick, and I'm not sick, I'm just fine, I like it this way. When I drink, I stop worrying about everything and everyone and I don't have to think about anything at all and that's fine by me. I'm not doing anyone any harm."

"That's where you're wrong, Julia. It's not only ruining your health, but it's affecting mine and Maisie's. She's having a job coping with it all. You remember the young English policeman friend of hers? Well, he and Maisie found this place for you and if you want a normal way of life or something near to it again, then you must go."

"I'm not going anywhere except England. So, clear off!"

Wakening to all this chaos I thought to myself, *'Here we go again. Another difficult day ahead.'* I met Dad leaving the bedroom, which stunk of booze. Mum had stopped drinking vodka and was now on brandy, whisky, and any other concoctions she managed to get hold of. We found out that she'd got one of our neighbours from the complex to do shopping for her, and her requirements included copious bottles of anything cheap, along with some of the hard stuff. The neighbour felt sorry for Mum and was only too willing to buy it for her. It was quite a time before Dad realized this was happening. Mum's help in getting hold of the drink this way apparently had only just begun, thank God. And, when he asked her to buy less gradually so that she didn't have to withdraw from drinking suddenly, she agreed to help out and do so. But, what we didn't realise was that Mum had stockpiled the stuff, well hidden, and if anyone went into her bedroom, she was like a banshee, keeping everyone well away from where she had squirrelled the bottles. She allowed no one near it, protecting her secret supply as if it were a newborn baby.

A smallish ambulance drew up to the house at about eleven in the morning. Dad began to shake so I stood close. As the two paramedics came in, I told them that Mum was upstairs and not in any frame of mind to leave her bedroom.

"Not to worry. We will sort it out," said the first paramedic who'd come in speaking in French. He was corpulent and looked strong enough to cope with what was about to confront him. The other chap spoke some pigeon English. He was around thirty, tall, with thick black, curly hair and smelt of Galois cigarettes. He reassured us by saying, "We are used to sorting out these issues, she will be fine eventually."

The second saddest day of our lives was seeing my mother, being forcibly removed from home and being pushed into the ambulance. She was screaming and lashing out at them with her fists, then kicking at their bodies, until she was eventually overpowered. Then, she held her hands to her face, hung her head in defeat and started crying. Dad couldn't bear it any longer, so he went back indoors. Neighbours came out to see what all the commotion was about and I again wept uncontrollably. It was simply the most shocking sight. *Why on earth could they not have sedated her before leaving the house, thus avoiding this debacle,* I wondered?

I watched the ambulance draw away until it disappeared from view and went inside to where Dad was standing. I put my arms around him and held him for a while. Eventually, he turned to me and said, "This is going to be the worst Christmas ever, girl."

"Dad, it's time for you to go back to work now, it will help in more ways than one." We were advised not to visit for at least a week, to give Mum time to settle in.

That afternoon, after eating barely anything for lunch, Dad got into his work clothes and set off back to the estate. I decided to go down to the farm. When I arrived, Ralph had not left the house. "I hoped you'd come. How did it all go, Maisie?" he asked.

"It was awful," I told him as I started to cry. "I hope never to witness such horror again."

"Where is that boyfriend of yours? Was he not around to help you?"

"I think I've lost that boyfriend. Wait, which one do you mean, Toby or James? By the way James is a friend, nothing more than that. If you mean Toby, it was over before it even began. He got so angry with me because I couldn't stop laughing over a scene in a restaurant he took me to. He told me I was still 'just a child', and I haven't heard from him since."

Ralph stood in front of me, took hold of both my shoulders, looked me straight in the face and told me I was lovely. Then, he kissed me full on my lips. I was flabbergasted at this and had to pull away as I needed to be able to breathe again.

As I pulled away, he took a step backwards and, looking worried, he said, "I'm so sorry for doing that, Maisie, it was a spur of the moment thing. It happened because you are so beautiful and fragile right now and I wanted to, I suppose. Nonetheless, I should never have taken advantage of you at a time like this. And, I must tell you, it's the boyfriend's loss, not yours."

"No worries there, Ralph. I've been wanting you to do that for a long time, but knowing you were married, I didn't think it would ever be possible."

"You're very young, there are many years between us."

"Yes, I know that. But, more important is the matter of your wife back home. What do you think she would have to say about you having extra marital relationships?"

"Well, up to now I haven't even thought much about it. Anyway, not long back I learned that she wants a divorce. It would seem she has not been as celibate as me."

"That makes things a good deal easier. There's nothing to stop us now." With that statement, I jumped back into his arms and we held one another tightly. Even though this man was a farmer and still in his farming clothes, he smelt amazingly fresh. Perhaps it was his aftershave. I clung to Ralph and we kissed again.

"Where's your brother?" I asked.

"He's away for the day. Gone to Bordeaux to see an old friend, probably a woman. He has a penchant for them, as I think you're aware."

"Well, that means there's nothing to stop us. Do you want to go to bed with me, Ralph?" I looked at him with doleful eyes.

"You know I do. But, what about your policeman?"

"There was never anything more than a kiss and cuddle between us, it wasn't meant to be."

With that remark, we both dashed up the long, wide staircase to his bedroom. A quick look around told me it was not used to a woman's touch. The bed was huge, a king-size; I think you could have had a party on it. As soon as we were through the door, Ralph closed and locked it. "Just in case anyone comes around," he explained.

I was nervous and excited all at the same time. I didn't know what to expect, as this would be the first time for me. He, on the other hand, was experienced. He whispered in my ear, "Don't worry, it will be fine. I won't do anything to hurt you."

I hadn't let on that I was a virgin, but I think he must have assumed I was. My clothes were taken off bit by bit and then he laid me on his bed, which was freshly made with clean linen, as his home help had been there to clean that morning. *Had he asked her to, especially in case I came to see him that afternoon,* I wondered? The sheets smelt wonderful. He undressed in front of me and that did make me concerned. He was a big man and I had never been touched before. We explored each other all over, then he kissed me everywhere, which I found so exciting I could hardly contain my aroused emotions. Then, he very gently put his hand between my legs and parted them. Then his fingers wandered up to that soft place and he pushed the lips of my vagina apart. For a moment, I wondered what would happen next. It didn't take long before I found out. He took my hand and put it around his penis. It was the first time I had seen one in the flesh, let alone held one.

My whole body was beginning to tremble and I think his was, too. He helped me to understand that he wanted me to rub my hand up and down his shaft. Then, suddenly he forced my hand away from holding him and from being on his side, he brought his body over and on top of mine.

All the time we were making love he talked to me, helping me relax and to try to enjoy my first experience of lovemaking. It didn't hurt anything like others had told me it would, as the experience was helped by his continual whispering and gentle caressing. I loved him, but was unsure if he felt the same way about me, however, no way was I about to tell him I loved him. I knew the age gap was his concern, especially in the cold light of day. But, this moment was not the cold light of day, and he enjoyed me; of that I felt certain.

When it was over, he took hold of me, pulled me to him and said, "You are the most wonderful girl. Have I made you happy?"

"Oh yes, I am that, Ralph. Did you realize I had never had sex before?"

"I thought that might have been the case. Now, I don't want you to have any regrets about what has just happened between us. If you decide that you don't want to have a relationship with me I would understand. Your father might not be too happy about it. Perhaps it's best if we keep it quiet, just between us."

"I'm more than happy to do that, and I don't think that I shall be wanting to go to bed with anyone else after the loving we've just had."

He kissed my lips and eyes, then my cheek. "We'd better get up. Do you realize it's five o'clock? Gosh that means we've been up here for four hours."

"How time flies when you're having fun!" I laughed.

We got dressed kind of slowly and then went downstairs where Ralph made me tea.

"What a gentleman you are to make a girlfriend tea after making love to her," I complimented him.

"And, why may I ask, would I not do so?"

"I only had my brother and now only my father as role models, and I have never seen Dad or my brother make tea for anyone. They are both the old-fashioned types, expecting to be waited on hand and foot, especially if a woman is around. Since Mum's been ill, I kind of fit into that role."

"You poor girl, as if you haven't had enough to cope with."

"I don't really mind. What about my poor father, losing his son and, to all intents and purposes, his wife? I can't imagine what he must be going through. Dad's not one to talk much about himself."

"Do you want me to drive you back, Maisie?"

"No thanks, I'd like to walk, I've got lots to think about."

I said nothing, just walked over to where he stood and kissed him on the lips. When I pulled away, the smile we gave each other spoke more than words ever could.

As I wandered home slowly in the pitch dark, I was so glad I'd put a torch in my bag. My head was full of all I must do for Christmas and in preparation for Aunt Mary's arrival, as well as the wonderful experience of the afternoon. I'd always wanted to be close to Ralph. He looked good, smelt good, even if he'd worked on the farm all morning.

He must have showered and changed, again in anticipation of my arrival and he spoke beautifully, that had always mattered to me, I felt it said such a great deal about a person and their intelligence. And now no longer a man with baggage, or at least was soon to be divorced.

I decided to let him make the next move and promised myself not to break my resolve. The other thing playing on my mind right now was how my brother had died. I had the strongest desire to find the answer to that question. Tomorrow I would go back down to the police in town and insist they tell me.

Yes, I felt very alive and grown up at that moment. I'd become a woman that day. When I got home, the house seemed so empty and even though I felt happy about events of the afternoon, the silence was concerning. Dad had been home so much of late and Mum was always around shouting or swearing at him or just being mean. Now, there was silence, just silence.

I made tea and thought about preparing supper. Dad would come home hungry—at least I hoped he would. He was looking thin and ill lately, his appetite had taken a downturn. I decided to make him something I knew he liked and we'd have a peaceful time together this evening. I made his favourite 'winter stew' as Mum called it. This was a slow-cooked beef meal with horseradish and garlic, curry powder and baby shallots, and lots of various seasonings. All these wonderful flavours fused together made a super meal in the winter. I started to prepare it and Dad was not home until eight, not quite as long as it should have taken to be cooked. But it was fine, by the time I served it up with mashed potatoes, and a bottle of Merlot. I hoped that Dad wouldn't notice anything different about me, for I didn't want him to know about this new relationship. We both enjoyed the silence and each other's company for the first time in such a long while.

I worked very hard preparing for Christmas, making sure that we had enough food and drink and time to visit Mum, who was beginning to show a few signs of recovery. We were told she had a long journey ahead before she would be well enough to leave the clinic, and not to build our expectations of her improvement too high. Dad was pleased that all the residents welcomed him back with open arms and were so grateful to see that the estate neglect was getting sorted. I had no idea what they'd have had to say about a seventeen-year-old having an affair with a much older man.

Dad and I had our Christmas Day alone and went off to visit Mum in the afternoon, taking her gifts of her favourite perfume, Coco Chanel. I had also bought her a new nightie, in her best-loved colour, pale pink and silky, along with her favourite bath oil. It had cost me most of the money I'd saved for presents. Mum was happy with her gifts and told us so. We let her know that her sister, Aunt Mary, was coming over soon and that we would bring her straight over to visit.

"That's nice, dear," she said to me. "Remind me would you. Who is Aunt Mary?"

I told her she was her sister and then swiftly changed the subject. Mum looked so small in the large functional hospital bed. We stayed for a couple of hours then she tired and the chatting stopped, so Dad and I left, saying we would return tomorrow. She didn't seem to be missing home.

We got home and Dad lit the wood burner. We both sat by it and warmed up for a while. There was a chill in the air and for the first time since our arrival in France a hard frost had settled. We felt the cold now and needed extra layers of clothing. That evening, we had been invited to Ralph's farm for drinks. We accepted, and I was nervous and a bit tongue-tied when we first arrived. That didn't last long, mind you, as there were so many people and everyone seemed happy and enjoying this festive time. However not many from the site. Ralph hadn't befriended them or they him. Gange started his staring act, which I desperately tried to avoid by standing behind the visitors without causing a scene.

Ralph smiled in my direction from time to time, however, I could not quite read him. I tried not to think too much about what we'd done, as I didn't want to imagine that it might never happen again. The alcohol flowed as did the food, beautifully presented by Lauren, the home help. She was a shining star for the brothers. Without her they would have struggled to keep everything together. Things had quieted down a bit on the farm but lambing was just around the corner and they were beginning to gear up for that. They had about 150 ewes most who were about to lamb around the same time. After about two hours, I could see Dad indicating to me he was ready to leave, but all I wanted to do was stay.

"No worries, love," he reassured me. "If you want to stay, I can take the car. I'm sure one of the boys will drive you back later."

"Thanks, Dad," I said gratefully. "I know you're tired. I won't be late. We have another busy day tomorrow, going over to number one. Remember, we've been invited there for lunch, then we're off to see Mum. What a lively Christmas we're having, after all."

Dad, still in his fifties, seemed to have aged enormously over these last months and he was exhausted. Now would be a chance for him to catch up on the prodigious loss of sleep he'd suffered throughout this terrible time, and worry of Mum's contributory illness. We said our goodbyes and I asked Ralph if he would take me home later.

"I think I could just about manage that, young lady," he said with an ear-to-ear smile. Then he clandestinely brushed my hand as he walked past to go into the kitchen.

I was so happy he didn't think any less of me for giving myself to him. The party continued until late into the night, by which time everyone still there was inebriated. A few were walking back home, but some about to take to their cars. The police over here were extraordinarily hot on drinking and driving, and although the roads around the farm were clear more often than not, the police would be lying in wait, especially at this time of year. Fortunately, Ralph had been careful about his drinking, more so when he knew he was to take me home. Gange, however, had made an utter fool of himself, flirting outrageously with a couple of the married women. I was delighted, as it took the pressure off me. I so hoped that Ralph hadn't said anything to his brother about us. I couldn't have faced him if that were the case. On the drive home I found out that he hadn't mentioned the fact to a soul, and that he had no intention of so doing.

"What happened between us stays just that. It only needs to be you and me who knows what we feel, no one else," he reassured me.

I was relieved beyond compare, and I grabbed his hands and thanked him for being the man he was.

"Why were there so few from the site there tonight?" I asked.

"I haven't encouraged the friendships as we're so busy on the farm and no one actually put themselves out to be my friend. So I took that as a hint."

I did not think that was a good reason as I recalled the warm welcome given to my family when we first met. Who would not have been influenced by that?

It then became Boxing Day which was also enjoyable. Dad seemed refreshed, looking better than we'd seen for some time. We ate a super lunch, wonderfully concocted and presented by the boys, who took great delight in showing off their culinary skills to the rest of the neighbours.

We drove to see Mum a day or two later. She wasn't so well, and I sought out one of the nurses to ask what had happened, as Mother seemed very sleepy. She told me that she had stayed up during the night, screaming out and hallucinating and so they had needed to sedate her. "Night times are the worst for her," she explained. "She seems to become disorientated far more at night than in the daytime."

"We've never seen her as comotosed as now, though," I said.

"That's because she needed a larger dose of the drug to calm her down. More than usual."

I went back to the bedside and told Dad the reason for Mum's state. We decided not to stay too long and left after half an hour. "It was a long way to come for a thirty-minute visit Dad," I told him. Back home, we sat and watched the new television Dad had bought, in an attempt to enjoy Christmas a bit more—I knew he had paid a great deal of money for it. Stuff like that wasn't cheap over here. It was lovely to have a TV again. I soaked up all the programmes, in English of course, although my French was adequate enough to understand quite a bit in the French channels. The English ones came through an hour after transmission in the U.K. Dad fell asleep in his chair. I woke him at eleven and suggested we go up to bed. I went up and ran a bath with oodles of bubbles and had a delicious soak before falling asleep in the bath. When I woke up, the water had gone cold.

Dad got up early the next day to go and meet Aunt Mary. She was coming into Angouleme airport at eleven-thirty. He came up with a cup of tea for me. "Are you coming with me or do you want to have a lie in?"

"I fell asleep in the bath last night and when I woke up it was cold and I was freezing, so I haven't had much sleep," I murmured.

"You stay where you are, Maisie, and I'll go and fetch her."

By the time they arrived back home, I was up, dressed and had started to get food ready. At the best of times, Aunt Mary was not the easiest going person. I realised her life had been hard, and losing her young son in the garden pond was the likely cause for her bitterness and dislike of people. She always made her feelings clear on all matters. Her husband of twenty-two years had left her for another woman and her resulting angst was all consuming. She'd never got over it.

In she came in a feisty flurry carrying gifts galore. I went over and welcomed her, gave her a hug and kissed her cheek. She never actually kissed you, just offered the cheek for you to kiss.

"I'll take your cases up, Mary," Dad said. "We have the room all ready for you. Maisie's done so much to make this Christmas bearable."

"When will we be going to see my sister?" she asked. "I don't like the sound of where she is. Are you sure they're caring for her properly?"

I couldn't help but interject. "As sure as eggs is eggs there is no way we could care for her at home. She is still being detoxified, Auntie, and you need to know that she may not recognize you. She asked us who you were the other day."

"Right, well we shall see. If I get there and feel she's not getting the proper care she needs, I shall have something to say and likely something to do about it."

"And what would that be, Auntie?"

"She may need to come home to be cared for."

"But, Dad and I are not equipped to care for her at home. She was becoming very aggressive and disruptive and Dad had to give up work to care for her. That was without much success, as alcoholics become crafty and find places to hide drink that we could never dream of."

"It takes years of drinking to become an alcoholic," Aunt Mary told us.

"Mum did have a good grounding for it before Dan's death. She would always drink at least half a bottle of wine at night with the evening meal. It was after Dan died that it became totally out of control. Would you like some tea, Auntie?"

"Yes, that would be very welcome."

Dad came back into the kitchen and asked our guest if she wanted to go see Mum before or after lunch.

"Makes no odds to me, as long as I do get to see her today."

"What have you planned for lunch, Maisie?" Dad asked. To be quite honest, I've nothing planned. That remark caused a tut from Aunt Mary who pursed her thin lips as she did it. I busied myself in the kitchen while she unpacked. By the time she descended the stairs, she had changed her clothes and looked reasonably presentable. She was smoking a cigarette.

"When did you start that habit, Auntie, I'd no idea you smoked."

"I've done it for years now on and off, helps to keep me calm."

The house had never had cigarette smoke in it since the day we came here. Dad kept sniffing the air and the whole place stank of strong tobacco. It was horrible, we said nothing as life was difficult enough without going out of our way to augment it.

I had managed to defrost some lamb shanks we were supposed to have on Christmas Eve. As she moved around the downstairs floor she noticed that Dad was nowhere to be seen, and demanded to know his whereabouts. I told her he'd gone to do a couple of small jobs for one of the neighbours. But I knew he was escaping the smell.

"But child, it's still the Christmas period, for heaven's sake!"

"Auntie, as you already know, Dad had to give up work because Mum needed constant care. We have had no money coming in for the last two months. So, he will do anything asked of him just to put food on the table and petrol in the van."

"Very well, Maisie. What can I do to help you out?"

"Why don't you go and sit by the fire?" I said. "It's lovely and warm in there. The huge wood burning stove throws out the most amazing amount of heat." We had plenty of wood, as it was in abundance around here. When trees had either blown down or been copsed by the farmers, they were only too glad to give firewood away.

"Would you like more tea, or something a little stronger?" I asked her.

"Yes, I think I shall have a sherry, do you have any?"

"I'm sure I can rustle some up."

Luckily, we had some sherry that had been brought over from England with all our belongings. I took the sherry through to her and poured a little for myself, then sat down close to the fire. We talked for a while.

Dan's name wasn't mentioned.

CHAPTER NINETEEN

The Visit and Beyond

"My Mama said life was like a box of chocolates.
You never know what you're going to get."
~ Forrest Gump.

We drove over to Perigueux after lunch, and our visitor only found the Brussels Sprouts to complain about: she said they were underdone. We took Aunt Mary up the clinic's long, winding staircase onto the second floor to where Mum's room was. She dashed inside, took one look at her sister and said, "Good God, Julia, what on earth has happened to you? What are they doing to you?"

With that outburst, my mother looked anxious and perplexed and had difficulty focusing on this new arrival. "Who is that?" she asked Dad and me. "Do I know her?"

"Yes, Mum, it's your sister, Mary over from England." Aunt Mary hastily left the room to find a member of staff. Two nurses in uniform came back into Mother's room, looked at their charge and asked Dad if he would accompany them back out. We all followed, and we were taken to one of the opulent offices. It was a comical scene. The nurses were as flustered as Aunt Mary was. "You must understand that your, er ... What relative, did you say you were?" asked the more senior of the two nurses. Dad and I both agreed that this lady was the best nurse there, even though she had a bossy 'nursey' attitude at times.

"I'm her sister," Aunt Mary replied. Her voice rose to a half-shout. "And I have never, ever seen her looking so dreadful!"

"She has been very ill and is still working hard to combat her demons."

"What are you talking about? Demons? What demons? What nonsense! My sister has never had demons, as you call them."

"We use that term for the drinking difficulties," said the older looking nurse, both looked annoyed about the whole kerfuffle. They were unused to being challenged in such a way. Dad said very little, as was usually the case, especially around a pugnacious woman. He was not used to pushy, overpowering women and neither was I, but, I had no intention of keeping quiet.

"Aunt Mary, I must ask you to be quiet, and listen to what the nurses are saying. They are doing all they can to help Mum, and you shouting and carrying on is not going to help one bit."

Dad interjected at this point. "The girl's right, Mary. If you don't stop this nonsense, we shall go straight home."

I was amazed to hear my father being so bold. In fact, he was the gentlest natured of all the men I knew, with the exception of my new-found friend, Ralph.

"I shall go in and talk to Mum," Dad said. "You two wait out here and come in after me."

Aunt Mary was furious and made no attempt to hide it.

When we went in to see Mum, Dad asked her, "Mum, do you know who's here to see you?"

"No, dear. Who is it?" she timidly replied.

"It's your sister. Would you like to speak to her?"

"Oh, yes, that would be nice."

I left the bedside and went back into the waiting area just across the hall from Mum's room, where the two nurses were still doing their best to placate Aunt Mary.

Dad walked in. "If you do go in to see her again, you really must be pleasant, Mary," Dad said. "No yelling or carrying on. It doesn't help the situation at all." Dad went in with her, as did the nurses. I kept well out of the way this time. When they all came out, the delicate atmosphere was tangible. My aunt and father both looked annoyed, each for different reasons, when they left Mum's room. I offered to drive us home. "Thanks, love," Dad said. "I think that would help and I could do with a stiff drink."

"Do you want to find a bar somewhere here, Dad?" I asked. "Or shall we wait 'til we get home?"

"There will be no drinking while driving is going on in my presence. I certainly couldn't bear the stink of it in the car," Aunt Mary announced imperiously.

Dad chose to remain unresponsive to this remark. The journey home was slow, silent, and tortuous. That was until we walked through our front door.

"Now, I'm going to say my piece whether you like it or not, Jack," Aunt Mary began. "You two are far too close to see things the way they really are. Julia is obviously not getting over whatever is wrong with her. It has to be more than just the drink. She needs to be in a proper hospital. Not a place for head cases."

"Stop right there, Mary," Dad warned. He walked over to where she stood and pointed his finger in a threatening way. "You weren't here when things became so bad that Maisie and I were unable to handle them. It broke my heart to see my beloved wife in the state she was and to watch her deteriorate so fast. We could not see the way ahead until a young policeman, who is English, became friends with our Maisie, and it was he who got the help we so badly needed. It's not going to be a quick fix, either. In fact, she may not come back here until the spring."

"That is totally unacceptable! I think you must have her home and the sooner the better. Remove all the alcohol from the house and she will recover far quicker in her own home than in that place."

"You don't understand how bad the situation is, Mary. And if you are going to make it more difficult for us here than it already is, I think you'd better leave." Dad was adamant.

"Indeed, I will do just that. Maisie, please go and get my things down and I shall call for a taxi."

"You've no need to leave now," Dad apologised. "I can take you to the airport later in the week. Stay a little longer. I'm sorry I said what I did, it's just that… it's such a stressful time."

"That's why I came back over here Jack, to help the two of you out. But, now I know I'm unwelcome and I wish to leave."

"Do you know how much a taxi will cost you to get to the airport, at this time of year? They'll up the price immensely." This was the first thing I had said since getting home. I'd kept quiet up until now, as Aunt Mary was clearly determined in her stance. Dad had dealt adequately with all of Aunt Mary's nonsense. My interference would only have added fuel to the fire.

"I can take you to the airport if you like," I said.

"No, thank you. I shall wait here until the taxi comes. He said it would be about an hour."

I was glad she had said that as I had not passed my driving test yet, that would give her something else to have a go about. I drove the car from time to time. I was soon to take the test.

"Auntie, do you know if there are any flights going back to the UK today?" I asked her.

"I don't care if there aren't any. I shall just wait until there is one. And, if I come over here again it will be to see my sister and her alone. I might even take her back home to England with me."

Her words were so cruel. My father and I had been through such trauma, through the worst events imaginable for any human being.

The taxi arrived. I got all of Aunt Mary's things together and she left us without saying another word. Dad and I stood there mouths wide open. I looked at him and said, "Come on, let's go out for something to eat. I don't want us to just sit here and mope. What an awful person that relative of ours has become."

We tried hard not to think too much about the day's events, for it had been the worst possible idea to bring Mother's Sister over here. But, neither of us dreamt we'd see such a demonstration of selfishness as we'd both witnessed.

CHAPTER TWENTY

My Love

"Respect your emotions while also training them. They can be great servants, but not leaders. When they lead, chaos follows."
~ Ryoko

I couldn't wait for the next time I would be alone with Ralph. I said nothing to Dad, as I didn't want him fretting about what we were up to. For me it was the promise of fulfilment, which was all the sweeter for having been so long deferred.

New Year's Eve came and went, and Dad and I spent it alone. But, I still couldn't fathom the reason why we hadn't heard from Ralph. It was over a week since I'd seen him.

"Maybe we should ask them to come over to us tomorrow and celebrate the New Year, love?" Dad suggested.

"What a good idea," I rejoined. "Except instead of 'them' let's go with just Ralph. Shall I call and see if he can come over?"

The phone seemed to be ringing at their end, but there was no reply. So, I left a message, saying we were going to have drinks in the afternoon of New Year's Day. It was most strange, as one of the brothers always carried a mobile phone when out in the yard or the fields. They had a gadget that transferred their calls from the land-line to the mobile. I was concerned and said to Dad, "They're not responding, I wonder why that is? Maybe the phone's out of order."

"Well, I've left a message so let's wait and see."

It got to three in the afternoon and I told Dad that I was going down to the farm to make sure all was well.

"Do you think that's a good idea, love?" Dad asked. "They may think you're being a bit pushy?"

"No worries, Dad, I won't be long. Hopefully I'll get a lift back, if they're home, of course."

I donned a hat and coat, as the weather was now exceptionally cold, the coldest we'd known since arriving here. I walked briskly, almost at a trot, to help try and keep some warmth inside, and it worked. Then It dawned on me that they might have gone away, maybe even home to England. My heart skipped a beat at the thought of that. *Would he go to see his wife and try to talk her out of the divorce? Was he not interested in having a juvenile girlfriend and all the trappings that go along with such a thing? Who would be caring for the animals?*

As I carried on walking, the grey day seemed to implode on me. What cheered me up, though, were the hedges dripping with silver icicles. Then I saw Ralph walking along the lane with his dog, Benny, ahead of me. I called out, "Ralph, it's me!"

He seemed not to hear at first. Then he stopped and turned around to follow Benny, who had made a dash in my direction. When Ralph noticed me, he waved vigorously and called out, "Hello sweetie, how are you?" Benny was bouncing up and down with excitement, he jumped up with his huge feet almost reaching my chin, then licked me all over the face and nibbled gently at my hands, as was his habit.

"I'm fine, but, how are you?" I asked him anxiously. "I've been trying to get through to you for ages. We wanted you to come to us on New Year's Day for a bit of celebrating."

"I'm so sorry. I turned the phones off because there has been some trouble, concerning Gange and a business back in the U.K. Nothing for you to worry your little head over."

"What was it about?"

"He may have to go home." Ralph said.

"Oh, that's odd as I thought he was enjoying living off of you over here. The ultimate freeloader."

"That's rather a harsh thing to say, Maisie. Why do you say that?"

"I'm afraid I dislike him, you know that. I told you before that he stares at me constantly. I want to talk to him about it and about my brother and his disappearance."

Ralph changed colour, and his pallor scared me.

"What's the matter?" I asked him with concern. "You don't look well."

"I don't think it would be wise to talk to him now. Gange is preoccupied with some business venture he's got going back home and I think it may be failing. And you must know he is a great help to me on the farm."

I said nothing more as we walked together back to the farm. He took my hand and I felt loved and strong again. It had started to rain hard just before we made it back to the house.

When we got inside, Benny was soaking wet and smelled horrible. He then proceeded to shake his body so hard that all the wet on him hit me and Ralph. We looked at each other, seeing the futility of it and laughed out loud.

Ralph went to get some towels. I dried the dog and, as I looked up, there in the doorway in complete silence stood Gange, looking down on me. I got up and patted the dog's head, then went over to where Gange stood and summoned up some courage, from who knows where, and said outright, "Why is it that you cannot stop staring at me the way you do?"

With a smug grin like an angry vulture he muttered, "Don't be silly, I've far better things to do than stare at you. What an imagination you have, but, I should make allowances because you're still just a child, aren't you?"

"You were just staring at me while you were standing there in the doorway!" I raised my voice. "Are you unaware of what you're doing?"

Ralph came back downstairs after changing into dry clothes. I didn't notice I was still wet at that point, for I was on a mission now, determined to find out more about this odd man and his bizarre behaviour.

I turned away from Gange and walked into the lounge, not making eye contact with Ralph as I thought he'd be annoyed that I'd verbally tackled his brother when he asked me not to. The recently lit fire was heating the room up nicely. It was so comforting as we sat in the cosy armchairs. Gange bought in some hot tea. I hesitated to drink it, for fear of what he may have added to mine.

"Do you think you'll be able to come over to ours later tomorrow? To celebrate the New Year and hopefully a better one than we've just had," I uttered in a rather aloof tone, looking only at Ralph.

"Yes, of course we shall come over, Maisie. How is your father?" Ralph answered.

"Dad's fine. He's had a chance to recover a bit from the stress Mum caused. Now that she's getting the treatment she needs, it's like a huge weight has been lifted off his shoulders."

"That's good news."

"Yes, but there's bad news, too. Aunt Mary came over to stay for the second time. We took her off to visit Mum and she behaved appallingly. She was horrible to the staff, moaning about the lack of care she thought Mum was receiving. When we got home, there was an almighty row between her and Dad, after which she ordered a taxi to the airport and off she went, with a few suggestions as to what Dad and I should do if we were anything like decent human beings."

"That's awful. How could she be so rotten? It's beginning to get dark, Maisie. Would you like me to take you home?"

"Yes, if you don't mind. Are we OK for tomorrow?"

"Yes, we are," Gange said in a rhetorical kind of way.

On the way home, Ralph and I were glad to be alone together. He put his arm around my shoulders while slowly driving with the other hand through the misty twilight countryside. Without taking his eyes from the road he said, "It would be nice to see you again. I miss you and want to make love to you."

"So do I. When do you suggest?"

"Maybe we could meet up somewhere."

"I have an idea," I blurted out. "Why don't you come to the house when Dad's out working? He often needs to go into town or visits Mum alone. That would give us time."

"Yes, let's make some arrangement to that effect as soon as possible."

The opportunity came the following week. Dad said to me that morning, "This afternoon I'm going into Ribérac to get some gear I need for work and then off to see your mother." School had recommenced after the Christmas break, so I calculated that if Ralph met me from school, we could get back, make love, and get on with our daily duties well before Dad got back.

As I walked to the school gates, Ralph was there waiting in his fancy car, not the Jeep type thing. Helen said to me, "Oh, is he waiting for you, you lucky thing? He's so handsome, but so old, Cherie."

I told her to shut up and said that he was a friend of the family and that we had some important paperwork to get sorted over Dan's death. That shut her up. I dashed to the car and jumped in with aghast enthusiasm.

"Just look at you in your uniform, it's so alluring," he said enthusiastically. "I can't wait to get you to bed."

"We need to be careful and hide the car and take the risk of putting it in the falling down garage behind the house, then the neighbours curiosity won't be awakened. Let's hope it doesn't collapse today." Most of them had returned to France, and they'll be on the lookout for a bit of gossip. Our liaison would give them plenty of ammunition to help keep the tongues wagging for weeks on end."

As we drove back, I told Ralph that I'd not long back had my seventeenth birthday.

"Why didn't you tell me about it before now?"

"Because I thought you would still think I was too young to start a relationship with and so I kept quiet."

"What would you like as a present, darling?" he asked smiling.

"I would like a long love-in session with you, and some perfume."

"Which perfume do you like?"

"Anything by Chanel, I don't care what. I just love all of the stuff."

When we arrived back home, I made sure the coast was clear and up the stairs we dashed, tearing at each other's clothes as we did so. He fumbled for a while with my bra strap, and I helped him out in the end. When we were both naked, we flung ourselves onto the bed, small as it was, but sufficient for our needs and we made love until we were both exhausted. Then he turned to me and said, "You are taking precautions, aren't you? Because I don't think either of us want the patter of tiny feet around now, do we?"

"It's a bit late to think of that after the event. I, my love, have thought of everything and am on the pill. I went onto it when I thought that I might be forming a deeper relationship with the policeman."

At that moment, I heard a car draw up outside. I went to the window and saw to my horror Dad had come home. It was only just after six-thirty and I was sure he wouldn't be home until later.

"Ralph, get up! It's Dad. I don't want him to know about us yet. And definitely not like this."

We both got dressed, but unfortunately could not make it downstairs in time to beat him getting indoors. He met us both coming sheepishly down the stairs.

"Hello, you two, where on earth have you been?" he asked innocently.

"Hi Dad, I was showing Ralph that piece of pottery Auntie gave me for Christmas."

I don't think he believed me for a moment.

Ralph said, "And how are you, Jack?"

"I'm well, thank you for asking, son. Are you going to stay for supper? I expect Maisie has been cooking me up something nice." Ashamed, I looked embarrassed. "Well, I was just about to start it, Dad. Do you want anything in particular?"

"No. Strange, you usually have everything under way by the time I get back from visiting your mother."

"How is she?" I rushed to say, changing the subject.

"I won't stay, thank you all the same, Jack. I need to get back to see to the animals. It won't be long now before lambing begins," Ralph stumbled.

"Right you are, son, then I shall say goodbye. I need to change." And with that he went upstairs. I panicked, as I couldn't remember if I had closed my bedroom door.

"Bye darling, for now," Ralph whispered. "Let's meet up again soon. Next time we meet up, I shall have your belated birthday present with me."

Dad came back downstairs and gave me a look that said, 'I know exactly what the two of you have been up to.' I cooked our meal and when we were sitting at the table eating, he said to me, "I hope you know what you're doing, young lady. He's a nice enough chap but he's old enough to be your father."

"Dad, he makes me happy. And our friendship has only just begun and I don't suppose it will get serious."

"Maisie, you are still so young, hardly old enough to be worldly wise now, are you?"

"Don't have a row about it. It's early days and at the moment, I'm in a happier place than I've been for months."

Dad chose to add no more to the conversation, and I realised that my words about being happy, indeed resonated with him. We didn't say that word very often.

CHAPTER TWENTY-ONE

Collusion

I dusted the main rooms, dining room and kitchen, then hoovered all over including our bedrooms, fervently. Even though it was still February, the sun had shone all day and was just beginning to fade and settle at six-thirty. I worked myself up into a frenzy, dashing around, fitting in as much as possible before starting supper.

Tonight I planned to keep it simple: baked potatoes with baked beans. We both enjoyed that, and if Dad wanted some bacon, I would grill him a couple of rashers. I had put on a bit of weight since Christmas, down to overeating, drinking, and basking in the glory of my new love. That was the effect my lover had on me. We did not meet as often as I would have liked. But, his life was so full and demanding and I had both school and domesticity to cope with. I was due to take my final exams in May and soon afterwards would be leaving my schooling years behind forever.

Trying to juggle education, cooking, cleaning, visits to Mum in the clinic (an hour-and-a-half round trip plus however long the visit happened to be) as well as making love with Ralph on the few opportunities arising, was no mean feat. I also felt I ought to seriously consider what I was going to do with my life. Dad would frequently ask me, *"What are your plans for the future, Maisie? It's about time you chose a career for yourself. When I last saw your teachers, they talked about how talented you were and how you should be thinking of going on to University after finishing school."*

I didn't think it was the right time to consider further education. There was too much happening and the thought of leaving my new-found friend had no appeal whatsoever at the moment. Dad had come to terms with Ralph and me being more than just friends. Although I suspected he would have preferred me to have a boyfriend closer my own age. But, he was kind enough never to mention it.

"Dad, if I wasn't here, who would look after you, what with Mum still away and you working all the daylight hours?" I pointed out.

"We shall have to cross that bridge when we come to it," he told me. "I will try to get a job in Perigueux. I'm good at maths, so, perhaps I could train as an accountant. A number of accountancy firms are scattered around there."

"I would still prefer it if you went on to university, as I'm sure your mother would. No one else in our whole family has ever gone to a university, and it would make us so proud, Maisie."

Yes, he wanted me to go, but the dichotomy was he also wanted me to stay and help with Mum. I knew that was in the back of his mind.

I thought it better to keep away from the subject for now, as I wanted to ask Dad if he would come to Ribérac with me and see if we could at last find out how Dan had died.

Down we both went. I didn't bump into Toby and was pleased about that. I knew it would be difficult for me to hide my embarrassment if I saw him again. As usual, we had absolutely no luck in finding out any more information.

I believed that they all had colluded with each other in some sort of conspiratorial way and that they were dragging their heels in slow deliberation. *How could they be so cruel? What had they to gain by keeping details from us? Dan was our family, and surely, they could empathize with us. They had families of their own, how would it affect them if they had no knowledge of the cause of death of a loved one, if they were ever unfortunate enough to be in our position?*

CHAPTER TWENTY-TWO

Confrontations and Revelations

"Chance will let you choose your path.
Fate already knows which road you will walk it on."
~ Ian Segal

Before too long we had a visit from one of the detectives working on Dan's case. When I went to the door I had a suspicion today would bring news. Why I should think that, I don't know, never having been blessed with psychic powers.

"There is a psychopath at large and his murder of a man near to Bergerac bore a similarity to the killing of Dan," we were told.

"And, what may I ask is that? Do you realize that no one has ever told us how Dan died?"

"Well, if you really wish to know details, I will tell you. But, be prepared to be upset."

"Son, please tell us what happened to him. It's better we know."

As the details of how Dan met his end were being relayed, Dad went white and I turned away, as if this news was not about my brother and not on my radar. I had a surreal out-of-body experience, not allowing such disturbing news to sink in.

"Oh my God, that means he must have suffered considerably before the end. I just cannot believe it. Why has it taken you so long to divulge this news?" Dad asked.

There was no reply forthcoming.

We think the killer may live in the Bordeaux region. Someone, somewhere will talk, they always do. I know this has been a considerable shock."

Dad interjected with, "I don't want my wife to ever know about the news you've just given us. She's in no fit state to hear such details about her dear boy."

"Oh my God, sir," I added. "Do you really think that he is the same man who killed Dan?"

"What makes you think it's a man?" He said looking at me in a strange, narrow-eyed way. "We don't know for certain, but there is a strong possibility that the murderer is a woman. There are some factors pointing to that fact."

"Tell me more," I pleaded. "How on earth could a woman kill a tall, strong young man?"

"There has to be savagery about her. And, she or he would have to be insane, and very powerful. The sort of person who's in the gym every day, building muscle, gaining strength to be able to handle the body afterwards."

"I can hardly believe a woman would be capable of that." I told him. I realized that was a stupid statement on my behalf; there have always been women who were capable of killing and, in the moment, when adrenalin released their strength comparable with that of any man, or so I've been told.

"You'd be surprised. The things people do to one another would horrify you. Dan was also stabbed in the back and, had he lived, he would have been paralysed as the knife severed the top vertebrae."

******

This cache of information might just be sending me in the right direction. It had to be a man. A few days later, I planned to go straight down to the farm and have it out with Gange. I knew this would not be appreciated by Ralph, who appeared to have a considerably misguided strong bond with his brother.

******

When I got to the farm, I had to go halfway down into the main farmyard where Ralph was busy concentrating around the pens where some of the sheep were already lambing.

"Ralph, I have no choice, I must talk to your brother again. I know you're not happy about it, but I need to know what he knows, and I must know if he was the man by the canal who scared me so."

"Maisie, what are you to gain by doing that?" Ralph asked me. "He is only going to tell you what he wants you to know. I think you'll achieve absolutely nothing by confronting him. He is a difficult man and in a bad place right now. Remember, I told you about some business venture of his back home that seems to have gone wrong."

"I won't rest until I've spoken with him. So, please don't try to stop me. I know you have my best interests at heart, but, I need to know. I think he knows more about Dan than he's letting on."

"Well, if you must, you must. Do you want me to be there, too?"

"No, I can manage. Thank you for loving me, my dear friend." That last remark came out a bit suddenly, for he had never told me he loved me. *Oh, crickey have I overstepped the mark again?*

"I'm not sure that your father approves of us being together," he remarked.

"Dad and other people will just have to accept it. It's not their business anyway. Where is your brother right now?"

"There's no time like the present to strike. I'll go down to the barn and ask him to come up and let him know you want to talk with him."

"Thanks, Ralph."

Gange shortly came sauntering up through the fields, saw me and gave a huge smug grin as ever then called to me, "Hello, madam, I understand you wish to talk to me?"

"Yes, that's correct, I do. Shall we go indoors?"

"If you wish, whatever your little heart desires." His arrogance persisted with his uniquely thinly veiled distaste.

We moved through the kitchen, into the lounge. I sat down as far away as I could from him without being too obvious. I asked him about the last time he was out with Dan. The answers came thick and fast. He went all through their afternoon together and the various timings. He seemed to know all this information as though he had been rehearsing it. He'd probably practised for the police's benefit. I then asked him if he went out again that night.

"No, I worked on the farm until well into the evening. I recall it was totally dark by the time I went in for supper. It was mid-November, if I remember correctly, and the farm was dramatically busy."

"Did Dan tell you where he was going after you left him?"

"No, but I had the feeling it was to be with a woman."

"What made you think that?"

"Well, there was a lot of men's talk going on between the two of us and naturally women were a regular feature of our conversations."

I then proceeded to ask about the canal back in England. Had he been there back then when I was still a child? He denied any knowledge of what I was on about and just muttered something about being in India at the time. When I reached the subject of his continual staring at me whenever we were in each other's company, he hesitated before saying, "Well, a cat can look at a queen, can't he? You should be flattered that I find you alluring. You've had that out with me before, why bring it up again?"

Maybe Ralph was right. I should have expected that he would say nothing of any use to me.

I thanked him for giving me his attention.

When I got up to leave, he came over to where I stood and attempted to kiss me. I pulled away urgently and told him to pack it in. He stopped, for which I was thankful, then went out to find Ralph. I relayed all the conversation and his brother's action at the end of it.

"Oh, he did, did he?" Ralph said angrily. "The sod! I shall have words."

"No, don't say anything," I told him. "It was easy for me to get him to stop and I don't want him to know about us."

"You're my girlfriend, and I don't appreciate the idea of him trying it on with you!"

"Well, he doesn't know that, I hope. You haven't told him, have you Ralph?"

"No. I was tempted to one night, but managed to stop myself. To be honest, my sweet, I want to let the whole world know about us and shout it from the hilltops."

I leaned towards him and kissed him on both cheeks. "You know something? You are the most wonderful person I have ever met. Now I need to find out more regarding Dan. I don't really know where to go from here. Until the police are prepared to tell us more. I'm stymied."

"You need to be careful. Just remember there's a killer out there who doesn't want to be found."

"Instead of stating the obvious, why don't you offer me some helpful advice?"

Ralph did not respond to my curt, unnecessary remark. Instead he just kissed me 'au revoir' and set off back to where the sheep waited for him and said he'd call me tomorrow.

Gange came back in from the yard and called to me, saying, "Oh, Maisie, I've just thought of something regarding what you said when you asked me if I went out again on the night Dan was killed. As already said, I didn't. But Ralph did!"

Further Challenges

"We cannot change the cards we are dealt, just how we play the hand."
~ Randy Pausch

T he dawn was breaking when I tried to wake, my eyes still full of sleep, not wishing to be disturbed. As I raised my head from the pillow I threw the duvet off my hot body. I still could not quite believe what I'd heard the day before. So, Ralph, the love of my life, went out again on that appalling night last year. So, what, how does that affect anything? Gange was a craftmaster at hyperbole and I was convinced he said it to distract attention from himself. Nonetheless it bothered me a bit and I tried to establish the best way to approach the subject next time we were together.

Mother lingered on at the clinic in Perigueux. According to her doctor not making as much progress as they felt she should have done at this point.

And there was my intrepid Father, working hard at the beck and call of the residents with all their complexities. I worried about him for when his days' work was done, at least three times a week he would visit mother, and always on Sunday. I found it to distressing seeing her look the way she did right now and limited my visits to once a week.

I felt a consistent nag deep down partly due to forthcoming exams and other issues. I remained confident as did Helen and we faired better by studying together. The other trick we practised was to write the hard to grasp subjects in large print on paper Sellotaped to the toilet door. Each time we paid a visit we would read the subject over and over and gradually the difficult to comprehend facts began to sink into our vacuous grey matter.

The next thing of great importance was taking these wretched exams. It was strange but over the past two weeks I hadn't thought about Dan as much as usual. I knew I had to take my studies seriously as failure was not an option. Helen had her life completely mapped out and it made me envious that she was so organised. Things at home for her had become grim as her Mother found out about the affair her husband was having.

"The atmosphere is becoming intolerable and I cannot wait to leave and get myself to Paris. I know that a new chapter in my life is just around the corner," Helen remarked.

I had put in an immense amount of study into perfecting my written French I had not studied the language seriously for long. However, Helen and I only communicated in French these days, assuming that making this effort would be well worth it.

I rang Ralph and told him that I would not be able to see him for a while as I had to buckle down to my studies. I also chose not to mention what Gange had told me about the night Dan was killed. He understood as I knew he would and told me he'd miss me.

The examination start day arrived and Helen and I sat nervously beside each other talking and putting our writing materials together for the first day of finals. We covered a number of subjects that day and the following week we had maths, English language [a doodle for me and Helen] then the dreaded French language oral exam, the one we both knew would be difficult. It wasn't as bad as I imagined, however Helen was distraught. She was convinced this would be her best subject until she opened the paper and the look of horror she directed at me said '*I don't know the answers.*' Her mother came to fetch us from school and she broke her heart as soon as we got I the car.

"What am I going to do?" Helen cried. "If I fail this exam all my hopes for going to university in Paris will be a pipe dream.'"

"Stop it, Helen," her mother half shouted at the girl. "Don't be so dramatic, save your tears for when you get the results."

"How do you think you got on, Maisie?' I was asked.

"I'm not too sure, the English will be fine for both of us, but the French language was worse than expected," I lied.

"There you are, Helen, Maisie had problems with it as well."

"Thank you, Mrs. Treadworthy for the lift."

I said farewell to Helen, kissed her and told her not to worry as we were in it together.

It was now Friday and I had plans. The next day, I was to take my driving exam. Now I must say that driving in France has proved to be a very different kettle of fish to learning to drive in England. There are many rules and regulations to be adhered to. I was so lucky not to have been stopped when I drove at Christmas when unqualified. If I had been caught, I would have been in serious trouble, but it was a risk I was prepared to take. It is twice the price of the U.K. I had to buy the twenty hours of formal tuition with the perfective and test application at a cost to my Dad of 13,000 Euros. He made it clear that this was a one off with the comment to me, "You'd better pass first time as I shan't be paying for it again."

Fortunately, the instructors don't put your name forward unless they think you will pass first time. It would be in the two parts. I wasn't too worried as I had a good deal of practice with Dad and Ralph, which had given me confidence.

The day came and I passed. I drove to Ralph's farm. It was fortunate I found him in the house alone.

"Hello, my darling," I quickly uttered. "Guess who's a clever girl and has just passed her driving test with flying colours?"

"Well done to you sweetie, that's fabulous news, I think we should celebrate. How about tonight, what are you doing this evening? And what is your Dad doing this evening?"

"Nothing, were you thinking of eating out? Dinner and making love after?"

"How'd you read my mind?"

He wrapped me in his arms and kissed me on the lips.

"I know of a fabulous little place just opened between here and Perigueux, it seems popular and has good reviews. I'll give them a call and see if I can make a reservation for four of us. Is that alright with you, Maisie?"

"Yes, that sounds like a great spot."

It was funny, Ralph was more relaxed than I'd seen him before. I liked to think that I also had something to do with that. It was mid-afternoon and I stayed until about four, I just loved his company in and out of bed. There was no chance of the bedroom today as Gange was working near the house.

"How long now before you finish up those dreaded finals?"

"They still keep coming, I've already taken a few, but there's worse on the horizon. Anyhow I don't want to talk about them. I want this to be a happy day. I can drive!"

Ralph had managed to get a table for the four of us for that night. Gange being included definitely hurt the celebration, but oh well.

"Want me to drive?" I asked. "Pick you guys up?"

"No, you certainly will not, this is a night for you to celebrate. Unlimited wine. No responsibilities. We'll come for you about seven."

"Lovely for me not to have to cook too," I said.

And with that he bent over to my face, took it in his large, work worn hands and kissed my lips tenderly.

I smiled thinking about those kisses as I drove towards home. As I turned a corner, perhaps a little faster than I should have, I couldn't stop in time to avoid a huge tractor coming from the other direction.

All I remember hearing was the massive noise of the vehicles colliding and the airbag being released, then nothing.

Nothing at all.

When I finally regained consciousness, my head had started to ache alarmingly and as I walked down the narrow lane I felt extremely sick, a few steps further and I vomited profusely. I felt desperately ill and needed to sit down by the roadside for a while. I'd not been there very long when I heard a voice say:

"Hello young lady, are you O.K.? You seem to have had an accident."

"Yes, I think I did, not sure where I am, I live in the Chez Mouzey complex."

Then I felt my speech begin to slur.

"You're not too far from there. Would you like me to help you home?"

"Yes that would be go—," I then realised I didn't know how to say the words. My head hurt so badly and my eyes would not focus. As I stood I felt myself falling and that's the last I remember.

Apparently, I slipped into unconsciousness. The next thing I saw was a uniform. Where on earth was I? Was I in the hospital? My first foggy thought: *'Good, that must mean I'm O.K. and not badly hurt.'*

The next person I saw was another uniformed nurse, I was mortified when she told me what had happened. She told me I'd been hit by a tractor.

"You're a very lucky lady, as you sustained a serious head injury. It so easily could have killed you. You also have a broken leg and arm on the right. It was your right side that took most of the impact."

"Oh, my God, what about my parents! Do they know what's happened to me? We were all going out tonight to celebrate passing the driving test. What happened to the other driver?"

I started cracking up, laughing like a child.

"The driving test. I passed it. I passed the test."

I started laughing more hysterically.

"I passed the test and I got hit by a tractor. Here Maisie, here's your license—*crash!*"

I laughed even harder and the tears started to fall. The nurse put her hand on my shoulder.

"Easy there. Catch your breath. Your parents know you're here and your Father comes in everyday to see you. The tractor driver was fine and uninjured, and I'm told he thought you seemed to be alright as you walked away."

"He comes in every—how long have I been here? Have I missed the exams and there's so much and there's so much happening to me at the moment and I need to be fit and well. "You've been here just over a week, and you are going to recover but it will take some time for you to be back to normal again. Any head injury takes time to recover, and you do have some memory loss. Exams are the last thing you need to be worrying about."

"I *absolutely need to get studying!*"

"Bones will heal as they do and in one so young the process will be quick. We hope that your memory loss will not last too long," the nurse said. She ignored my plea for studying. "That needs time and lots of rest."

"I can't rest, I have my Mother to care for and I look after my Dad. I cook for him as Mum's in the clinic."

"Maisie, that's good, that's good. Do you remember anything else about your Mother and Father anything else at all?"

"Oh yes. I remember something else. I do. I do. I can picture it."

"Yes? That's great! What is it?"

"I got hit by a tractor!"

I started cackling like a hen again. A mixture of laughter and tears. The nurse gave me a sympathetic smile.

"Alright, why don't you lie down," she said. "Let's get you some sleep. Your Dad will be here soon."

Apparently, while I was sound asleep, Dad spoke with the senior staff and asked how I was doing and when could I return home. I heard them speaking in the room. I kept my eyes closed.

"She will be in hospitals for some while because her head injury is proving to be more serious than we thought. She is going to need to be transferred to the major trauma unit in Bordeaux. As you know she does not recognise you right now. The Doctors are hoping that will pass and her memory loss transient."

"Oh dear, we have had so much misery in our family since we came over to France, now this," I heard Dad say. "She took her driving test and I have to tell you I don't think the accident was her fault. She wouldn't have been going fast she never has when learning and she hated speeding on the roads. I know it wasn't her fault."

That afternoon I woke up and had the most tremendous headache and could not focus properly. *Where the heck was I??* At that moment of me trying to pull my thoughts together, someone in a uniform passed me.

"Hold on there. Where am I? Why am I in a bed? What sort of place is this?"

"Ah, there you are my dear, you're with us again," the person in uniform said. "Can you remember what happened to you?

"What do you mean what happened to me?"

"You have been in a car crash with a tractor. Can you recall anything of that?"

"No, I bloody well can't. Couldn't possibly have been in an accident I can't even drive yet."

With that remark, the uniform beat a hasty retreat. I seemed to be in some sort of hospital bed, I knew what they looked like alright as I'd been seeing someone who was in the hospital recently.

What the devil is going on here? Where am I? I need to get away from this place.

"Hello Maisie, how are you feeling my love?"

Who the hell is talking to me in this familiar way?

"It's Ralph my dear I'm here for you, can you remember what happened to you?"

"No, I can't. Something to do with an accident, or so I've been told, but I know nothing about it. And who are you?"

"Surely you're pulling my leg, Maisie. Or perhaps things are worse than I thought. It's Ralph, pet, surely you remember me. You must. You and me, well, we are a couple."

"What are you talking about, I'm not a couple to anybody. I don't like it here I need to get home."

"I will go and get help for you."

With that, this stranger who called himself Ralph left me and I attempted to get out of bed. I had great difficulty in pulling myself up enough to get out of bed, getting my legs over the side of it was virtually impossible.

"Help me! Help me! I need someone to help me."

I could hear myself screaming out those words and oh, how it hurt my head. Each syllable felt like a needle poking at my temples.

The uniform came back.

"Help me to get out of this place, please, I need to get home now."

"Do you know where you live Maisie?"

"Of course I do, and so do you, so help me to get up please."

"Tell me where you live?" said the uniform.

"I live in Hythe, in England, Kent to be exact."

"That's where she lived before they came over to the Dordogne," I heard someone tell the uniform.

I looked over to see who it was.

"Oh, it's James, James! I've wanted to see you for so long I have tried to get in touch with you I needed you to be here with me as I need you to see someone and tell me who you think they are. It's so good to see you James, how I've missed you. Come over here so I can say hello properly."

By this time, I was half in and half out the bed. The uniform was trying his hardest to push me back into the bloody bed and I was pushing as hard as I could in the other direction. James was here, now everything would be fine.

"I should go, she clearly doesn't remember who I am," the man I thought was James said. "I do hope this is temporary, I couldn't bare it if she doesn't recover."

"Don't worry, sir, she will get better with rest and time. That's what she needs just now," the nurse said.

"How long is it likely to take before she sees life the way it really is?"

"That's very hard to answer, every patient is different. Some recover quickly and others take longer. Don't you worry, she will be well looked after here."

"James, where are you going, come back I need to talk to you. There is this man—"

And with that I seemed to fade away somewhere, I suppose I went to sleep, it's all unclear. The next time I woke—I'm told a long time after—my Dad was sitting by my bed.

"Hello dear, how are you feeling now?"

"I'm fine, Dad, I want to go home. Get me out of this strange bed. This strange room."

My father's eyes were filled with tears and he took hold of me.

"Thank the Lord you have come back to us," he said, burying my face in his chest.

Helen stepped into the room next. To me, all I thought was, "Oh, there's Helen." But to Dad and the nurse, this was a major step in the right direction for me to recognise someone from France.

"Good Lord deliver us, Maisie, is that you?" Helen said. "You look terrible, I've never seen you so pale."

Dad made an attempt to stop her from continuing.

"She's not been in the sunshine for a while, you know." Dad said. "I think you look great honey."

"I know that James has been here, but I didn't get the chance to talk to him," I said. "I think they gave me something to put me out and now he isn't here. Helen, where have you been? I thought you might have come sooner."

"I'm sorry, love, but the exams have taken over everything else."

"I need to get back to school and finish them too! Will I be home soon Dad? And do you know where James is?"

I'd find out later everyone was doing a mental checklist in this moment. Helen: Check. Exams: Check. James: Ok, she's not fully back yet. But hey, these are signs of progress. Dad, the one who never gave up on me or anything, attempted to keep building on it. I imagine this must have been what so many trips to see Mum were like. The patience he's developed is something I will probably never have.

"Well, I haven't seen him here," Dad said. "But Ralph has been in to see you many times and you don't seem to remember him."

"Ralph? Is that one of my teachers? That makes sense, we were talking about exams. Helen, did Mr. Larabee come by? Did I forget his name was Ralph?"

"Um," Helen started to say.

"That's enough for now," the nurse said. She adjusted my bedclothes. "We don't want her to get too tired. The signs are very good she is beginning to remember things. Maisie, you've made a lot of progress. But we don't want to rush it. Let's get you some more rest. We can have visitors again tomorrow."

CHAPTER TWENTY-FOUR

Recovery

"Hope is being able to see that there is light despite all of the darkness."
~ Desmond Tutu.

Today they got me out of bed. I was feeling better and so glad as I seem to be able to remember more clearly. Dad keeps coming to see me, but not James and I can't think why he doesn't come back. After all I've had a bad accident and he's my friend who I thought cared for me. Maybe he'll come today. The male nurse told me that I should be able to go home soon. Can't wait for that to happen. To see the sea and the Canal again.

"Hello Maisie, and how are we today?"

"We are jolly fine thank you," I said, playing along. I really did feel a whole lot better.

There was this handsome man standing in front of me, very tall, slim build with a smell of farmyard about him."

"And who may I ask are you?"

"It's Ralph, my darling. Don't you remember me at all?"

"No, I don't but I wouldn't mind getting to know you. Do you live in Hythe?"

"Actually, Maisie, we're in France right now. You moved here last summer. Your Father has a job at the English complex in St. Severin. Your whole family came over with you."

"No, I don't remember any of that, please stop it. I know I had an accident and now I have the most dreadful headache so just leave me alone."

"Come on, you're so close! Exams, right! Your school exams. But you just passed your driving exam and I think you may have been leaving the farm, my farm, when you were going around a corner not far from us and you hit a tractor."

"Was this by the canal?"

"No, Maisie, it was in France. Where you now live."

This man named Ralph lost his cool a bit. He left shortly after. The following day I was transferred to the hospital in Bordeaux. It was here that they operated on my brain, apparently I'd had a bleed which clotted and the clot had to be removed. I was there some time before being transferred back to the local hospital.

I overheard the nurse talking to my Father. Into the room hurried a dynamo of a woman wearing a bright yellow shirt. She looked a bit like the sun in the sky.

"Now, Miss Patterson, I understand you are to go home today," the sun lady said in a booming voice. "I need to give you some advice before you leave about the dos and don'ts following a head injury."

She went on and on in French and I understood everything she said. Dad and I departed and thanked the buxom lady and the uniform. Apparently, I was not to move around too quickly. I do recall being told that if I go unconscious I was to call the hospital immediately.

It was a beautiful Spring day. The sun was getting warmer now. The birds were chirping away to their little hearts content and the flowers were desperately trying to push up through the cold earth in an attempt to reveal their glory to the world. As we drove home the farmers were busy on their land getting ready to sow seeds of their next crops. I felt strange, I hadn't remembered so many farms before or quite so much countryside. And I didn't like the fact that I had a huge bald patch on my head. Even my long hair would not cover the baldness completely.

As I got out of the car, I looked over toward the front door. It looked as though someone had painted it a different colour.

"Dad, when did the door get painted it used to be blue?"

"Oh, I did that at the end of last year. Do you like it love?"

He asked me in such a gentle way I started to cry. I didn't seem able to control the tears from falling. My eyes were swollen and red from the onslaught. Later that night, when I was alone, I would pray to God to help me and my family get all that was on the wrong road right itself again. And that is exactly what I did.

When we stepped indoors, everything looked strange to me.

"Where is my rocking horse? He always stood in the corner. Right there, Dad. Where is he?"

"We got rid of him when we left England last year. We didn't see the need to have your little kid toy anymore."

At that moment so much became clear. I actually did remember that entire conversation happening. We were standing in the corner, and it wasn't this corner. It wasn't this house. Because we're now in France, ok, that makes sense. The move. The ride in the car with Dan and Mum. Dad working for the folk on the site. So much was flooding back at once. That room was not this house. And Mum was at the table, Dad was on the couch. I picked up Freddie the rocking horse and said, "Dad, I think I'm finally ok with letting my 7-year-old girl toys go. It will have a better home with James' sister." Dad got up, put his hand on my shoulder. "Proud of you, Maisie." Mum laughed. "Well, it's about damn time," she said. And then Dan. Why hadn't I seen Dan yet? And where was Mum? Well, she was getting help. The drinking problem. But where was Dan. Where was Dan?

"I gave Freddie away," I said out loud. "We're in France, Dad. We live in France."

"Yes! Maisie, that's fantastic. We'll laugh about it later. Asking me about your rocking horse. What a hoot."

"And Mum, I understand she couldn't make it to the hospital. But where is Dan? Did I miss him?"

"Maisie, come over here, I have something I need to talk to you about," Dad said. He took a deep breath. Actually, you know what, another time. We'll talk about it another time."

Oh, how I wish this part of my memory would not have recovered. But there was no stopping it now. I remembered the night we found out. I remembered the trips to the police station. I finally remembered Ralph. And Gange. Dan didn't visit me because he's no longer here. I knew the truth, the memory was back, but how I wanted to believe, how tightly I held onto that last shred of hope that maybe, just maybe, my mind was playing tricks on me. Maybe this was a nightmare during all those hospital sleeps.

"Dad, tell me I need to get some sleep," I said. I started to cry again. "I have these terrible images in my head that Dan was murdered. Please, tell me I'm crazy. Please, tell me this were just me dreaming, please."

"I'm afraid that what feels like a horrible nightmare is the way our life really is," Dad said. "We've been through hell. More than hell. There hasn't been hardly one good thing that has happened since we moved away from home. And yet, Maisie, you were my rock through it all. The one part of the family not in shambles. But of course, in this cursed year, that too could not last. There's your accident. I thought I'd lose my mind seeing you another day in that bed. You are all I have left, Maisie. Dan's gone. Who knows if we'll ever have your Mum back," his voice faltered. "But I've had to keep on going. I can't wallow. I need to be here for you and Mum. But Maisie, I need you. Even more than you need me. We are in this mess together and I promise you I will never let go."

CHAPTER TWENTY-FIVE

My Friends

"If you cannot find peace within yourself, you will never find it anywhere."
~ Marvin Gaye

When I was left alone at home, I felt a bit afraid and unsure of everything around me. Dad told me I may have visitors as the neighbours knew I was coming home and told me to be honest with them if my head started to hurt. It was okay to ask them to leave.

It must have been around five in the evening when the doorbell rang. That was unusual, people usually knock the old brass knocker that adorned our heavy wooden front door. *Hey, there's another memory.* Any time a memory returned, it felt good, like I was going in the right direction. The nurses said I would remember more when I got home and that my recall may well be hasty.

In trepidation, I went to open it and there stood an Indian gentleman who was beaming at me astonishingly.

"Good evening to you, my dear. How are you?"

It was Mr. Banerjee, my friend and mentor. I was so pleased to have recognised him immediately.

"I am so sorry not to have come to visit you when you were in the hospital, but we have been away quite a long time in London and my wife, well, she was in no hurry to get back here. Oh Maisie, you look so well, and we heard that you had an accident."

I went over to him, put my arms around his neck and held him close.

"Yes, I did, not sure how long I was in the hospital, but it seemed like a lifetime. The trouble is now I don't remember so well, but I do remember you, Mr. Banerjee."

The conversation carried on for some time and I felt quite weary when he finally said I must go now and let you rest. *It's okay to tell them your head hurts.* I didn't want him to go, but I really did need to lie down. I went upstairs again and straight to bed. Night was drawing in and I felt terribly tired and afraid. How could my Father have left me alone when I had been so ill? I didn't sleep a wink for a couple of hours and then the doorbell rang. I leapt out of bed like a gazelle, rushed downstairs. I was desperate to talk with anyone.

"Maisie, you look great!" Ralph said, greeting me at the door. For the first time since the accident, I looked at Ralph and saw him.

"Ralph, I'm sorry about my memory. I—"

"You don't need to say anything more. Hearing you say my name was plenty."

He leaned in to kiss me. I was thrown off at first then thought, "*Oh, yes, it would make sense for us to kiss.*"

Dad came home at that moment and I was glad as I didn't want more of this kissing.

"Good to see things are back to normal," Dad said "Sorry to interrupt, but are you going to stay for supper? I don't have much in the cupboard. Would some bread and cheese do. I've also got some salad and quiche?"

"Thanks Jack, I would love to stay."

"Why don't the two of you go into the other room and I'll get things together."

It was an embarrassing liaison, as I didn't know what to say to him. There were lengthy, embarrassing silences. At last Dad called us through to the kitchen.

"When do you think Mum will be coming home?" I asked.

"Hopefully, within about a fortnight, I do hope so. Those journeys are getting me down now."

Ralph left after supper and I couldn't help noticing that whenever our eyes met he smiled at me, just like an old friend would do. It was still hard to get used to. The kiss goodbye was as foreign to me as the kiss hello. I wondered if the feeling of love would return like an old memory. I helped Dad clear the plates and kitchen paraphernalia.

"Maisie, it's so good to have you home again. I've been lonely for the past weeks while you were away."

"Well I'm back now. I mean I really feel like me again."

With that said I went back upstairs. Almost the second I stepped into my room I heard the phone ring.

"I got it!" I called out.

I jogged over, picked up the receiver.

"Hello?"

"Maisie, hey. I've been trying to call for days, what's going on?"

It was James. And this time it was the real one, not me confusing Ralph with somebody else.

"James, hi! How are you?? It's good to hear your voice. I have so much to tell you. I mean so, so very much. My life has been completely thrown out of whack."

"Well, why don't you tell me in person."

"What?"

"I'm at the airport. Surprise!"

"You're kidding?"

"Not at all. I called a few weeks back, your Dad told me what was up and I wasn't gonna stay here in England while you were in hospital. It was hard to get the money together, but I made it work. So uh, could I get a ride or should I get a taxi? I'm guessing you're not exactly hungry to get behind the wheel again."

"Yeah, not so much. I hate to say it, but maybe a taxi?"

I thought about asking Ralph if he'd pick James up and it took me a few seconds to realize that probably wasn't the most girlfriendy thing to do.

"Taxi's good for me. See you when I see you."

When I came back downstairs, Dad asked me how James was getting here. He offered to go and pick him up. I didn't want to be alone in the house again.

"A taxi? I feel like a bad host. He flew all the way here and we couldn't even pick him up."

"Dad, it's ok."

"Well, I'll set-up the bed for him in one of the spare rooms. I'll put a heater in there to air the place. I'm glad he could make it. I'm so looking forward to seeing him again."

My feelings for James seemed unusually strong right now. I had given up on normal. Normal was no longer a word for my family, and I don't think it could ever be again. But James being here, my dad here, both these men who meant so much to me under the same roof, I don't know, perhaps there was a little bit of normal starting to come back to me. If not normal at least safe. Comfortable. A little bit of peace. My mind was wrapped up in what it would be like to see James again. As I thought about the taxi arriving I didn't even realize how little I'd noticed Ralph's leaving.

CHAPTER TWENTY-SIX

My Angst

"Kindness is a language which the deaf can hear and the blind can see."
~ Mark Twain

I was far more relaxed and composed with James around. I cannot tell you how important it is to me that my friend has come to stay. Things were different, too. But in a good way. We sat closer to each other. There were times when he'd put his arm around my shoulder. We didn't talk too much that first night he arrived because it was late and we were both tired. But for that hour or so we did we sat on the couch holding hands. And it didn't feel weird at all, it felt so natural. James started to unpack the following morning.

Maybe it was part of the post-crash effect. I was more comfortable sharing how I felt and wearing my heart on my sleeve. .

"It's good you're here, James. I've thought about you and missed you so much!"

"I'm just sorry I couldn't get here sooner," James said. "I should have been there for you in the hospital. Do you remember what happened when you had the crash?"

"No, not much. Although since I've been home a lot has returned. So how long will you be able to stay this time? Any girlfriend you need to get back home to?"

"Well as long as it takes I suppose, that's if you don't mind me sharing the board and lodging. And no, I don't have a girlfriend, at the moment."

"Good Lord, do I mind if you share the house? Not at all! Selfishly, I want you here as long as possible. I want to get back on the case. With the accident and stuff that followed I haven't had time to think much about Dan's murder. And I feel guilty about that. What kind of person does that make me that I can go a whole day and not think about my dead brother? It makes me sick to the stomach when I think about it. We have to get back to solving things."

"Maisie, you were in a freaking car accident. Give yourself a break. You're not being selfish, you're healing. And I don't know about going after the case again. When I think about it it's like, what are we going to find out that the police haven't? Just doesn't seem like there's anything we can do better."

"You're assuming that they're actually trying to solve it. Let's go out for a walk."

We were about 10 minutes into our walk when this lovely black and white dog came rushing over to me. He seemed to know me. I bent forward and started to stroke him and suddenly it dawned on me, it was my Benny. Benny ran out in front of us as if to say *Come with me you two!*

"What's with the face Maisie?" James asked as we approached the front door. "You look perplexed."

"I'm not sure why something is chipping away at me, can't think what it is."

"Hello darling, you must be feeling better."

And with that Ralph came over to me and tried to pick me up off the ground. I resisted then he ushered us into the house, pushing Benny away from me, saying "Leave her alone you silly boy, she doesn't want you slobbering all over her."

We followed Ralph down the hallway and into the lounge. James took my arm for either reassurance or just this continued touching we were doing this whole trip. Either way was fine by me. Ralph spoke to us nineteen to the dozen about the farm and the lambing and told us all about the ups and downs of the cold weather and how it affected lambing and how some had died this year as it was the coldest winter he'd experienced since first coming to France.

As I sat down in the lounge I noticed Ralph looking at me and he beamed the widest smile. He went in to kiss me.

With that, his brother came and stood very close to both of us and said, "Ey, ey, what's going on here then. She's young enough to be your daughter and how come she's only just recognised you? Surely that's a sign that she wasn't sure about it in the first place."

"Why don't you shut up Gange, and go back where you came from," Ralph said.

"Oh, do you mean leave here? Yes, I can do just that and I've been thinking it's time to be going. But now I've got second thoughts. Must make sure that you two get sorted out. How could you be so stupid as to fall for a teenager? You must be mad."

"Well, looks as though it runs in the family then," Ralph interjected.

I resisted and said "Do I know you?" It was half joking and half out of defense.

"James, she used to call me your name when she was in the hospital," Ralph said to James.

"That's funny," James said. "Hey, I'll take that as a compliment."

"Tell me about your travels, James, have you been to many countries?" Ralph said.

"Yes, I have been to the States, India, Taiwan and Singapore, and was about to go to Africa. Then returned to England and have been working as a journalist. But plans have changed and now I'm here."

"What do you intend doing now you're here then?" His tone was almost like a TV attorney, peppering the witness with questions. "Actually, hold that thought. More coffee folks? I fear I need to go back down to the animals too, check for a second."

Ralph was still looking over at me and when our eyes met he again gave me the broadest and kindest smile .

"Maisie, can I have a word with you, quickly."

"Sure."

I followed him into the kitchen.

"I know it isn't a big deal, and you were trying to be funny with Gange, but can we stop the 'do I know you' jokes?" Ralph said. "Seeing you in the hospital and having you look back and not recognising me, or call me James, that was hard on me. I don't want to remember back to that time, ok?"

"Oh, good Lord Ralph," as I went over to him and gave him a bear hug. "I've never seen you so sensitive. I didn't mean to upset you."

At that point Gange came in to where we were and said to me, "I take it you remember who I am Maisie? Are you better now?"

"Here's what I remember," I said. I moved away from Ralph and walked right up to Gange, stared right at his greasy ugly face. "I remember that I never want to be in the same room as you again, ever."

I don't know where I got the nerve and such confidence to stand within slapping distance of him and tell him what I really thought, but I have to say it felt so good to put him in his place. I turned my back on Ralph and walked out of the kitchen.

"Come on James, let's go home," I said.

"Maisie, wait," Ralph called out, jogging out after me. "You only just got here. We haven't even had a chance to talk."

"Ralph, I don't want to see your brother, I don't want to hear him, I don't want to be in the same room as him ever again. And if that means you and I can't be together, then so be it."

"Where's all this coming from! All he asked was how were you doing. He was showing he cared."

"Then why doesn't he come out here like a man and defend himself? I'm tired of you covering up for him, Ralph, I'm tired of everyone covering up for him. If he has something to say then let him say it. And, until he does, then yes, I am going to believe he killed Dan. You hear that, Gange, I know what you did and we're going to lock you up for the rest of your miserable life."

I put my two hands in a cup around my mouth and called out as if I were a mother saying to her kids, "Dinner's ready!"

"Gange! Gange! Where are you? Come out and play, Gange. *Gaaaaange!*"

"Well, clearly you're not fully healed," Ralph said.

"Come on, let's go Maze, let's get you home," James said.

"Gange, Gange!" I yelled again.

"I shall see you again soon," Ralph said. "I'll come to the house and we can talk there. Thank God you've come back to me and I will be patient."

"I will not be coming back until you boot him off the property," I said. "And that is final. That is not going to change."

As James and I left we heard a terrible row start and could still here the shouting after we were well away from the farm.

"Not sure that was the best idea," James said.

"I couldn't help it. That's the first time I've seen him since the accident and the second I looked at those lifeless eyes I knew without question he killed my brother. I'm tired of playing nicely. And if he attacks me, well, then the police have no excuse but to step in."

"Yes, but Maisie, if he's dangerous, then an attack may not be something you bounce back from."

"I will never go to that farm again."

As we walked home, I did feel a little anxious. The ramifications of my challenging Gange were starting to sink in. I kept looking over my shoulder, expecting to see him running after us. I wanted to call the police. I wanted to talk to Toby again. I wanted to tell him, "Please have a car outside our house, I think I've provoked a murderer."

I can only hope they catch him before he catches me.

CHAPTER TWENTY-SEVEN

Remembering

"And now you don't have to be perfect you can be good."
~ John Steinbeck

James and I got back to the house. Dad was still out working. We were hardly in the door when the telephone rang.

"Good evening, Doctor Arnuad here," he said in the purest French.

"My Dad's not here at the moment and I think it would be better if you were to talk with him," I replied in my best French. "I've been in hospital myself after an accident and not been home for long and I'm only just getting my memory back."

I got off the phone and saw James smiling, shaking his head a little.

"My word, you are proficient in this new language. How wonderful is that?" James said. "I'm very impressed, and good for you."

I may not be in trouble with my exams after all," I said. "I must see if I can find Dad and get him to call Doctor Arnuad. It sounded urgent. I hope nothing's wrong. James grab a drink I won't be long"

"Nah, I'll come with you."

We stepped outside.

"Dad," I called from the top of the hill. I almost laughed about how I was using the same voice I did in Ralph's house about an hour ago. "Dad, the phone just rang and the Doctor has called. Can you call him back? It sounded somewhat urgent."

"That's fine love, I'll come right in."

Dad walked up and gave James a pat on the back, almost as if greeting a son.

"I could use a break," Dad said. "I've been here an age trying to get the bloody pool cleaned properly. The residents are going to want to start their laps soon. You know how health conscious they are. Good for them I say. James, how are you feeling? You regret flying over here yet? Has Maisie been showing you around? Being a good host?"

"Being a *great* host," James replied. "And I'm impressed with how she's changed since the last time I saw her."

"How do you mean?" Dad said.

"Yeah, I'm interested to see how this is going?" I asked.

"I heard her speak fluent French on the phone. She sounded like a real French person. And then over at that guy Ralph's place, she totally ripped that Gange to pieces. It was cool. She's tough. You've got a French speaking tough girl there now, Mr. Patterson."

Dad wasn't amused. He looked at me with a serious and callous stare.

"For Pete's sake, Maisie, stop this nonsense once and for all. I don't know how she's got all that stuff in her head about that man. Gange has been nothing short of a friend to us and I won't hear this carry on. Now you've been yelling at him! What exactly did you say?"

"I told him what I should have told him long ago," I said without missing a beat. "I know he killed Dan and if he wanted to defend himself then he should have done so then and there when he had the chance."

"Maisie! James, tell me she's joking."

"Well, technically she was shouting at Ralph, but Gange was obviously eavesdropping from the kitchen," James said.

Dad let out a big sigh.

"I'm gonna need to go over there and apologise. I can't believe you did this, Maisie."

"Apologise? What am I, eight-years-old? You have to go and vouch for me?"

"Well, if you're an adult, then you can go, but someone needs to."

The three of us wandered back to the house in silence. Dad went to the phone. I went into the kitchen to start supper.

"I don't think you should be cooking yet," James said.

"I shall get us some cold meats and salad then. That alright by you, James?"

"What, you don't trust me with a knife?" I said. "I can do it no problem. You're about to be impressed with another new skill: I've become quite the French chef."

"Shall I make a Charlotte Rouse, James?"

"That sounds nice, what is it?" James said. "And by 'sounds nice' I mean I have no idea about what you just said."

I laughed playfully then hit his shoulder. James continued working on the potatoes while I looked for the right pan.

"Hey, I do want to talk to you about something though, Maisie," he said. "Don't you think that guy Ralph is a bit too old for you? You're young and you don't want to throw your life away on an old bloke, surely?"

"I wouldn't say he's too old," I replied. "If I didn't know you better, James, I'd think you were just a teensie bit jealous."

"I wouldn't say jealous. I just think I'm a better catch."

"Wow, speaking of new found confidence."

We laughed, together. Then we looked into each other's eyes for a lingering few seconds and smiled. Everything felt so warm and right between us. I don't know if Ralph and I were ever this natural. Ever this effortless. For a few seconds, I might have even put the dinner things down, walked in front of James, not go in for a kiss myself, but see if he would. Instead, I chose to change the subject. Before I could, though, Dad walked in.

"It looks as though mother is coming home at last, it could be as early as the weekend," Dad said. "I'm not sure she's really ready yet. She wanders off at times and says peculiar things making no sense.

Do you think we'll be able to cope with all that? How long are you going to be here James?"

"I've no plans at the moment, but the last thing I want to do is outstay my welcome. I've taken unpaid leave from work as I didn't know how Maisie would be."

"You won't be doing that at all, son. It's great having you here and you know that Maisie wants you to stay."

"I wouldn't complain having you around longer," I added in. "Perhaps we could go off to university together."

"Oh, so I'm going to the same university as you now?" James said. "I don't think so though, love, my education days are over now."

"Yep. I think it makes sense. You need a university qualification I think."

This made Dad go quiet and a strange look crept over his face. He then turned to me and said, "How do you think I shall be able to manage mother when she comes home, without some help?"

"What on earth are you on about?" I asked. "I'm not talking about going immediately. I don't know what I'm going to do yet anyway. But I figure it will be university. That's always been the plan. You and I talked about it, Dad."

I felt a little lightheaded as I looked back at him, eyebrows scrunched together.

"And that's a damn selfish thing to say, Dad. Why should it be me giving up my life because of Mother? You surely don't expect me to stick around here just to look after you and her do you?"

"Look after—stop it Maisie, what on earth's come over you! I've not known you to think that way or at least you never seemed to view us as a burden to you before. I really don't recognise you."

"Well, I'm sorry everyone is so taken aback by me finally voicing my thoughts. It's time I did. I need to be thinking about me for a change, figuring out my life. It can't be all you and the family, or what's left of it."

"Go to your room! I can't believe what I'm hearing. How dare you speak to me like that. You've changed so much since the accident."

"*Go to my room. Go apologise to Gange.* Maybe we should bring back the rocking horse because you obviously still think I'm a little girl."

"Maisie," James said. He put his hand on my shoulder.

Dad stormed out of the room and went upstairs. I just stood looking at James, frowning.

"That was a bit harsh, don't you think?" he said. "Your Father's clearly concerned about your Mum returning home. He's probably imagining it won't work and the task ahead is an impossible one. He just wanted your help at the start. What about your farmer friend? I had the distinct impression that the relationship was serious, or at least on his part. Are you changing your mind about him?"

"Maybe I am changing my mind. I like Ralph, I really do. Or I really did. I don't know. But what's the future there? Gange as part of my family? The man who killed my brother as my brother-in-law? No thank you. And you're right. Ralph is old. I didn't really notice it 'til now, but who knows, maybe he starts slowing down and I'm left taking care of him, and my dad, and my mum, what a hell that would be! I want to take care of myself for a change. And I don't want to live out here in the sticks anyway. Come on, let's go and eat."

Dad came down when I called him to say supper was ready.

"I went too far before and I'm sorry for that," I said.

I wasted no time getting into an apology. I didn't want to hurt him. I could live my life without Ralph, but I didn't want to lose my dad.

"But Dad, I have thought a lot about what I would do when I was better and back to my regular life and you need to know that I don't intend to be in France, or at least not these parts."

"I thought you told me you were thinking of going to the university in Paris with Helen?" he said.

"Yes, I was thinking about that, but I'm not so sure anymore. I didn't mean to be rude before, I just wanted to establish that if or when I do leave, and you are back to work as before, you will probably need someone to stay with her."

"And just how do you think I shall be able to afford that? The complex committee has already met and decided that some of my pay should be deducted because of the hours lost in trailing from one hospital to the other visiting you and your Mum."

"Are you serious! I can't believe they would do that!"

I hit my hand on the table, almost landing on a fork.

"You know what, let's stop talking about it now, Dad, so we don't ruin dinner. Let's eat in peace and when the time comes we will work things out I'm sure."

After we finished dinner, and had the dirty dishes cleared away, James pulled me to one side.

"Maisie, we will need to have a conversation soon about what the future looks like," he said.

"What the future looks like?" I asked. "For as much as I know an asteroid could hit France tomorrow and wipe us all out. That would go with the year I'm having. What do you mean the future?"

"Well, you know, the future of us. And I don't mean like us, us. But how long am I going to stay here? What does it look like when your Mum gets back? Are you still with Ralph? Are you single? Is there anything going on with us more than just good friends?"

"That's a lot of questions, James," I said.

"Even having just one answered would be helpful," James said with a smile.

"I don't have answers right now!" I said. My tone and volume even surprised me. "Ok? Ralph wants me to be with him and I don't want to be there. Dad wants me to be here with him, and I do want to help, but I don't want to be stuck here. And then there's you. I want you here, but you keep talking about leaving and heading home. The people I want to be here aren't here and the people who want me here I don't want to be with. So no, James, I don't have the answers. I'm going to bed."

I ran away and went straight to my room. I stayed there for as long as I dared. As I lay on my bed, I began to wonder about the way I'd behaved. I yelled at everyone in my life today. That wasn't me. I don't think my nature had ever been cruel and selfish and on reflection on my outburst to Dad, I was ashamed. What had he ever done wrong? Absolutely nothing was the answer. Then to lash out at James?"

I came downstairs, which were still bleak, dark, and uncarpeted as they had been since the day we moved here. I almost slipped. That near slip pushed away any potential apology. I was back to Hurricane Maisie.

"Dad, why have we still got no carpet on the stairs? Surely we could have put some down by now?"

"Are you going to pay for it? Be that the case go right ahead and get the job done."

And there I went, off again.

"It's carpet, Dad. How can we not afford carpet! I don't work yet but I'm planning to change that as soon as possible."

"No, you know how I feel about your education. Focus on that. I have told you often enough, if you wish to have a mediocre job then expect a mediocre life along with all that brings with it. I don't wish to argue with you anymore, so you do what you like."

"Do what I like! One moment you tell me I can't go to university, now you're telling me about getting a job and helping out is a mediocre life? You're right about that part. It absolutely is a mediocre life. And that's putting it kindly!"

Then I knew Dad would assemble the stone walls of silence he was good at building up around himself.

I turned to James.

"Come on, let's go out."

CHAPTER TWENTY-EIGHT

A Newcomer

"It's not what you look at that matters, it's what you see."
~ Henry David Thoreau

I looked up and out of the kitchen window as James and I went to the door. I thought I saw someone creeping around the house. Maybe it was just a shadow on the wall. Then the doorbell went. I answered it to find a young man about mid-twenties standing there. His looks were unremarkable, overweight and dressed quite smartly for these parts.

"Bonjour, madam, I am looking for a Maisie," he said in a strong French accent. I replied in French and he looked surprised. I told him that was me and how could I help. He said me he was curious about my health and that he was the man who had found me after the crash in the lane and he wondered how I was getting along.

In French I said, "Do come in. It's nice to meet you. It's been a while since I was ill."

His English was not so good; telling me he had been asking around this area since the event. He told me his name was Franz.

"That's not a French name is it."

"No, it's German, my Father was from Germany and Mother French, we come from Bergerac."

"That's a long way from here, how did you get here?"

"I have a car, but I left it down the road a bit as I thought I'd have better chance of finding you if I walked and indeed that has proved to be the case."

I noticed he fidgeted with his hands all the time he spoke to me. And had difficulty standing still. In fact, he seemed to be as nervous and restless as a fox, on the move the whole time.

"Thank you Franz for rescuing me that day. I ended up in the hospital in Bordeaux and was there for some time. I had some sort of brain disturbance, a bleed I think which resulted from the accident and they operated on my brain. Look just here."

I lifted the rest of my long hair pulled over the scar.

"That must have been awful for you. You poor thing. I'm so very glad I've found you, Maisie, I did not think I would meet up with you again."

"Would you care for something to drink, maybe tea or coffee or even something stronger?" I asked.

"Coffee would be fine, I don't drink alcohol."

He looked a bit embarrassed as he said that. And I must admit I found it strange to meet someone living in France who did not drink.

"What do you do for a living Franz?" I asked while making the coffee.

"I'm a teacher, in Bergerac."

"Is school out today?" I asked.

"Yes, It's half way through term."

I gave him his coffee and then said I just need to pop upstairs a minute. And up I went. Straight to the bathroom, in front of the mirror, fussing with my hair and putting a little makeup on my face. I dashed back down to find Franz sitting in the living room. I grabbed my coffee and went into the room where he sat.

"I see you're making yourself at home?"

"I'm so sorry, I do apologise, far too forward of me."

"No worries, tell me about your job. Who do you teach and what subjects?"

He led off into a mammoth account of what he taught, who he taught, what he thought of teaching. So on and so forth. He stayed for what seemed like an epoch. Then we shook hands politely, and he said It's so good to find you looking so well and fit now.

"I was afraid you might die as you looked so desperately ill," Franz said. "Did you know that a passerby came along, someone from here, where you live, they had a phone and called for help? I do hope to see you again one day."

And with that last remark he turned and left. James had excused himself when I first met Franz. I think he thought he may be in the way if he hung around. James spent most of the time in the bathroom during the visit. We spoke of the goodness of some people and thank the Lord for it. I was ready to reach the end of Hurricane Maisie. I wanted to be kind again. I wanted to be me again.

CHAPTER TWENTY-NINE

More Troubles

"Never be fearful about what you are doing when it is right."
~ Rosa Parks

Dad and I settled back into a loose sort of routine, and then mother was discharged. Our relationship wasn't fully mended, wasn't fully back to normal, but we were headed in the right direction by the time she came home.

It had been some time since I'd seen my Mother and when I did it was a shock. I had a job recognising her. She had lost a considerable amount of weight, her hair had thinned badly and turned completely white. The staff told us that was down to the treatment. *Had they used some form of Chemotherapy on my poor Mother, surely not, that could hardly be the treatment for alcoholism.* She was also pale and looked so sad.

She seemed to recognise me and was aware of the accident and the following drama.

"Hello Mum, it's good to have you back home," I said heartily. Dad had his arm around Mum's waist to steady her.

Time has passed at glacial speed and on a number of occasions Dad and I discussed what we would do when Mum came home. He'd been told she would need a lot of care and attention. And was not to be on her own for any length of time. Our discussions now were far more civilised. We had reached an agreement that the only way forward was to see how Mum reacted to being home again. How much of our influence was needed to keep her on the straight and narrow and neither of us talked about me finishing my exams.

He had muted that when Mum had settled back in she may want to work again with our neighbours and take up her old job.

I had my doubts about that. No sooner was Mum sitting down and drinking a cup of tea than Dad said, "I'm off now ladies, work to do, people to see, places to go."

This took me by surprise and the reality of the full weight of responsibility expected of me began to sink in. He'd just made it crystal clear that I was to be the caretaker; today and probably for the foreseeable future.

"Mum, do you want another cup of tea or do you want to go back to bed?"

"I don't really know what I want to do, but Maisie how are you feeling? You've been through so much lately."

"I'm well again, Mum. Enough about me, how do you feel?"

"I'm not sure how I feel, they've told me I must never drink alcohol again. And have me on this stuff called antabuse. It's horrible and leaves an awful taste in my mouth. Just like metal."

"Will you always have to be on the drug, Mum?"

"Yes, I think for a long time anyway."

"When I look back I cannot imagine how I could have become so dependent on drink," Mum said. "Hard to feel like that was even me now. Your poor Dad has had so much to cope with almost from the day we arrived here. Perhaps we should think about going back to England.

"He won't want to do that, he couldn't find work there before, so he won't find it now," I said. "Anyway, I suppose our lives will settle down again."

And with that I helped her upstairs to her bedroom. I put freshly ironed cotton, bed linen, the set with little blue flowers onto her bed.

This was the set she loved most. I tucked her in and said, "Have a nice sleep."

"That's nice dear, thank you for being here. You will be here when I get up, won't you?"

I nodded. *Not sure I have any choice in the matter.*

As I slowly went downstairs, I thought about my lot in life and what it had in store for the foreseeable future. It looked as if Dad had me down to be nurse, general cook, and bottle washer and the injustices of it all made me feel sick.

I hadn't mapped my life ahead in the way it was panning out. Surely my Father wouldn't expect me to give up my life to always be there at Mum's beck and call.

The phone rang, it was Ralph.

"Hello sweet pea, how are you? Is your Mum home yet?"

"I'm not so sure how I am, Ralph, don't exactly know what the future holds. It seems I'm to be Mother's carer."

"Look, I have a few more chores to be getting on with here and then I can come over if you'd like that."

"Yes, I would like that, I need someone to talk to."

"Is James not there anymore?"

"No, he still is," I said. "He's going for a run right now. Why do you ask?"

"Oh, no reason," he said. "I'll be about an hour."

Three hours later the doorbell rang. James was back and showering, Mother was up and out of her chair trying to help me with the meal. I told her not to worry that I would do it but she was insisting, so I gave her the potatoes to peel. I instantly recognised that she had trouble coordinating her hands. The water and the potatoes were flying everywhere making a plethora of puddles on the tiled floor. She really didn't seem to know where to begin. I thought it wise to leave her to get on as best she could.

"Hello there, Julia," Ralph said when he saw her. "There's a sight for sore eyes before me if ever I saw one. Look at the pair of you. Julia, you look so well."

"I'm only just back and still adjusting to it all. It does seem strange to me right now." I indicated to Ralph that I wanted to see him in the lounge, I dried my hands on a wet tea towel and we left Mother for a moment.

We kissed momentarily and he took my hands.

"You sounded worried on the phone love," Ralph said. "I got here as soon as I could. Sorry I was so late, I thought it'd just be an hour, but I had about everything that could go wrong go—you know what, doesn't matter, anyways, are you ok?"

"I don't think I shall be able to stay in the house day in and day out Ralph, surely Dad doesn't expect that of me, or maybe he does. What do you think?

"It's early days for your Mum. Perhaps this is the way for now, but I think your Dad must get a carer to help in the long run, that's of course if she needs it. Perhaps she'll be alright as time goes on."

"Yes, of course you're right, I suppose I'm worrying unnecessarily, and still recovering myself. God knows if all our bad luck is ever going to end."

"Yes, I will. Your Father isn't going to expect you to stay as a carer all the time. You've still got the exams to finish."

"Before the car smash, Helen and I talked about going to Paris to university, get a degree and then decide what to do. She has gone already."

At that point, Mum came to find us.

"I can't seem to get it right dear, I mean doing the spuds, I can't grip the handle."

"Don't worry, Mum, I'll do it, come and talk to Ralph for a while."

He was good with Mother, spending his precious time making small talk and winning hearts and minds. He was good at that. I finished the food preparation and went in to join them.

"You two seem to be getting along well."

"Yes, we've been discussing all that's happened since you arrived in France and your Mum has talked to me about going back to England."

"I have to be going. Maisie, Julia, I'm glad to see you back home. You know where I am. If there's anything you need just call. You must come and see us soon I'll get Lauren to make us a nice dinner."

I followed him out into the kitchen and to the front door. He held me tightly for a while, I was nervous that Mum would see. I didn't feel like loads of explanation right now. As Ralph walked away from me I felt a shiver through my spine and wondered why on earth I found myself with a man so much older than me. He was indeed handsome, but he was also a bit too clingy, especially since the surgery. I didn't want to be burdened with something all consuming. I wanted to take some time to talk things over with James too, see what was going on there. And Ralph must have picked up on something between me and James because it was clear he resented James' presence.

I went to where Mum sat looking at her hands inquisitively, she turned to me and said. "I've got lovely hands, haven't I dear? They've always been my best feature you know. What a nice young man that Ralph is.

Young man? If you say so, Mum.

Dad came in after a long day. It was mid April and not dusk until around eight.

"Hello, hello, have you two had a good day together? I'd forgotten just how much work there is on site this time of year. Everything is growing like crazy and the tenants are no less demanding than they ever were."

Dad walked over and kissed Mum on the top of her head. I went to the kitchen to take a look at the spuds.

"Hello love, you're looking better," I heard Dad say as I left the room. Then he called out to me from the kitchen. "What's for supper Maisie?"

"Wait and see I think it's called," I said sarcastically.

"Mmmmm, sounds scrumptious," he replied in good spirits. "I shall look forward to that then."

At about nine we sat down for supper together for the first time in months. Everything jogged along well with questions and answers flowing from one to the other. We were having our pudding when out of the blue and to our amazement Mother said the craziest thing I've ever heard her say while being sober. Or drunk for that matter.

"I know who killed Dan," she pushed her pudding bowl forward. "It was me. I couldn't help it. I knew he was seeing that married woman and I didn't like it one bit. And I killed him."

Dad and I sat open-mouthed looking at each other and back to mother in sheer amazement. We could not comprehend what she had just said.

I left the table and went around to where she sat. Putting my arms around her shoulders.

"Mum, do you realise what you've just said?" I laughed and tried to make light of it.

"Of course, I do," she continued. "I told them in the clinic but they didn't believe me, I kept telling them and still they didn't. They just said I'd feel differently when I got back into my own home with the family. But I knew differently."

I now knew the reason the staff at the clinic were keen to see Mum soon after discharge. By this time Dad had composed himself and stared at mother. James gave me a look that said, "We should go outside, this isn't going to be pretty."

James took my hand in his under the table. It had been awhile since we were holding hands like that.

"You do know, Mum, that if you're not kidding then we shall have to tell the police about what you've just said to us, don't you?" I said.

"Well of course you must, in fact I was going to ask you to take me down there tomorrow."

Dad got up from the table walked round to where I was with Mother and nudged me to follow him into the kitchen, which was cold, he partially closed the door leaving enough of a gap that we could see what Mum was up to, although James was there with her.

"You don't think she's telling the truth, do you?" Dad asked. "We should brush this off as some sort of side effect from the treatment, yeah?"

"It's one hundred percent a side effect," I said. "Remember they had mentioned that she sometimes rambled a bit and was not always aware of her surroundings and thought it was due to the drugs."

"What on earth are we going to do? What if she calls the police and reports herself? They can't brush it off. They'll take it seriously and ask more questions. Should we get rid of the phones?"

"Do you really think they'll believe her?" James said, joining us in the kitchen.

"They have to take any claims like that seriously," Dad said.

"They didn't take any of my claims about Gange seriously," I said.

At that moment, we heard her moving about and thankfully heard the door to the kitchen open, not the front door.

"What are you lot whispering about?" Mum said. "What I've said to you happened and if you want to tell the police let's go down there right now. The clinic people didn't believe me and that's why it's not been done before, but I told them ages ago."

I failed to see why Dad had not been informed of this revelation. Dad didn't know where to look or what to say, he just started wringing his hands and kept touching his forehead as though his head hurt. He walked over to Mum.

"Now listen, Julia, I think you may have things muddled up a bit. We've been to the police constantly over these months and they are no closer to finding Dan's murderer than when you were first ill."

"Yeah, because they didn't think to ask me. I know what I'm talking about and it was me, that's why I drank as much as I did and got ill in the first place."

She was getting red in the face and angry and went to get her coat on. Dad held his head in his hands and was forcing back the emotion I knew he felt.

"I don't know what to do, love," Dad said. "This is all getting beyond me."

It dawned on me that I needed to take charge with James' help, so I took hold of Mum's arm and led her to the lounge and sat her down taking a seat as close as possible without being intimidating.

"I think the best plan is for us all to go to bed, then in the morning we will go to Perigueux and see Doctor Arnaud, see what he has to say, then we can go to the police and have a word with them about what you told us tonight," I explained as calmly as I could.

"I don't think we should waste any time," Mum said. "It's got to be said and the sooner the better. I should be locked up forever. I should go to prison for what I've done. No, worse than that. I don't deserve to live. They should fry me."

"Julia, please!" Dad shouted.

"How did you kill Dan with your bare hands," James asked, stepping in as the calm voice of reason.

I looked at James with a, "What are you doing? Don't egg her on," expression, which he returned with a look of confidence. *I've got this under control.*

"Don't be stupid, I'm not strong enough for that. I got a knife and stabbed him repeatedly. He was laughing at me when I lunged at him, thinking I was joking, and then he picked up real fast that this was no joke. He started pushing me away when he saw I meant business, but it was too late."

"And where exactly did this happen?" James asked.

I don't remember details, but it was me and I need to let the police know then they can stop looking for anyone else."

"They will ask to see the knife as evidence," James continued. "Do you know where you put it?"

I finally understood what he was doing. He was poking holes in the story, maybe as a way to reassure me and Dad that she wasn't telling the truth.

"I don't know," Mum replied. "Probably hid it somewhere, maybe threw it away. They can examine the body though, they'll find each and every stab wound."

I stepped in front of James, rubbing his back as I passed by. I put one hand on Mum's shoulder.

"Come on, let's all go up to bed," I said. "I don't think there's much more to be said tonight."

CHAPTER THIRTY

A Confession

"No good thing is failure and no evil thing success"
~ Unknown

I didn't sleep a wink and kept getting up and going downstairs, pacing the floor and making hot drinks. James came down at one point and tried hard to help me see reason.

At first light, I looked out of the undressed lounge window and saw Helen who was taking the neighbour's dog for a walk. Dashing out of the house and over to her calling her name, she came towards me. I more or less fell into her arms and relayed the latest saga of our sorry family.

"Do you think you could see that Dad's alright?" I asked. "He's taken this very badly and I don't want to drag him around with me today. I have to take Mother back to the clinic. He might even decide to go to work to take his mind off things. I thought you were in Paris?"

Helen was so kind and understanding and said that she was home that day and would look out for him. I went back indoors and Dad was up. Looking dishevelled and concerned.

"Listen, Dad, I will take care of things today. You go to work or do what you want to do. I'll see to Mum."

224 | Joy M. Lilley

"You are still recovering yourself, don't you think we should go together?"

"No Dad, James and I will sort things out."

I went up to Mum's bedroom and she was still fast asleep.

Mum, come on, I called you earlier. You know we have to go back to the clinic this morning, the doctor wants to see you again."

"I've only just come away from there, I'm not going back. The place I need to go is the police station, then prison. And they should lock me up and throw away the key."

"Mum, the hospital can help you. They can help to get you better. The police station, if what you say is true, you will be gone forever. Would you rather go there than the hospital?"

"It's what I deserve."

I felt my breath hitch in my chest and turned away from her.

"Come on, it's time you were dressed. Do you want me to help you, Mum?"

"No, I'm quite capable of doing that myself, you have no need to trouble yourself."

With that I left her room and went back down the stairs to where James sat with a cup of coffee he'd made himself.

"Do you want one, Maisie? I'll make one for Julia too."

"Julia. You said that so casually like you two were old drinking pals. But thank you, yes, can you make one for me. I don't know how long she'll be. It's nine now and we must be there by twelve."

"Has she said anything about the murder today?"

"Yes, she's right back at it. Asking to be locked up. There's no way it's true. It has to be the treatment she's been on. I mean after the accident, I had all types of problems with my memory. Add all the chemicals, I could see how this might happen. After all, she's been in that clinic for over four months. Who knows how the treatments she had could have affected her mind. As if there's not enough to worry about now we have this lot to deal with."

I took the cloth from James' hands and out to the scullery. I took a deep breath and called up to Mother that we were leaving for the clinic.

"I thought she was able to drive now so why isn't she taking me?" I heard Mum say to James.

"She is supposed to rest for another week or so," James said. "That's why I offered. Shall we go to the kitchen? I'll make you a cup of tea. You might want some breakfast before we go?"

"Yes, I will have some cereal," she said curtly as she came into the kitchen where I was doing the dishes from the night before. She sat down at the kitchen table and without hesitation said to me, "And what may I ask is wrong with you? Nobody tells me anything but James has just said you're still unwell."

"I probably could drive today but, given everything going on, I wouldn't trust myself behind the wheel."

"Don't trust yourself, what's that supposed to mean?"

"If I'm not focused. Here. Let me make you some toast Mum."

"No, I said I want cereal. What have we got? And I'll have a whiskey mac with that."

James and I looked at each other. We couldn't tell if she was kidding. Deciphering any truth out of that woman's mouth was going to be impossible.

The journey to Perigueux took longer than expected as tractors hogged the road as if a pageant extolling the virtues of Spring was pervading our streets. Mother said nothing even though I tried to make banal conversation. James made the occasional comment mostly about the surrounding countryside and weather. I was glad when we arrived. I hated long silences and embarrassing pauses.

"Come on, Mum, let's go right in here."

We were dropped at the front door and James seemed to be gone for ages trying to park the car. In the meantime I asked Mum, "Do you recall the Doctor who attended you for these last weeks?"

"Of course I do, his name is Doctor Arnuad," she said without hesitation.

Almost on cue, Doctor Arnuad walked into the room. No hellos. No how are yous. No good morning. Mum just went right into it.

"I told her, Doctor, I told her about what I'd done and that I must tell the police."

"Did you now?" he replied calmly. "And did your daughter believe you?"

He looked at me and gave me a wink.

"I don't know, she hasn't said much. I don't care if she did or didn't but if you lot don't take me to the police I shall take myself at the first opportunity."

I just stared at him and mother carried on ranting about how shocking it was that a mother should kill her son.

With that, Dr. Arnuad rang the bell which sat on his desk, clearly for such occasions as this.

"You called, Doctor?" a nurse said.

"Yes, would you mind taking Mrs. Patterson into the lounge and make sure she gets some coffee. Thank you."

"Sure thing. Julia, how are you? Want to follow me for a coffee?"

Mother got up in a rush and followed the nurse.

"I wanted you to come back here today as I thought maybe these ramblings were for our benefit and that maybe when she got back into her home it would stop, clearly not," Dr. Arnaud said.

"Has she been saying this sort of thing for long?" I enquired.

"Yes, well, since she's been home. She's convinced that she murdered Dan."

"Unfortunately, some of the drugs used in treating alcoholism can cause the recipient to hallucinate. And, as Julia's been with us longer than I had hoped and a longer course of treatment was required, this could be the reason for her reaction. Do you know how she slept last night? Did she sleep?"

"Hard to say. I think she did."

"I think the best course of action is to take her along to the police and let her tell them. By now they should have found enough facts about the case and be able to reassure her, and you, that what she says cannot be true. To be honest, I think the sooner the better. I will reduce the drugs she's on. However, they are strong and will take some time, usually about one month before the effects are seen."

"Dr., I have questions; did Mother never say anything of this murder nonsense to my Dad? And why did you not begin to reduce the drug you think may be the cause of this behaviour before now?"

"I cannot say if she spoke of it to your Father. He has not indicated this to me on his many visits. And, as for not reducing the treatment earlier, well the reason for that is she was responding so well to being cured. Also, it's only in this last week that it's become an absolute obsession with her. I'm sorry, Maisie, but I do have more patients to see. Why don't you go along with what she wants and then I will see you both in two weeks' time? She's not guilty. There's no harm in her confessing to a crime she didn't commit."

I said goodbye and thanked him, but felt deflated and unsure of what to do for the best course of action. James had been patiently waiting in one of the plush rooms associated with the building. I told him everything I could recall and he was as astonished as me.

"Well, if that's what we have to do then let's go along with it and take her on the way back home," James said.

"I just don't know," I said. "Do you think she'll be up to that when she's hardly out of the clinic?"

At that moment, Dr. Arnaud called out to us.

"Here is a new prescription for your Mother. I have altered the dosage. Make your next appointment for two weeks at the desk before you leave. I know things appear bleak at the moment but this will all pass, try not to worry. She's been in much worse shape than this before, and we got through that."

We all slowly walked away from the clinic.

"Come on Mum, we're going to take you to the police. There you can make a statement to the effect of what you say you've done."

"Good, it's about time we did that. After all, I shall need to confess and then do my time. How long do you think I shall be in prison for?

I didn't even have the energy to answer.

"Come on Maisie, let's get it over with," James said quietly to me. "I don't think it will take very long to sort out."

We got Mother into the car and both looked at each other over the car roof as if to say why on earth are we going along with this nonsense. I sat there trembling in the passenger seat. All I could think was what on God's green earth would the police think. We drove yet again in silence apart from Mum's singing quietly to herself. She loved the songs of Abba and a stream of their top repertoire came full of musicality from the back seat. James turned to look at me as he drove and smiled a smile that said, 'Don't worry, I'm here with you.'

As we got closer, a scary thought entered my head.

What if she is telling the truth?

CHAPTER THIRTY-ONE

Imprisonment

"Tell me and I forget. Teach me and I remember. Involve me and I learn."
~ Benjamin Franklin

Mum had fallen asleep by the time we arrived in Riberac. "Seems a shame to rouse her, doesn't it," I said. "We could just go straight home and forget all about this."

"No good putting it off as we shall only have to come back another day," James said. He put his hand on my elbow. "Let's go in and get it over with."

"Ok, you'll go in with us, yes? I can't face it alone."

"Of course I'm coming in with you. I will be there, Maze."

We managed to wake Mother without too much of a struggle.

"Where are we going now?" she asked.

"We're here now, just like you wanted," I said. "It's time to tell the police what you did."

"What are you talking about?" Mum said. "Do what? Tell them what?"

And then she began laughing so hard that she seemed unable to stop. I wondered if all this was just a game to her. Was she so out of it that she didn't know what she was saying? My mind ran riot and I stood outside the police station looking into space fearing the inability to identify reality from fiction. James put his hand on her back.

"They might have some new details about the case," James said. "Let's go in."

As soon as we were inside I went up to the desk and asked if Toby was on duty.

"No sorry, he's not here anymore. He returned to England in February. His tour of contract ended. How can I help you?"

I was sorry to hear that Toby had gone, because he knew all about Mother so that would have made life easier. Someone new on the case might take her words to be more serious than they actually were.

"My Mother wishes to confess to something very serious," I said. "She's delusional and the Doctor said to come here and prove once and for all that she's making this up."

The young uniformed officer took one look at us all and then at Mother and a grin crossed his face. After he composed himself with an embarrassed cough, he asked if she spoke any French. I answered no and asked if they had an English speaking officer on duty.

"I think we have, just a moment I will call up to one of the offices and ask if Charles is on, I think he is today."

He held the phone until someone on the other end answered.

"Hi, it's Dennis. Is Charles on today? Oh, thanks very much."

He hung up the phone, looked over at me.

"Right, we're in luck Charles is coming down. Now come with me and wait in here. You will be more comfortable."

Down we sat looking at one another and wondering what Mother would come out with now that she had the opportunity to officially speak up. I was worried that she would turn around and say that she'd no idea why she was there and what did they think she was guilty of. How embarrassing that would be. But then again, I would rather have that embarrassment than hear her launching into confessions again.

We waited for nearly half an hour before anyone came to speak to us. We had finished the coffee that provided plenty to drink and Mum managed to eat the whole plate of biscuits. In came a short stocky fellow of about thirty at a guess. He was no oil painting, but had a charming manner and came over to us and held out his hand to shake ours. As he did, he asked if we were the Patterson family and what could he do for us. He then told us his name was Charles Persimmon and he was a senior police officer at the station.

I spoke first saying that I'd hoped that Toby would still be around as he was in full knowledge of everything that had happened at the time my brother was murdered.

With that, Mother burst out with, "I did it, it was me!" in a very loud, uncouth way. She then proceeded to tell Charles all about how when and where she took her son's life. And in such a 'flirty' kind of way.

Tears welled up in my eyes at the thought that what she was saying could possibly be true. Surely not, she would never be able to do anything so heinous. She didn't know anything about Dan's affair until after his death. Which completely contradicted her story.

Charles, took it all in and wrote down what she said in a black leather bound folder. He encouraged her to talk and said very little. James and I became more and more surprised at the minutiae of her revelations. At the end of it all, Charles stood up and said, "Right, Julia, we need to temporarily arrest you on the grounds of what you've told us."

With that I stood up immediately from my chair.

"I wish to speak to you in private if you don't mind."

"Of course not. Come with me, I will find somewhere private."

The private place he found was no more private than flying to the moon. People kept coming and going and the noise was deafening.

"Sorry it's so noisy. Lots going on today being Saturday."

He ushered me to sit down. As I did, I couldn't help but notice how cold and austere this place was. Was it a ploy to make me be careful of what I was about to say?

"What did you wish to say to me young lady?"

That was disconcerting for a start. Why do the police have this condescending attitude? Making me feel like a child.

"I have to say that my Mother is not well, what she is telling everyone is complete nonsense. There is no way she would have harmed her son, she has always been a strong family woman and in no way would ever be able to murder someone."

"That is for us to establish, it shouldn't be too difficult to find out if what she tells us is fact or fiction. We don't have too much to go on but what we do have will soon make it clear if she is letting her imagination run away with her."

"Never mind about imagination, she has been in the Perigueux clinic for more than four months to help cure her alcoholism and only just been released. She'd began to talk this way over the last couple of weeks apparently. She's on strong drugs. The Doctor told us that she's possibly hallucinating because of them. I wanted you to know all this so that you can put what she says into perspective."

"As I told you, we have the ways and means of getting to the truth behind what she says. Now I must get back to work. Goodbye for the moment and I should have some good news for you very soon about your Mother. It shouldn't take long."

I walked away with Charles and into the lobby where James was waiting.

"Where's Mum, James?" I asked.

"They have taken her into custody," James said. "I asked them to wait until you came back but they refused."

"What!? Charles, bring her out. Now! I'm not even allowed to say goodbye to my Mum? Was she upset? Did she go willingly? Charles, bring her back out, please!"

"Like I've said, it's not going to take long to prove if she's lying," Charles said.

"There's no if! She isn't telling the truth. Simple. Now please bring her out."

"We will call you soon," Charles repeated.

"There's no soon! There's no soon with you people. My brother's been dead for months and you've all done nothing. Nothing has changed. There have been no leads, no anything. And when I told you about Gange, nothing there. Well, there's your real lead! Why don't you arrest him! Why is it my Mum gets taken seriously but I don't? And now you tell me you're going to call me tonight? Tomorrow? When, Charles. I need a date and time. When am I going to see my Mother again!"

I felt James' hand on my elbow again.

"Here, let's get some air," James said.

I couldn't yell, I couldn't even talk in the car. I just cried my eyes out. Hysterically crying making horrible sounds. Making a mess of snot and tears. Wiping my nose and eyes with the back of my hand. James didn't try and stop me. He didn't say "There, there." He kept his hand on my knee and drove the car steadily.

Dad came home around seven that evening. We had the dinner ready, mostly done by James. I was still in shock. Less tears. But still not functioning in any sort of capacity.

"Dad what would you like to drink tonight? Shall we have a bottle of wine between us."

"I thought we were supposed to be cutting down on the booze, for Mother's sake as well as our own."

"I have to tell you about what has happened today."

"That's fine love. Is your Mum in bed?"

"No Dad," I said. Tears came into my eyes again. "She's been arrested and is in prison."

Dad turned a rather strange colour. His usual rich tan turned to grey. He turned away from me as if to walk outside. Then he suddenly came towards me and stood so close It was intimidating.

"This can't be true, Maisie. Of course she didn't kill Dan, there is no way she could have done such a thing. How did you let this happen? Why did you take her there in the first place? I can't leave the house for one day."

"Dr. Arnuad told us to!" I shouted back.

"I'm calling him right now. Ah! Maisie, why'd you listen to him? Why didn't you speak to me first? Why was there such a rush to get there? And how can the police be so stupid?"

"I suppose they were left with no choice, Dad. After all, she thinks she did it and until they prove otherwise, which they told me would be easy and quick to do."

"I can't believe they would put a woman who is still under the Doctors into a prison cell. I must go to her right away. Are you coming?"

Dad was in a panic. He went to his keys then his coat. Went over to the phone then got his shoes. He didn't know which way to turn first.

"Why don't you leave it until tomorrow, Dad," I said. "It's getting late now and Mum's very likely asleep. Don't forget she has put herself in this position so she's not going to be frightened, is she?"

"Of course she is! She's in a prison cell, Maisie! This is real. This is a very real situation. And wait until tomorrow? Why couldn't you have listened to your own advice. Why did you go there? She's probably trembling, and crying, and very frightened right now. She's not well, Maisie."

"Go down there if you wish, but I doubt they'll let you see her," James said. He was trying to provide that third party voice of reason.

"We shall see about that." Dad said. "I shall kick up such a bloody stink they'll have to let me see her."

And with that he flounced out of the house nearly tripping over the doorstep as he went.

"What about your supper?" I called after him.

"You think I care about that?" Dad yelled back "Put it in the bloody bin."

I felt quite sick at that moment, standing in the doorway of our rickety old house watching my Father drive away as though he was in a car chase. I feared his haste would result in an accident. Yet another trauma to bare. I turned and hugged James who had been so supportive, even in his silence.

Dad was gone for several hours. When we heard his car return, he didn't put it in to the car port but left it outside the front of the house. The door slammed hard and when he came into the kitchen his face was like thunder and he was so red I thought he would have a stroke.

"What happened Dad?" I asked plaintively.

"You may well ask what happened, nothing bloody well happened that's what. It took all my powers of persuasion for them to let me see her and then it was for only five minutes and with a cooper there all the time. She's still talking stuff and nonsense about Dan and hard as I tried to tell her it would have been impossible for her to have done such a thing, she won't have any of it."

"Come and sit down and take the weight off," I said. "Do you want anything to eat now?"

"What is it with you and this dinner? I don't have any appetite right now. For pity's sake just shut up about bloody food."

With that he went upstairs. James and I chatted for a while and then went to bed.

"Are you warm enough James. I've tried to make the room as comfy as I can."

"Yes, I'm fine. Good night love. Try to sleep."

The house was quiet. I crept downstairs to get some water when I heard footsteps outside. My mind immediately raced to Gange. I could imagine him creeping around late at night. Instead it was Franz.

"Good Lord, Franz, what on earth are you doing here at this late hour?"

"I was in the vicinity and I thought I'd look you up. Sorry it's so late, it's later than I thought. I've been ill and had some time off work."

"I'm sorry to hear that. What's been the matter?"

"I've had a virus of some sort, left me feeling extremely sick and have been in bed for a few weeks."

"I'm better now though, and will soon be ready to work, however it's just in time for the school holidays."

"How long does it take you to drive all the way over here?"

"It's not that far really, the road was clear and it has taken me just under the hour."

"You must be thirsty; can I get you something to drink?"

"Yes, please I'll have a lemonade spritzer, please."

"I haven't heard of that one, what is it?"

"Everyone's heard of a spritzer, where have you been girl? It's white wine with lemonade half of each and served in a long glass with ice and lemon."

"Well you see I am not everyone, and I really have never heard of it. Anyway, if I remember correctly, you said you didn't drink."

I didn't like this guy, he was dominating, and I was not used to being around people who behaved in that way. I just thought to myself I will get him his bloody spritzer and then tell him to leave. That of course didn't happen. Thankfully James joined us in the kitchen.

"James, this is Franz, come visiting again."

"At this time of night? It's nearly eleven."

"And who may I ask are you sir." Franz responded as he clicked his heels together.

Strange but he looked kind of attractive in the dim kitchen light. He stood tall and had a kind of Germanic pride about him. Definitely not the sort of man I personally found attractive, though.

"Don't you think it's a bit late to be calling on someone?" James said.

"You don't know how long I've been here," Franz answered "Anyway, I am about to leave as I don't wish to impose on you any longer. And it takes quite a time for me to drive back to where I live."

"And where do you live?" asked James.

"I live in Bergerac."

"Good grief, that's miles away from here, how come you were out here and this late, mate?"

"Oh, I like to travel and drive all around the Perigueux region, on quite a regular basis."

"I really do need to get to bed now, Franz," I said. "Thanks for calling. Perhaps you will ring before you come next time."

"I certainly will as long as I have your telephone number."

"Yes, here it is" I quickly wrote it on a bit of scrap paper in the hope he just might lose it."

"Oh, I see. I thought you were trying to get rid of me. Now I know you're not."

I just smiled and thought, *if you only knew what I was thinking young man and if you have any designs on me other than friendship you can stick them right where the sun doesn't shine.*

When Franz left, James finally lost his cool. He had been such a rock for weeks, seen so much happen, but apparently Franz was the final straw.

"Bloody roll on, Maisie, why are you entertaining a creep like that and at this ungodly hour?"

"I heard someone creeping around the house and went out to look. Don't have a go at me and don't forget he had something to do with my rescue. But have no fear, he gives me the creeps and now more than before."

"It would not surprise me if he didn't have something to do with Dan," James said. "He's a weird bloke."

"What? Now you sound as crazy as Mum. What on earth would his motive have been? I think you're barking up the wrong tree there."

"I'm tired of sitting around here as your friend from home. How do I know this isn't another Ralph situation?"

"A Ralph situation? I haven't talked to Ralph in days, James. And wait, why would it matter if it was a Ralph situation?"

"Well, is that what this Franz thing is?"

"James, were you not okay with me and Ralph?"

He came over to where I stood, looked me straight in the eyes.

"Maisie, I'm in love with you. I think I always have been and it's been confirmed since I came over this time. Everything that's happened since I've been here has been horrible and messy but it hasn't pushed me away at all. It's just made things more clear to me. I don't know how. I don't know what that means for my future, what that even looks like. I don't know how I'm going to make it work, but all I know is I want to be with you. And I want to know if you feel the same way. Or if I'm just your friend from home. If I'm—"

I lunged at him. Threw myself into his arms. We started kissing passionately. I pushed him against the wall and he pulled me even closer.

"Wait, wait, sorry love, this is too much right now," I said, catching my breath. "That doesn't mean I don't love you, James. I think I've always loved you too. Way back to our bike rides and canal trips. But there is just so much going on and I need to be clear headed to help get through it all."

We held each other for a while, then we went upstairs to bed, separately.

CHAPTER THIRTY-TWO

Toby's Return

"When we are no longer able to change a situation,
we are challenged to change ourselves."
~ *Victor Frank*

I woke up early in a confused state. First was this overwhelming feeling of joy and completeness as I thought about James and the revelations of last night. And that kiss. Oh, that beautiful kiss. Then reality crept in. My Mum was in jail. Those thoughts pushed James away and I was back to an anxious mess.

I got up and dressed hurriedly and went to find Dad.

"Good morning, are you feeling rested? You look much better than you did last night," I enquired. "That odd bod turned up late last night, you know Franz the one who found me just after the accident."

"Was that a nice surprise?" Dad asked.

"No Dad, it wasn't. I couldn't wait to get rid of him, only a weirdo would turn up to visit at eleven at night."

"I'm O.K. I think we both have to go down this morning and see what's going on. They can't keep her there for long. This wouldn't have happened if we'd been in England you know."

"Dad, if we'd been in England, Dan would still be alive, so you're right none of this would have happened."

"It's too early to have a go at each other," Dad said. "Let's call a truce for the day, at least the morning. After we've eaten and got ready we can go and see what's happening."

I popped in to see James before we left. He was still fast asleep.

"Hello, dear," I announced as light and playful as I could. "And how are we this fine day?"

He stirred, saw me and made a grab, pulling me down on top of him.

"James, pack it in. Dad's waiting for me to go down to see if Mum's coming out."

"Oh, alright. You are a spoil sport."

"Yes I am. And your breath stinks."

And with that I left saying that we should be back again soon.

As we were leaving the house, Helen came over.

"I was just coming to see how you're getting along and thought you may care for a walk a bit later," Helen said. "I have something to talk to you about."

Dad yelled at the top of his voice from where he stood waiting for me.

"I'd better be going," I said. "Let's catch up later."

I ran to the waiting car, Dad had the engine running.

"Dad, it was my friend Helen. Did you have to be in so much of a hurry?"

"I most certainly did. Pardon me for thinking that you'd be a bit more concerned about your Mum than you appear to be."

"Of course I'm concerned about her, but there are other things going on in my life as well as Mum and her antics."

"Yeah, well, there's nothing else in my life and there shouldn't be anything else in yours until your Mother is back home. A little more respect for me and your Mother wouldn't go amiss, Maisie."

I realized this wasn't right, I shouldn't have been picking a fight. We called a truce. When we got to the police station, we walked to where Charlie was sitting and asked about Mum. His face changed and he looked at us with sheer antipathy.

"The boss would like to see you in his office. Could you follow me."

Dad looked perplexed. Although he had picked up some French he was far from understanding anything put together in a sentence.

We hurried behind the officious desk officer who almost had the pair of us running behind. It seemed as though he had little time for us or the business we were about. I failed to read what was in this man's mind. Why was he treating us this way?

We entered a room where I was so amazed to see Toby sitting behind his desk.

"Good morning, Mr. Patterson. And how are you, Maisie? It's good to see you again. Please do sit down," Toby said beaming his broad grin.

The desk chap was then dismissed in French. We settled in to our seats as I stared unbelievably at Toby.

"Toby, what are you doing here? They told us you'd gone back to England."

"I did, but they wanted me here to help move this virtually immovable case forward. So here I am."

Toby looked us straight at us.

"We have a conundrum here right now don't we? Let me start with the good news, let you both breathe a much needed sigh of relief. We have some proof that the fingerprints on the knife used do not have your wife's on it."

"Thank the Lord for that, can we take her home now?" I almost yelled.

"Then there's the not so good news. I'm very concerned about her mental state and believe that at this moment she is unfit to be at home with you. With this fixation in her head she is likely to still think she killed Daniel, so will keep coming to us unless she's treated further. We feel she should be back in the clinic and I'm sure the Doctors will agree with that."

What the hell does he know about my mother and her treatment? He's now putting himself on the pedestal of playing Doctor.

"That's for us to deal with, thank you," I said. "We are well aware that her mental state is not as it should be and we will sort things out."

"Just a minute, Maisie," Dad said. "Toby was trying to help us. And Toby, I cannot express enough how thankful and grateful I am that you're back to help us."

With that I got up and moved over to the door, turned the handle to leave when Toby got up and jogged over to me.

"Maisie, you're alright now?" Toby said. He led me back to where I'd been sitting.

"Your Mum will be out shortly. I've got it under control. Your father is right, I am only trying to help you in this bleak situation."

"You didn't know about the accident I had," I replied.

"I did know of the accident, Maisie, we were told about it. Tell me what else went wrong?"

"Pity then that you decided not to come and see me when I was in the hospital. I saw plenty of uniforms trying to get statements about the accident. But I never saw your face. Why would that be? I had to have a brain operation."

Dad butted in.

"Please forgive her outburst, Toby, she's not at her best yet son, she has been very ill and still has some recovering to do."

I could stand it no more and left the room and walked out past the desk chap, who gave me a vacuous stare. I waited by the car for Dad to appear.

"That was an unnecessary thing to say, Maisie. He was trying to be helpful. Yelling at him for not seeing you? I thought you ended it with him?"

"Don't forget, Dad, I do know the man and helpful is the one thing he is not."

"Look girl, we've got enough to cope with at present so just you stop your nonsense and help things along rather than hinder it."

I said nothing more as I knew deep down he was right and that I was behaving like a spoilt child. But I was so utterly confused, mixed up and unsure of anything. Maybe it was down to the accident. Who knows. I just wanted to forget it all.

The police wanted Mother to stay until the next day. Apparently there was more paperwork needing completion. We were asked to come first thing in the morning to collect her. When we got home I told Dad I was going over to see Helen as we had things to discuss about my future and what I hoped to do with it. Dad looked at me amazed, he was still under the impression I would stay at home and care for mother. How wrong he was.

Helen was waiting for me and looking at her watch as I approached. She complained I was late and that she must leave soon to catch her train to Paris. She was to be interviewed for entrance into the Sorbonne.

"I'm so sorry Helen, there was little choice as Mother is still being held at the police station and then I had words with that policeman I went out with for a bit. Then Dad got funny with me and it's altogether a bloody mess."

We chatted for awhile, mainly about what we thought the future held for us. I told her what was happening at home and that it seemed that Dad was expecting me to be general cook and bottle washer around the house.

"I fear my education and any chance of university may be a long way off. Dad and I keep arguing about it. It's making us both unhappy, Helen."

"That's totally unfair, there is no way he should make you put your future on hold. What can the man be thinking of?"

"He's thinking of himself all the time right now," I replied bitterly.

"Well, you must stand up for yourself Maisie and make sure that he understands you have to leave. He will find the way forward. He will have to ask the neighbours to keep an eye out for your Mum when he's at work"

"I know you're right, Helen," I said. "But it may involve bringing in a paid carer. And as you know there's not much money around."

I had the distinct impression that my friend's future looked a whole lot rosier than mine. We said fond farewells, I wished her good luck and we agreed to meet up again in a few days when she'd tell me how everything went.

It was with sadness I left Helen. The thought of her not being around, my friend who had always been so loyal and kind. Who came to see me many times when I was in hospital. I had to get myself together and stop stressing about the paradoxes of life. After all, if I wasn't around Dad would have to get on with Mum and her troubles.

With the promise of Mum only being a day from being home, I was ready to cool things off with Dad. Try to regain some sort of peace. I met him in the living room.

"Okay Dad, let's be friends. I don't want us to carry on like this. I know I'm not behaving as I should and I do feel bad about it. But we know why it's happening and I think we need to talk about it. How we shall cope. Also, we must get in touch with the clinic to talk about Mother's mental state and readmission.

"Maisie, you don't have to apologise for anything. And I should not have lost my temper with you. No daughter should have to go through what you've been through. And yes, I know all about what we need to do regarding the hospital. I will call the clinic later."

"I think you'd better do that now as time is getting on and it will be nursing staff only around and no Doctors."

"I shall do it right now, Maisie, if that pleases you."

I don't know if he meant it to be good natured. *If it pleases you.* To me, it sounded like Dad was clearly still angry with me and being sarcastic. *How could the pair of us be changing so much?*

Moments later I heard him speaking on the phone.

"What do you mean you can't take her back? She is unwell and will be too much for us to manage here. The police don't want her to be going there every day and complaining that they need to arrest her. You have to help us Doctor, you really do."

The conversation continued for a while and when Dad came off the phone, his grey pallor returned and he looked totally drained.

"Tell me what they said, Dad."

"They have no beds. As soon as they do, she can be readmitted. They don't know how long that will be though as they are full with many sick people who may be long stay."

"That's just not good enough! We can't manage her in the state she's in here."

"Don't panic, we shall think of something. I must go to bed now and we'll talk about it in the morning."

CHAPTER THIRTY-THREE

Uncertainty

*"Unless you cross the bridge of your insecurities
you cannot begin to explore your possibilities."*
~ Tim Fargo

My relationship with Ralph further deteriorated. It had been weeks since I saw him. And I thought about him less and less. Mother was back in the clinic. Dad had resumed his chores around the site and everyone seemed to be happy that the status quo resumed.

In the end, Ralph asked me if all was well between us. I told him that I was unsure about everything at the moment. So much was going on in my life that I found it hard to even think straight.

We talked for what seemed like hours and, if I'm honest, I was a bit scared of how he might have reacted. I really had nothing to fear. I told him of all the latest events with the exception of my newly found love for James. I felt that would be hurtful and just a step too far. Funny thing was that the way he reacted made me feel bad and I actually felt a great fondness for the man creep over me when he said.

"My dear girl, I quite understand. You've been through so much, more than most could bear without going under."

He then suggested we needed to have some time apart, at least until I got my head around all that was happening.

I had returned to school and it was agreed with the headmistress that I could take the last exam in June. Helen had been successful at her interview for the Sorbonne and left for Paris soon after and was getting used to being away from home. She told me she was surprised to feel as homesick as she did at first, especially as she'd staunchly been looking forward to leaving.

Dad started to talk about getting someone in to look after Mum in the daytime when I left home. That was a major breakthrough. I thought that maybe someone on site had a discussion with him about me being young and needing to stretch my wings. Perhaps it was my lovely friend Mr. Banerjee.

I had an appointment to see Toby to try to get the police to reopen (or perhaps open for the first time) an investigation on Gange. I don't know why I did so, but I dressed myself up to go and talk with him. Maybe I wanted him to see what he was missing out on? I did have some new high heels, at least 3 inches and could just about stay upright in them. The dress came with me from England. A floral waist tight, with a wide leather belt in black, holding me in and making a good job of showing off my waistline. Why was I trying to impress Toby, that episode was over and done with. And now I was in love with James. How fickle am I?

I drove myself down to town for the first time since the accident. When I arrived, he saw me walking across the forecourt. He opened the station door and came out. Holding his arms towards me and smiling.

"Do come in Maisie, it's good to see you," Toby said. "You look great."

"Is it awkward seeing me again?" I asked rather bluntly.

"How do you mean? Since we were going out for a while?" Toby asked.

"Don't worry, I have no designs on you in that direction. In fact, I have found a very nice girlfriend who I'm hopeful I shall marry one day."

That came as a blow from the blindside, but why on earth wouldn't a good-looking guy like Toby find himself someone to settle down with.

I was ushered into a cold office, the weather was heating up over here and although I'd had little chance to sunbathe, I must have been out in it enough to give my skin an impressive golden glow. I couldn't help but notice Toby looking me over more than once. He tried unsuccessfully, to do it clandestinely.

"Right, let's get down to business, I believe from what you said earlier that you had what you thought might be a new lead."

Pity he was now in a relationship. How could I be thinking that when James and I had at last declared our love for one another? He seemed to have grown up probably as much as I had, that was appealing. However I still hadn't seen any of that previously lacking sense of humour.

He asked me if Ralph and I had been lovers. I was a bit shocked he came out with that, although Heaven only knows why. Why was I ashamed of what had happened between Ralph and me? I'd been in love with him. Indeed, I was still only seventeen and if I'm honest my Father and even Ralph were conscious of that fact and I know it concerned them. But me, ever headstrong went forward into that relationship with my eyes wide open, or so I thought at the time.

The conversation between Toby and me continued, culminating in Toby's agreement to go and talk to Ralph.

"I shall take samples for DNA. I don't think Ralph had his taken at the time of the incident."

"I think he'll be shocked to find that he's a suspect in the case, as well as his brother."

"I hope to be able to go to his farm today, he lives quite near you I believe?"

"Not that far away. I think it's about a couple of miles, as the crow flies. How do you know that he lives on a farm?"

"If you can recall correctly I visited his brother there when Dan was murdered. Do you remember that?"

"Yes, of course I do, it had just slipped my mind. Just like so much is slipping away from my mind of late."

I didn't seem to be improving in that direction as much as I would have liked. The Doctors in Bordeaux had told me that memory loss was to be expected, and that I was young, and that in time I would be back to normal. It wasn't correcting quickly enough for me though.

"Also, I want to know how you are so certain that mother had nothing to do with it," I enquired.

"That's easy to answer. It would have been unlikely for a woman to have carried out such a ferocious attack. And, as we told you and your Father before, her DNA was nowhere on your brother."

It didn't take long for Toby to pay Ralph a visit. I kept well out of the way and told him I would be at home if he cared to call on me on the way back to the station, I'd be glad to see him. Toby later told me everything about the visit, so much so it almost felt like I was there.

"Hello Gange, I believe that's what they call you?"

"Yes, that's correct, and who are they? Who are you? How can I help you?

"I have come to speak with your brother, if he's home."

"He's out on the farm and busy. But may I enquire as to who is asking?"

"Of course. My name is Detective Inspector Roi, I'm here in regard to the murder of Dan Patterson."

"Are you the one who came to interview me some time back? Sorry, I just didn't recognise you."

"There are one or two points that need to be cleared up," Toby said.

"I will go and see if I can disturb him. We are very busy here at the moment. There is a lot of livestock on the farm and he will be milking."

"Thank you, shall I wait here?"

"Well, you can't wait on the doorstep so you'd better come into the lounge. I shan't be long. By the way, you're English aren't you? Just like us. What brings you to a backwater like this?"

"I'm over here to gain experience of how the French systems work and we have an exchange going on and a couple of Gendarmes are working in London at the Met."

"Oh, that's a far cry from the local Gendarmerie."

"You may be surprised to know just how much crime goes on around these parts, and we're involved in cities like Perigueux and Bordeaux from time to time."

"Okay, I'll go and find the man."

Ralph came dashing over to the house and spoke to Toby then said he needed to clean up and would be right with him.

"Gange, would you get a drink for the detective?"

"What would you care for officer?"

"Nothing, thank you, or maybe just a cup of coffee if that's not going to be any trouble."

"Not at all."

And off he went to the kitchen to make coffee.

"How can I help you? What's it all about?" Ralph said as he walked back into the kitchen. He looked the officer up and down, held his hand out to shake Toby's and then ushered him to be seated.

"We need to get samples to eliminate you from a crime scene. The one in which Dan Patterson was killed." Toby, told me later that at this point Ralph went pale and said, "How can I do that Officer?"

"First and foremost, I'd like you to tell me about your movements the night that Dan Patterson was killed. It was a Sunday, the 21st of November last year."

Gange returned to the lounge with the coffee.

"I have not added sugar; do you take any?"

"No thanks," came the reply. He then left the room closing the door behind him.

"I shall do my best, but why on earth are your guys sniffing around here again. We went through all that last year. That was when my brother appeared to be in the frame," Ralph stated.

"New information has come to light and, as you know, we have to follow up every lead we get."

"Yes, of course, now let me think. I recall my brother and I had supper that night. He must have come in at about four. He had been drinking with Dan in a bar in Riberac. He said he left him there alone telling him he'd had enough and that it was getting dark and that he should come back and help me with the livestock. We had our meal and I felt the need to get away from the farm for a while. Sometimes being on my own away from my brother who can get on my nerves, takes a bit of a toll and I wanted to have an hour or two to myself. So, I took off and headed towards town."

"Which town would that be, Mr. Waterman?"

"I drove towards Perigueux, there is more going on over there. I was troubled about some personal happenings in my life and needed time to think. I can always do that when I drive."

"What personal things would that be sir?"

"Well, that really is my business and would have nothing at all to do with your enquiries."

"Let us be the judge of that if you don't mind."

"I do mind, but I have no intention of talking to you about it."

"Very well. Do you mind if I take some swabs from your mouth? It's for the DNA elimination."

"Not at all."

"I shall also need to take your fingerprints."

"Will I have to come down to the station for all of that?"

"No, I've got a portable machine in the car. I'll just go and fetch it."

With that Toby left the room. Gange popped his head around the corner and asked what it was all about.

"He's making more enquires about Dan's murder."

"Surely, he doesn't think your implicated now, does he?"

"Seems so, I've got to have swabs taken and fingerprints."

"A bit late for all that don't you think?"

Toby re-entered the house and came into the lounge, looking flustered.

"I am so sorry I've picked up the wrong machine. This one will not do the job. Would you object to coming down to the station tomorrow? We can get it done and over with then. And I think we shall need a blood sample, you would have to come to the station for that anyway."

"Yes, I shall do that."

Toby made his way to the front door, started to open it when Ralph said, "Hang on a moment. You know I had to go through Riberac on my way to Perigueux. I did pass someone running fast away from close to the area where Dan's body was found. I didn't think much of it at the time as he seemed to be shouting out to someone in front of him. I didn't see who. It didn't seem important at the time. But maybe there is something to it."

"Would you recognise them again? How old do you think he was?"

"It was dark, but at a random guess I should say he was in his twenties."

"Thank you, that could be helpful. It's a pity you didn't tell anyone this at the time of the incident. I may ask you to take a look at some mug shots and photo-fits we have down at the station."

"Anything I can do to help and I'm sorry I said nothing before but it had completely slipped my mind until now."

CHAPTER THIRTY-FOUR

Attempting the Changes

'You can't let other people tell you who you are.
You have to decide that for yourself'
~ Unknown.

After James left for home with a promise to keep in close touch and saying he would be coming back over soon, I gave Helen a call.

"How are you my friend?" I asked.

"I'm fine thanks, what about you? Are you feeling more like your old self again?"

"Yes, I think I'm headed in the right direction now and I'm certainly over the accident. Gosh, that's a long number to get hold of you on. Typically, French of course. How are you getting on up there, Helen?"

"I am doing alright. Mum and Dad helped to get this flat. It's lovely, wait 'til you see it."

"There's lots going on down here. Mum thinks she killed Dan. And is now back in the clinic. Dad has relaxed a bit about me leaving home and has tentatively agreed to bring a housekeeper in. Worry is that he's not sure how he's going to be able to afford it. The thing bothering me most is that I have gone off Ralph. Don't ask me why as I don't know. I thought I was in love with him once but now I know I'm not. But Helen, I have to tell you, remember James my partner in crime from way back? We seem to be getting it together."

"Never mind about Ralph, honey, far better that you're now fancying someone your own age. But we are young to get too serious with anybody, and there are plenty of fish in the sea. What about your Mum? How dreadful is that. You must tell me all about it when you come up here. By the way, when are you coming up?"

"Well who knows. Results are not here yet and I'm getting nervous about that, but there's something else afoot. Do you recall me telling you about the day I was found collapsed in the lane and someone came to my rescue? Well, he has found out where I live and keeps coming up, sniffing around. He's a geek type and half German and a bit creepy if I'm honest. He profoundly irritates me. He found me, from what I gather after a long search, as he wanted to know how I was doing and has at least a two-hour round trip to get to here. He must be mad."

"Nothing wrong with that Maisie. In fact, I think it was a decent thing to do. And it seems as though he's sweet on you honey."

"You're probably right about that. But I find him weird and worse of all he seems to be getting along splendidly with Dad. Enough of me. I want to hear all about you?"

"I've more or less settled in. I miss you though, I haven't made any real friends as of yet. There is this older professor who I quite like and he is definitely keen on me.

"What about the job?"

"It's more of a research role."

"What's the nightlife like? I hear it's wonderful?"

"I haven't done much of that yet. Don't forget I know no one up here and I'm not inclined to take-off alone. When can you come up and see me? Perhaps you could stay for a week and we can get to know the scene together."

"That sounds wonderful, but I think I'd better wait until life on this end has improved. When I get my results, I shall have a better idea of what I want to do in the future. What is your research about?

"I'm working with a forensic scientist, he's rather nice, but probably married. Like all the good ones."

"I hope Mother will be back in about a month and when Dad gets all the practicalities sorted out, I shall be more free."

"I'm so looking forward to seeing you, at the moment I wouldn't even mind seeing my parents, but I don't think that's going to happen. Mum's kind of becoming a recluse and Dad, well who knows what he's up to these days. Could you do me a favour, Maisie? Would you call in on my Mother? I'm worried about her, I think she's very lonely and a bit down right now. I asked her to come to Paris to see me, but she declined as she says it's too far for her to travel. I find that so hard, she's only fifty-five. No age to be shutting your life down."

"Yes, of course I will, I'll take some flowers round. I'll be with you soon. Time flies as we know. Lots of love, Helen, and keep smiling."

"Goodbye my friend, speak again soon."

When I came off the phone, I had the strangest feeling. Nothing I could put my finger on but it was an overwhelming sense of impending doom almost as though I was racing ahead of an unseen demon. Surely life had thrown enough at our family for now, what else was lurking around the corner to trouble us? I was clearly distressed about Mum and her latest antics. I asked myself if she would ever be cured. Dad once again had the freedom to do the job he came over here to do. And I had more time on my hands. No school, no Ralph, no James, or the German for that matter, and no one to think of except me and Dad.

Dad asked after Helen, and I relayed much of the conversation. I told him I'd like to go and visit with her in Paris and couldn't help but notice his less than enthusiastic expression. It was twilight outside. I loved the extra hour of light we had in the Summer months over here. It meant you could get more things done. Working as a daughter, housekeeper and general factotum, the role I currently played made me realise things had to change. Never before had I wanted my life to be back to normal as much as I did at that moment. I knew it was selfish, but I realised this way of life was not the life I wanted.

The Summer rolled on with relentless sunshine and little rain. This made life on the land so much harder and the local farmers and landsmen did much complaining. I loved the heat and was developing a deep golden-brown glow shining my skin and accentuating my blonde hair and I was told made me look more attractive by a couple of people. Nothing like a compliment or two to raise the spirits.

I tried to relax with a crafty, clandestine swim in the pool late at night. Unfortunately, I was discovered by the people at number six, not the best people to have caught me, and that put a swift end to that activity. The issue was that unbeknownst to me they had the responsibility of covering the unheated pool last thing at night.

Anyway, other elements of my being took over. My exam results arrived and I had done well. The envelope arrived early in the morning. I tentatively opened it pulled out the contents and to my amazement I had passed all exams with the equivalent of a distinction. How did that happen. I'd been so ill and depressed. I was ecstatic, I rushed out to find Dad. When I told him, he just flew into my arms and scooped me up saying "What a clever girl I have. Well done love."

He was so proud of me and I too felt pride in overcoming huge obstacles to pass exams I feared I had little hope of achieving. I must have retained more than I thought. When the next opportunity arose I said to Dad,

"I have to think about my future now. I would like to go to see Helen sooner rather than later and find out what's available for me in the city. That's if I decide to stay in France."

"You're not thinking of going back to England are you love? I would hate that and it looks as though Mother will be home quite soon. She is so much better and more like she was before the drinking."

My heart sunk somewhat. *Here we go again, he's delving into the realms of keeping me here. I had my doubts from the outset as to whether Dad's resolve would continue and that he'd try to persuade me to stay.* I decided not to answer and carried on with the banal job of preparing the evening meal.

It was going to be a difficult journey escaping this pattern of life. My thoughts had turned to teaching. I was virtually fluent in French now as at every opportunity I would converse in French with any French person encountered. The folks on site also spoke the language and Mr. Banerjee who I met up with often would help by nattering away in a language that I'd come to love. If my thoughts of teaching came to anything, I would want to go to one of the larger cities.

I knew I must cross the first hurdle of getting mother back and settled in. Then the `need to make arrangements for her care would be my dominating influence. When I broached the subject of leaving again, about the need to be getting on with things, Dad began to get quite upset and made it clear he didn't want me to go far.

"I honestly don't know for how long I shall be able to cope without you nearby."

"But Dad, we've had this conversation so many times and I thought the last time we'd reached some kind of agreement that I could leave. I think my results from the exams will lead me into a good career and with being bilingual I should be able to get sorted with a decent future. I thought you were all for that. Now I'm not so sure."

Dad said nothing more but the look on his face said it all. His head went down, he sat in the nearby chair and held his hands into his face. I couldn't speak, I was distraught and feeling desolate. When he finally lifted his face to me, tears were clearly visible.

"Oh Dad, don't do this now. Let's take one step at a time. Things do have a habit of sorting themselves out. Even when it seems there's no light on the horizon."

To add to the confusion Ralph came up to see how we were.

"Good to see you, Ralph," Dad said. "What have you been up to these days?"

"Nothing really changes. The farm is as always heavy work. The Government are putting more and more stipulations on farming. Little wonder there is such unrest amongst the farming communities. However, I still enjoy it and all the time that's the case I shall carry on. Gange, is thinking of going back to the U.K. so I shall need to look for someone to help me in his place. I've come to rely on him quite a bit."

I walked into the room right as he said Gange.

"Hello my dear, are you well? Haven't seen you for a while?"

"Yes, we are okay, thanks. Lots going on here as usual. I keep getting visits from the guy who saved me in the lane. He lives in Bergerac and makes the journey here quite often. And I'm thinking of going into teaching." All this came flowing out without much thought for Dad's feelings or anyone else for that matter. I felt embarrassed to be around Ralph now and I didn't have the courage to tell him I'd decided it was over for good.

"That's wonderful, have you had your exam results then?"

"Yes, and I did well, better than I thought I would. I want to go to Paris and visit Helen. We talk on the phone a bit and she's keen for me to visit. Do you know much about teacher training over here Ralph?"

"I don't, but we could find out together. Why not come over soon and we'll look it up on Google. Should be able to get some idea from that."

"Thanks, but I intend to go to the school. They have a career day later this week and that should give me all the details I need to make the first steps," I interjected.

Ralph looked sad and I felt guilty, but there was no way I was intending to go back on my stance. He was his impeccable, stoical self and appeared in control, with a semi-smile on his face. That made me feel a bit better. Then he said, "Where's James? I haven't seen him for a time either?"

"He went back to England. Did you know he took unpaid leave to come and see me? Let me offer you something to drink, Ralph. What would you like?"

"Coffee would be fine, thanks."

He was fully smiling now, clearly glad James had gone.

"I shall make it Dad, you two have a chat, won't be long." I welcomed the opportunity to get away.

"I'll have the same love." Good I thought, he's not showing his sadness in front of Ralph.

"Can't be long, Ralph, as work awaits. Couple on the corner want a trench dug for new fencing. Didn't think that was in my remit though."

"You'll have to be strong and not let them take advantage of you.

"Yes, you're right I should stand up to them more. But they've not had the greatest deal since we've been here now have they. I've had a lot of time off."

I noticed Ralph kept looking in my direction. He was now wearing glasses, that was new about him and he kept trying to peer over the top edge without me noticing. Perhaps he thought I couldn't see his eyes. I drunk my coffee as quickly as possible and then made an excuse to go upstairs.

He called out to me, "Bye, bye for now Maisie, do come and see us again soon, won't you?"

"Yes, I'll let you know what's going on and keep you in the picture."

"Bye Ralph, good to see you."

I looked back as I said it and gave him a huge smile.

Why, oh why on earth did I say that. Here I am trying to cool the relationship. I will have to be tougher and tell him straight it's over and that I don't want to see him anymore. That's the only fair thing to do. Mind you I might just get away without doing that as I shall take off to Paris and not let on when I'm coming back. I called on Mr. Banergee.

"This is the best news for a long while, my dear," he said. "You are a clever girl. I have always known it. Now what does the future hold for you?"

"I think I'm going in to teaching."

"What fun, do you know the subjects, and age group you wish to teach."

"No, not yet, in fact I haven't even thought about the age group."

"You must start to consider where you wish to train. If I may be so bold. Could I suggest that you leave here and head for the cities. Bergerac and Bordeaux both have grand training facilities."

"I was thinking about going to Paris. Did you know that Helen is up there and she tells me it's great and that I must visit?"

"Yes, that's another option you have. I'm very happy for you Maisie. You are young and life has not treated you well so far. High time you start to think about yourself. What did I tell you long back? That you could have the world at your feet if you studied hard?"

"Yes, you did and it's come to fruition. Must go now Mr. Banerjee, lots to think about, lots to do."

"Have you told your father?"

"Yes, and he's not happy about it."

I couldn't wait to get back indoors and call Helen with my good news. My conscience got the better of me and I decided to drive to Perigueux to see Mother. I felt so happy on that pretty drive as though a huge weight had been lifted that I was now thinking of me, instead of everyone else. When I arrived it had begun to rain hard. Much needed and the first we'd seen for nearly six weeks. I rung the doorbell and was ushered in. Mum had been moved to a side room yet again. I asked as to why this was and was told in no uncertain terms that she was disruptive and causing trouble for the other residents' as they were now being called.

She recognised me at once and leaned forward and put her arms around me and gave a tight hug. I pulled back and looked into her lovely face and we smiled at each other for the first time in many months. Her hair had been washed and set and her nails painted a pretty pink. She looked so good in that moment.

"Mum, I have some good news for you." I relayed the story of my exam success. She beamed even wider than before and took my hands in hers and said, "What a clever girl I have. How is your Father and where is he dear?"

"He's at work, Mum."

Mum, was more like her old self than I'd seen for ages. I was so glad as it would make my departure easier. I stayed and we chatted nineteen to the dozen and as I was leaving she said to me, "Take care my clever girl, look after your Dad and I shall be home again soon."

Before I left the building, I found one of the nurses and spoke of Mother's improvement. And enquired as to why had it been necessary to shut her away from others' company. I was told that most nights she tries to escape and that she could sometimes be aggressive with the other patients.

Of course, that put a different slant onto the happy visit I'd just had. There was no sign of aggression or delusion. If she did come home soon it would give Dad plenty to think about. That night, after supper, I had a long chat with Dad, which didn't go well, I told him about the visit to Mum and how well she seemed to be and that she was in a room by herself and when I told him the reason why he got quite angry. I impressed upon him that I must go away for training. He was having none of it and said I should be able to do it locally. I went into the greatest detail I could muster about how that would be impossible for the sort of teaching I had been thinking about. I didn't want to teach infants.

I called Helen.

"Helen, I must come and see you. I need to get away to clear my head. Its stifling down here, Dad is being difficult about me going in for teaching if it means going away to train."

"Of course, you will need to leave home, you won't get much of a training unless you come to one of the cities. Surely he can appreciate that, Maisie. You'd better get yourself up here as soon as possible, hadn't you? There's plenty of room for you. Then we can get stuff moving. Get your ticket and let me know when you will arrive."

"Helen, thank you for being such a good friend. I don't know what I'd do without you. When would it be suitable and I'll sort things out my end."

"Come whenever you like, I'm not going anywhere. In fact, the sooner the better. This chap who also lives in the house seems to be after me. Everywhere I go I see him. Hope I'm not being paranoid. Thing is he's quite ugly and a bit loud."

The call ended. I went over to where Dad sat and said, "I shall be going off to Paris to visit Helen next week, Dad. Just wanted to let you know. And while I'm there she will help me to find out about teacher training."

I gave him no time to reply, instead I headed for my room. Thinking it over when I got into bed I realised that was an unkind thing to do. However, I wanted him to know I was serious and not just playing with the idea.

The day came for me to go. I met with Mr. Banergee the day before and he was as excited as me about my adventure.

"Teaching no less, of course you will aim for the aggregation won't you? That is the most prestigious accolade you can achieve."

I had no idea what he was talking about.

"I do know that I would rather teach middle grade students or maybe higher education and not the infants."

"I am so pleased for you, Maisie. This will be the making of you my dear. A chance to spread your wings and to fly. I know you will be concerned for your Father. But you know parents have a way of coping when their young flee the nest. It's the way of the world. It has always been so and will be forever."

He then gave me a handful of notes saying: "That is for your trip. You go to Paris to your friend. Have a wonderful time and find out about all on offer. You've crossed the first hurdle with excellent exam results and now it's time to follow the continuum."

"Thank you, you are so kind. I'll tell you all about it when I get back."

I had to add part of my meagre savings to be able to buy the return train ticket. When I got home I started packing my small case, the one I'd brought with me from England. It was an old battered leather thing that looked as though it came from out of the ark. I knew I'd feel embarrassed taking it with me. But there was no money for a new one. The little I'd saved and the 100 euros Dad gave and the money from Mr. Banergee would have to last.

Dad came upstairs and said, "There is someone to see you." I hadn't heard the door knock.

"Who is it Dad, I'm up to my eyes, is it important? We weren't expecting anyone were we?"

He turned away and went back downstairs. I hesitated a little and then felt I should go down. I was surprised to see Franz standing there. Looking quite different than the last time I saw him.

"Hello, how are you Maisie?" Franz said coming over to plant an inevitable kiss. "Your Father told me you were going away?"

"Hello Franz. Yes, I am in the middle of getting ready so don't have much time. I thought I asked that you ring before calling?"

"Yes you did, I won't be long. Just wanted to find out how you did in your exams."

Dad jumped in and asked Franz if he wanted a drink. "You must be thirsty after coming all this way."

"Thank you, yes, and he almost clipped his feet together and stood to attention as he said it. I still couldn't figure out what looked so different about him, he looked better than before. I couldn't resist but burst out with, "What's different about you Franz?"

He looked at me quizzically and said, "Well I've lost a stone and a half and changed my hair style. I take it you approve?"

"Yes, it suits you." He had a thick head of brown hair that before had been unruly and dishevelled.

"I have to leave first thing in the morning to go to Paris. I'm staying with my school friend Helen."

"How fine that will be, now won't it? Helen, yes, did I meet her before?"

"No, I don't think you did. She lived on the site here, she'd probably gone to Paris before you came looking for me."

"What will you be doing in Paris, Maisie, may I ask?"

"You may. I passed the exams with good marks and then I made the decision that I'd should like to try my hand at teacher training."

"Oh, that must have been my influence then. I love teaching and it may be a good career for you, but then again maybe not,"

I was annoyed at this and fortunately the spell was broken by Dad's entrance.

"Thank you so much Mr. Patterson, that's most kind of you."

Dad told him to call him Jack. Which he willingly did. He then turned to me and started on about my intentions regarding teaching. He went on and on and in the end, I thought I needed this to stop so I said, "Franz if you don't mind, I have to go and pack and I cannot answer all you wish to know about what the future holds as I know so little myself."

"Well I know that," came the reply. "But my thinking was that I can be of help to you with the knowledge that I clearly have. I thought that would be to your liking."

"I'm sorry Franz I don't mean to be rude, but I know nothing right now, you'd be better off asking me in about a years' time. You'll have to chat to Dad as I really must get on."

"No problem at all, If I don't see you again tonight, do have a lovely time with your friend in Paris, won't you?"

As I left the room I replied, "I do hope so, that's my intention." I knew my tone was harsh I couldn't help myself. I just didn't take to his ghastly mannerisms. However, it appeared that he was pursuing me, so I'd need to find a way of putting him off. Perhaps my coldness did the trick.

CHAPTER THIRTY-FIVE

Freedom

"To handle yourself use your head; to handle others use your heart."
~ Eleanor Roosevelt

I woke early the next day so excited and nervous to be going on my first big adventure alone. Dad dropped me off at the station to catch the eight fifty train to Paris expecting to arrive three hours later. Helen would be waiting for me. An announcement came over the tannoy system to say the train for Paris was going to be an hour late. Most unusual for French trains as they are world renowned for good time keeping. I began thinking *This is scary. My brother murdered by someone unknown, my Mother still in a clinic with chronic alcoholism. My older boyfriend now on the wane and a new one waiting in the wings.*

I relished the fact I was free. My horrendous accident and the debacle that followed. God in Heaven only knows what's next.

As I neared Paris, I started getting butterflies, you know that churning feeling you get when you know little about the place you're going to. I was fascinated by what I saw from the train. Huge, architectural buildings, looking profoundly grand and austere. The roads were narrow with many closely planted tall trees lining the pavements. Badly damaged cars were back to back, some even touching each other.

Helen still had her phone turned off, I kept trying to reach her unsuccessfully. The train was just entering the main La Garde Station when I saw her facing away from me with her recognisable long blonde hair. She looked amazingly chic. As she turned and waved to me I rushed towards her as though the Mistral was blowing me there. We hugged each other.

"You look so lovely and grown up, Helen; how have you done that in such a short time?"

"It's Paris Cherie, Paris, is the place to change you forever and I'm happy here, I won't be going back. Come let's go get some coffee. You must be parched. Was the journey good? How long are you able to stay? You know you asked me to find out about teacher training. Well I've done some research and it looks as though it will be right up your street as they say."

"That's good."

"Yes, I met this guy at the University and he knows a lot about the training and is happy to come out with us one night and talk it through."

"That's fantastic Helen, thanks so much. And I'm only here for five days, that's all I could sort for the first time away."

"He'll be alright, I think parents just like to make a fuss to show they care."

"I know Dad fears caring for Mum alone and also the costs attached to hiring someone to help."

"Yes, it's hard but he'll find a solution, people usually do. Also remember there are kind hearted folk on the site who I feel sure would be happy to lend a hand."

And on that note, we wandered through the streets of Paris and into a café. I was fascinated to see tables and chairs outside on the pavements. Even some from gas heater above every table, which Helen told me are used in Winter so folk can stay in the fresh cold air. Then we got a taxi to where Helen lived.

"Wow, how fabulous is this, how did you find the place?"

"I didn't do it alone. I met this chap at uni, you know the one I told you about and he knew this place was empty and asked if I wanted to go and see it which of course I did. And here we are."

The building was modern and that lovely honey coloured stone. As we entered I could not believe my eyes, we went up to the fourth floor in a fast lift, I'd never been in the like before. The landing was thickly carpeted in soft lilac and grey diamonds dotted here and there. It was beautiful. Then Helen unlocked her door and in we went. "It's got two bedrooms so you can have your own room, not only that, it's got two bathrooms too."

"Helen, you've fallen on your feet. How on earth can you afford it?"

"I have to work, waitressing in the evenings. I don't get much time off. Mum and Dad gave me the deposit and then said now you're on your own. I have this whole week off though as I said I needed time with my friend. I hope the job will still be there when I go back. I think it will as they know I'm reliable and a hard worker. I must say, Maisie, you look to me as though you need a break?"

"Do I look worn out then, because I feel it sometimes."

"Well, we shall have a super time together. There are so many amazing things to see and do here."

"Why don't you go and shower in your very own space, you might want to change clothes and then I shall take you to a wonderful restaurant. It will be my treat and I know you'll love it. The chap I told you about took me there once. He's well off, from a well-to-do family. Money no object, you know the type."

"Helen, I'm just so happy to be here, it's going to be fabulous for us. By the way, where's my room?"

As I went in with Helen to my digs, I had to take a deep breath. I'd never in my life before seen a spare room like it. It was furnished with white modern chests of drawers. A walk-in wardrobe, large and airy. The walls were also painted white and there was grey carpet and grey accessories scattered around the room. My bedding was a soft, pale mauve and I just melted into the luxury of it all.

"How are you going to be able to keep up with the rent working as a waitress?"

"Not sure really. Mum and Dad have paid so far, even though they told me that wasn't going to last. I think they felt a bit sorry for me and had a guilty conscience about their only daughter struggling in Paris, trying to make a career and a decent life for herself. When the guilt wears off as it surely will, I'll have to move out. It is possible to live at the university but I'm not sure about that. It's full of silly, immature females that giggle a lot."

"So, you're not one of them? As I remember we did quite a lot of giggling and got ticked off for it. Don't you recall?"

"I know but that was different."

"I don't see how!"

"Now get yourself sorted out and we'll go eat."

"Right away ma'am, see you in a minute," I said saluting.

We found the restaurant, the food was exquisite, and I ate like never before. Small portions starting with amuse bouche, I'd never heard of that before. Helen told me it was a delicacy of some expensive taster that came before the delectable flavours of the nouvelle cuisine that followed. The evening was divine and I was treated to it along with wines accompanying each course.

Helen said that her new friend would meet us and have coffee before we left. An hour later in walked a handsome man who looked to me to be in his late twenties. This surprised me as Helen had plenty to say to me about Ralph and his great age.

"This is Francis, he teaches at the Sorbonne."

Pleasantries were said all round and coffee served, the atmosphere was electric as many folks from the nearby theatres were coming into the restaurant to eat. The noise got louder and I had trouble hearing everything that the softly spoken Francis said. I was beginning to feel tired and ready to leave. We exchanged a few more pieces of information about my proposed future, then said our farewells. How about we meet up tomorrow evening, I'm free then and we can go through the paperwork I have at home.

I liked Francis, there was something about his charisma that was charming. He smiled a lot and appeared to be a thoughtful man. Helen was obviously drawn to him. I just hoped that she wasn't getting too involved and that he didn't have a significant other back home.

Helen knew I didn't have much money, she understood the situation and said, "You have no need whatsoever to worry about that. Just enjoy yourself." We got back to the flat had a drop of brandy each. "Cheaper here than in the restaurant" she said.

"Let's call it a day. We need to be up early as there's so much I want you to see."

I slept like a baby and yet again Dan and Mother and Dad stayed out of my thoughts, giving me a chance of some peace. I felt so relaxed in Helen's company. We were up at eight, breakfasted, and ready for the off at nine thirty.

The sites were fascinating. The place was chock full of amazing buildings, structures, and street cafes everywhere. It occurred to me that the French people who owned cars didn't take much care of them. Maybe they were cheap to buy.Firstly we visited the Sacra Cur, Sacred church, in the artists area where all the artists and street players closeted themselves. Helen said do you like that picture, it was a scene in Paris of the Eiffel tower and interest of the streets leading to it. I said I did and she promptly bought it for me.

"There you are, now you'll always have a memory of our day doing the arty, farty, stuff."

"Thank you but you shouldn't have done that. It's just too much. You paid for supper last night. Tell you what, Helen, let's go and have a coffee, that will be my treat."

It fascinated me to see all the odd bods and talent.

"They hang out here in their droves," Helen told me.

We found an unusual cafe that appealed to both of us.

"What would you like, Helen," I said as the waiter came to take our order.

"Just a coffee for me please."

"Two coffees please."

"Of course mesdemoiselles, what sort of coffee would you care to 'av, could it be espresso, or even latte or cappuccino?"

Helen wanted Americano and I had to ask her what it was, she said it's a largish black coffee and you can have hot or cold milk with it.

"I shall have that please with cold milk."

The waiter came about half an hour later, when we were on the brink of leaving and brought our drinks. That's when the fun and games began. There were these two men having an argument. It was getting more and more heated. They were French and we tried our hardest to listen to what they said. It went something like,

"You rotten bastard, what are you, you pig. Taken my girlfriend, I challenge you to a duel."

At that point, the manager came and asked the pair to shut up or get out. They chose to get out and continued their angst on the pavement outside the café.

"Helen, do the French men still have duels? I thought that was archaic and ended long since."

"You're right it did. They get a bit excited over here. It's fun though to see the Latin temperament prevails."

We saw the Eiffel tower, I particularly wanted to go to the Musee D'orsay Art Gallery. When we got there the queues were immense snaking out onto the pavements.

After we'd tired ourselves out, we headed back to the flat. Sat down, made tea, and fell asleep in the soft and sumptuous armchairs. When we awoke we chastised ourselves for losing time, which happened to be the most precious of elements. I wanted to return to the Musee d'Orsay as by the time we got in we only saw a tiny amount of the plethora of paintings. Its sheer imposing size is in itself a statement of intent. There was still so much to see and we returned that evening for a deeper study of the arts. Helen and I had a great deal in common and famous artists had always been one aspect of our love of similar things. The next day we planned to go to the Notre Dame Cathedral, the Arc de Triomphe and the Luxembourg gardens, that left time for little else. That night we stayed in and ate a fabulous meal prepared for us by Francis. He was a magnificent cook and I wondered how he became that good. Did he learn the skills from his Mother or his wife?

Why was I so suspicious of people? I said nothing of these unkind thoughts to Helen. We had such a lovely evening talking about all we had seen so far and plans for the next day. Francis was to leave for the South of France attending a conference.

"Never mind sweetie, will you be back before Maisie leaves? She goes on Friday," Helen said.

"Afraid I'm away until Sunday. Not to worry, as I hope you will come visit us again, Maisie."

"Should the opportunity arise I shall be up here in a flash, I just love it. All the hustle and bustle. We'd better get on with the teacher training stuff, don't you think Francis."

"Yes, of course, and I can send some paperwork to your home. That will reinforce what I'm about to tell you."

The three of us made ourselves comfortable on the luxurious couch and Helen opened yet another bottle of wine. We had a fine old time hearing all that Francis had to say about teacher training. The year was passing and fast. I was looking forward to being eighteen, the age I must reach before I could start training.

"Where do I start," Francis said. "I'll start with primary and middle school level before I go onto the Aggregation, that's another kettle of fish entirely."

The glasses were re-filled. Francis went into great detail about what it would take to get from where I was now to a certified teacher.

"How long did it take you to get back to Paris?" Helen asked.

"Too long," Francis said. "If I recall correctly it was like two years, which at the time seemed more like a lifetime."

"I don't think it's done you too much harm, Francis, you seem pretty well adjusted to me," I said.

"Maisie, I cannot impress on you strongly enough that you need to think carefully about which route you are going to take. It's hard enough for a man, imagine how difficult it could be for a foreign woman. Now I really must be going, bye for now you two lovely ladies. I hope to see you again soon, Maisie."

"I'll see you out Francis," Helen said. She stood up from her seat. I listened to them doing a bit of billing and cooing at the door as they said their goodbyes.

"You seem to like him very much, but he is a bit old for you, don't you think?" I said when she came back.

"Funny that I can remember saying that very same thing to you about Ralph, if you recall. And I don't think you took it very well, so how do you expect me to now?"

"Oh, come on I didn't mean to offend you Helen. Are you one hundred percent sure that he doesn't have a wife tucked away?"

"If he does, he's hiding her very well. He spends a lot of time with me here, when he's not at work or at some conference or other."

"He goes away a lot, does he?" I asked cautiously.

We spent the rest of our time together trekking around more of the tourist sites. The parks in Paris simply amazed me. They were huge with the most beautifully kept glinting with colour flower beds the like of which I'd never encountered. This day we visited The Luxembourg Gardens, Helen told me that a fortune is spent on them each year to impress the visitors and for the locals pleasure.

When we were there one day we saw such a kerfuffle. There was a typically smartly dressed, dapper looking short Frenchman taking his little terrier dog for a walk. Suddenly a group of schoolchildren came into view eating ice cream cornets. The dog, who was off his lead, tore over and stole a little girl's cornet. Then overran the owner who tried in vain to remove the ice cream from his dog's mouth. He eventually succeeded. The little girl was screaming her head off in the distance. He looked from the ice cream to the little girl deciding whether to give it back to her or not. He decided against and threw it into a bin. The dog ran to the bin and tried hard as he may to retrieve it but he was unsuccessful and he barked and barked in disdain. The Frenchman took pity on the little girl who was continuously wailing over her lost cornet. And over he went to the ice-cream van and bought her another. This time his dog was on his lead and as the treat was handed over to her she was transformed into a smiley creature once more.

The scene was the stuff of the Monsieur Hugo silent movies. We couldn't have made it up. That afternoon we'd went to see the Arc de Triomphe, cut short because I had a train to catch. I was sad to leave this amazing city and my caring friend, but knew I must return home.

FINAL CHAPTER

After getting back to normality as I'd come to know it, Mother came home. Strangely there was no pomp and ceremony, no dramatic scenes, just my Mum. A young carer called Lucy had been employed by Dad and she was very good. He was happy to go to work and Mother relaxed more and more as the days passed. One day she called me into the living room where she liked to sit in her recliner chair.

"Maisie, I want to talk to you," she said.

I hadn't heard her voice like this before. It wasn't sad in the sense she was holding back tears or getting ready to break down, but there was a certain level of defeat. And the way she spoke was calming, as if she were reading me a bedtime story.

"I want to apologize to you and your Father for all the grief I've caused over these last eighteen months. I cannot believe that I would have behaved so badly. I, this might sound odd, but I think of that person, that monster I became, and it's hard to even say that she was me. But I need to. I need to say it, Maisie. I need to take ownership, so that I can truly apologize to you. Oh Maisie. And you never gave up on me! Your Father never gave up on me. I just hope that you can find it in your heart to forgive me. It's something I don't deserve and shouldn't even ask for. I shall speak to your Father when he gets home later, but I needed to tell you. I don't deserve to still have you in my life, but I will consider myself the luckiest woman on this planet for each new day I get to spend with you."

As we sat at the kitchen table she could not keep still. Her fingers fidgeting with the cup and plate in front of her. She was so changed but she was still my Mother. Looking back, I think I expected to find myself more conflicted in that moment. However Mum looked so sad and tired, the dark circles around her eyes told of inveterate grief and sorrow. Her face pallor showed the mask of someone broken beyond repair. The loss of self-respect was clear for the world to see and I feared to some degree of what our future would hold.

As if each step closer toward forgiveness I'd replay all the scenes of what she became, and how much she hurt me, and that would build up a wall. Prevent me from taking her back. I thought the pain from the past would be too much. How I'd never have that last year before college back. I'd never have Dan back, and sure it wasn't my mum's fault, but that whole year, that whole year and half, I thought I'd never want anything from that time again. Nothing to remind me of all the sorrow. I mean the police, the detectives, everyone else had moved on from solving the crime so I should too. Forget France. Forget mum. Forget everything. But none of those thoughts were there. All the pain, all the hurt, none of it was there in that moment. I looked at this woman across from me and all I could think was this is my Mother. And maybe it was reverse now, I would be the one taking care of her. That worried me still. But I just wanted her back in my life.

"Oh, Mum," I said. "I know how hard it has been for you and for all of us. Of course, I understand and forgive you. Life will never be the same for us again, not since we lost Dan and there will always be the knowledge that his killer hasn't been found yet. And that will always sting. But we shall have to adjust to that for the time being. Maybe sometime in the future they will find who killed Dan. Or maybe they won't and we just have to, I don't know how, live with that. As terrible as that may sound. Maybe we can both miss him and keep living. That memories of him will both hurt and bring a smile. We won't forget him but we'll keep on going. And you, and me, and Father, we'll figure it out. Together. One day at a time."

The End

Thank You

Thank you to Nonnie Jules, President of Rave Reviews Book Club. Also thank you to Deborah Bowman, CEO of Clasid Consultants Publishing Inc. Silver Spring. And thank you to Chris O'Brien, Founder of Long Overdue LLC.

Also by Joy M. Lilley

Figs, Vines and Roses

Times Pendulum Swings Again

The Liberty Bodice

All available on Amazon.com

Made in the USA
Middletown, DE
28 August 2019